THE BOY IN THE REEDS

An absolutely gripping Detective Jemima
Huxley crime thriller

GAYNOR TORRANCE

DI Jemima Huxley Series Book 7

Joffe Books, London
www.joffebooks.com

First published in Great Britain in 2024

Cover art by Nebojša Zorić

ISBN: 978-1-83526-553-6

PROLOGUE

At this early hour it was chilly inside the hide. It would soon warm up as the sun's rays kissed the exterior. The dampness would evaporate. The musty aroma would lose its potency, and before midday it would inevitably become oppressively hot.

For now, Siân Baker and Hannah Sutcliffe appreciated the warmth their padded jackets and fingerless gloves provided. The women had been neighbours for many years. Friends for the last thirteen of those, since bumping into each other at the Newport Wetlands and discovering a shared passion — their love of birds.

Twice a week, regardless of the weather, they'd set off together before sunrise to visit the nature reserve, where they'd spend hours in a hide. It was a well-worn routine. Coming equipped with flasks, sandwiches, binoculars, cameras and notebooks. Ready to watch the wildlife and record their sightings. Much of the time they only saw the usual birds. But there was always the chance of a rare sighting, and the anticipation of this happening made every visit an exciting event.

As the first of the sun's rays reached out in the east, velvety hues diluted. Siân never tired of witnessing this spectacle. Nature's banishing of darkness always felt like a rebirth, giving an injection of hope before the banality of the day-to-day routine. It was an occurrence unnoticed by those still tucked up in their beds.

The dawn chorus was glorious. As birds took to the wing, and plants unfurled, it was nature's most active time of day. Siân and Hannah were concentrating hard, searching for any birds which were unusual visitors to the area. Adopting their usual routine, they positioned themselves at opposite ends of the hide, to allow for maximum coverage. They gripped their binoculars tightly, intense concentration causing their more immediate surroundings to fade away. No two mornings were ever the same.

Hannah spotted movement in her peripheral vision. So low to the ground that she hadn't expected it. She'd panned past the area before her brain had time to register what she had just seen. Shifting her position and adjusting the sight, her jaw dropped. She wanted to say something, but no words would come. This wasn't the usual wildlife.

A small boy, barefoot, dirty, bedraggled, and clad only in a torn pair of underpants, was leading a woman along. She was barefoot and dressed in underwear too. They looked as though they'd escaped from a war zone: clearly traumatized and malnourished, their bodies covered in scabs and scars.

Hannah gulped. She opened her mouth to say something, but no sound would come.

She could see terror etched on the strangers' faces. God only knew what had happened to them. The boy was gripping the woman's hand tightly, whereas her fingers didn't have the strength to curl around his. Despite his small size and emaciated state, it was apparent that he had taken charge. He was forcing her to keep moving. All but pulling her along.

The woman's pace was flagging with every step she took. Her feet barely cleared the ground as she shuffled along. Blood trickled down the inside of her legs.

Hannah lowered the binoculars. She'd never been good in a crisis. It was obvious that these people required immediate medical attention, and Hannah needed to do something before it was too late.

Her bag toppled over, and the flask, which was the topmost of its contents, clattered to the ground and rolled across the floor before coming to a halt. 'Siân,' she muttered, but still the words wouldn't come. Without a backwards glance, she raced outside.

Siân huffed as Hannah's sudden movement startled the birds from the trees. As they took to the wing, others were alerted to their fear and within seconds there was a mass relocation. Survival instincts had taught them to distance themselves from potential danger. They wouldn't return until they felt safe.

Siân turned abruptly to face Hannah and was shocked to discover that her friend wasn't there. Aware of a continuing commotion somewhere nearby, she discarded her binoculars, grabbed her phone, and raced outside. As there was nothing seemingly amiss directly outside the hide, she stepped on to the main path and strained to see where Hannah was; looking in every direction until she saw her friend racing along the track as though the hounds of hell were after her.

'Hannah!' she called. 'Hannah!' But her friend ignored her and kept on going.

Before setting off in pursuit, Siân had the foresight to return to the hide to collect her backpack, which contained some basic medical supplies. Snatching the bag from the floor she headed back outside and raced off in the direction her friend had taken. Skidding to a halt as she rounded a bend she got a first glimpse of what Hannah had seen.

'You got your phone?' asked Hannah. She hadn't even turned around to see who had approached. All the while she was seeing to the woman, who had collapsed and remained unconscious.

'Yeah,' muttered Siân, as she pressed the button for the emergency services.

Seconds later, an operator answered. 'Emergency. Which service do you require?'

'Ambulance and police,' said Siân.

The boy knelt beside his companion, gently stroking her hair. Hannah reached out to touch him, but he flinched and scuttled back out of reach as though he anticipated pain.

'You're safe. We're not going to hurt you,' she said.

The child stared blankly. His lips scarcely moving as he whispered something repeatedly. Though whether it was a collection of words, or merely a sound which gave him some comfort, it was impossible to know.

'Who are you? What happened to you?' Hannah spoke gently, in what she hoped was a reassuring voice, but the questions went unanswered.

They'd lost the boy for now. He was physically present, but his glazed expression suggested that he had retreated to a safe space inside his head. His unintelligible mantra was no more than a low hum. Until specialist help arrived, there was nothing to be done for him. Both women knew they were out of their depth. This boy and woman were beyond their help.

CHAPTER 1

Detective Chief Inspector Jemima Huxley had spent the first part of the morning at court, waiting to be called to give evidence. It was a necessary part of the job but tedious and unproductive all the same. It was such a waste of time hanging about like a spare part only to be in the witness box for a quarter of an hour. She was glad to get out of there.

Her stomach had been rumbling for what seemed like an age, though she only had herself to blame as she'd skipped breakfast. She had reached the stage where she felt she could eat a scabby donkey. As she sat at her desk and chomped on a mouthful of tuna mayo sandwich, her phone pinged.

Glancing at the screen she saw that the message was from her sister, Lucy, and her heart skipped a beat. Common sense told her that there was nothing to worry about. After all, if it was some sort of emergency, Lucy would have called, not texted. But still . . .

As usual, Finlay, Jemima's toddler, was at Lucy's house. He was being looked after by Eloise, Lucy's live-in nanny. Eloise was employed to see to Lucy's brood, and had agreed to take on Finlay and ensure that James, his older brother, got to and from school safely.

Like many mothers worldwide, Jemima experienced an underlying sense of guilt about not being there for each moment of her youngest son's formative years. But she didn't have a choice. As a single parent, she needed to provide for herself and the boys.

While on shift, if she received a message or phone call from either Lucy or Eloise she couldn't help but catastrophize; all sorts of irrational fears would flood her imagination until she took a deep breath and told herself to stop being so ridiculous. It came from years of being told you weren't good enough. That people like her didn't deserve to be happy. It was also exacerbated by the awful situations she was forced to encounter. Every time she went on shift, she saw first-hand how a person's life could change in a moment, if you were unfortunate to be in the wrong place at the wrong time. It was a completely ridiculous over-reaction, and Jemima knew it. But Finlay, and James, meant the world to her.

Jemima's mouth was suddenly dry, making the act of swallowing the sandwich seem impossible. She reached for her cup of coffee to swill it down, only for the steaming liquid to burn her mouth. It seemed that the day was getting worse by the minute. A quick glance around confirmed the fact that none of her squad had noticed that she was acting like an idiot.

As she scanned the message, the tension drained from her body. Lucy was only reminding her that it was their father's birthday in a few days' time, and that they needed to decide on how they'd celebrate it.

Jemima had only just switched on her computer when Superintendent Torsten Olsen marched into the room. Throughout the time he'd headed up the squad, the man had made no attempt to bond with the team; personal questions were met with expressionless silence, and nothing could be gleaned from his office, where there were no photographs of family or friends on display. It was unsettling to know so little about someone you worked with. When push came to shove, would he have their backs? The consensus was that if

Olsen were to be cut open, they would find a circuit board and wires, where internal organs and blood vessels should be — they called him the cyborg when he was out of earshot.

'Gather round people!' It was an order to be obeyed. No attempt at even the most basic of pleasantries.

Sergeants Dan Broadbent and Gareth Peters were the first to oblige, quickly followed by constables Nancy Chen, Levi Jackson and Andrew Mackintosh. Jemima suppressed a sigh of frustration as she joined her team.

'I've a new case for you, which demands your immediate attention. Early yesterday morning a woman and young boy were discovered at the Newport Wetlands by a couple of birdwatchers.'

'Twitchers,' interjected Dan, and then remembered who he was talking to. He dropped his gaze, unable to meet Olsen's steely glare.

'Yes, Sergeant. As I said, birdwatchers, and I'd appreciate it if you did not interrupt me again.'

Colour quickly rose from Dan's neck to his face. He shuffled his feet sheepishly, every inch the naughty child.

'Now, where was I? Ah yes . . . There are a number of reasons why you will be investigating this incident. Firstly, this woman and child were barefoot and dressed only in their underwear. Garments that were no better than rags. Secondly, it was apparent that they were both malnourished and there was evidence of mistreatment. Thirdly, the woman was in a very bad way — a miscarriage, it seems. Unfortunately, she fell, and was unconscious by the time these birdwatchers reached her. Finally, and perhaps most importantly, she has not yet regained consciousness. As such a DNA test was done, and a match was found.'

Olsen paused for dramatic effect. Seeing every eye upon him, and knowing that he had their complete attention, he continued.

'It appears that the woman is none other than' — he glanced at the notepad he was holding, to ensure he got the name right — 'Tabitha Leysham.'

'Didn't she go missing about five years ago?' asked Jemima. She was glad he'd finally got to the point; she was already keen to investigate this case.

'It was actually eight years ago,' said Olsen.

'Who's—?' began Levi.

'I'm just getting to that, Constable,' said Olsen. 'Tabitha Leysham is the daughter of Lord and Lady Leysham. And before anyone asks the question, there is DNA confirmation that the child found with her is not hers.'

'As she didn't disappear from these parts, I'm afraid my recollection of the case is a bit sketchy. Are you able to fill us in on the background?' asked Jemima.

'I am indeed, Chief Inspector.' Olsen's lips twitched as he suppressed a smile. It was apparent that despite his aloof demeanour the man relished the opportunity to be the one in the know. He glanced back at his notepad, cleared his throat and continued.

'Tabitha disappeared without trace eight years ago when she was nineteen years old. At the time, she told a close friend that she was meeting an attractive, famous man; she refused to reveal his identity as she'd said she was sworn to secrecy. She'd set out in her car from the family home in the Cotswolds. The vehicle was found two days later, parked in an isolated beauty spot. There was no sign of foul play. Her disappearance was headline news at the time, and there was a great deal of speculation about what had happened. But despite an extensive police investigation, and a substantial reward being offered for her return, Tabitha's whereabouts remained a mystery.'

'Has the child said anything?' asked Jemima.

'Nothing that makes any sense. I've been informed that the boy is traumatized. Apparently, he keeps muttering something repeatedly, as though he's fixated upon it. One of the hospital staff thought it sounded something like, *"Beat the brave man."* Though it makes no sense. As things stand, it might be that he's trying to say something important. But I've no idea what. Then again it could just as easily be a collection of sounds that might give him some sort of comfort. Make of that what you will.'

'What progress was made by the team initially assigned to the case?' asked Jemima. It was a reasonable question as Jemima's team were being asked to take charge of things more than twenty-four hours after the woman and boy had been found, and nothing could be taken for granted. There were protocols in place, but it didn't necessarily follow that the officers in attendance had adhered to them. Sadly, barely a week went by without media reports about unprofessional practices by police officers which ultimately led to cases collapsing and criminals getting away with the crimes they'd committed.

It seemed that ineptitude and corruption were rife in every police force across the land. Which meant that hard-working honest officers not only had to tackle the criminals, but they also had to root out and clean up the mess resulting from officers who should have never been allowed to join the force in the first place. It made the task of an honest copper a hundred times more difficult than it used to be.

'Very little,' said Olsen. 'I've already asked the question and received an unsatisfactory answer.'

'Which was?' interjected Jemima. She could already sense her hackles rising.

'Apparently, yesterday was a busy day in that particular area, and was combined with an unusually high number of officers calling in sick.' Olsen's annoyance was apparent in his voice. 'It resulted in an inexperienced team, and by that I mean a PC and PCSO being the first on the scene. It was mid-afternoon before they managed to get anyone senior out there, and by that time any chance of preserving evidence had disappeared.

'Forensics were called in. I believe they're still at the scene and will be for much of the day. The entire approach was amateurish at best.'

'Did anyone send in a canine unit to search the area?' asked Jemima.

'No.'

'What about drones?' asked Gareth. 'Since the boy isn't related to the woman, it's possible his mother could be out there somewhere, and in need of medical attention.'

'Again, no.' Olsen looked and sounded glum. 'All I can say is that it was not their finest hour, and there will be repercussions. Lessons learned, as they like to say.'

Jemima thought it best to remain silent. The lessons learned trope was well past its sell-by date. Given the number of so-called mistakes that were made ad nauseam, it had long ago become apparent that lessons were never learned.

'I'll arrange for drones to scour the area, if that's OK with you, Guv?' said Gareth. 'If there is an injured woman out there, we might still be too late, but I think we should give it a shot.'

'Thanks Gareth. It's the right call.' Jemima knew that her sergeant would see the task through and deal competently with anything else that was required of him.

'Have Tabitha's parents been informed?' asked Jemima.

'Not yet. Her identity was confirmed less than an hour ago. Given the high-profile nature of her disappearance, and the lack of progress on the case at the time, it was deemed necessary to treat her reappearance with kid gloves. Despite the short time I've lived in this country, even I have come to understand the sensitivities that come into play when dealing with such a powerful and influential family. As such, I would like you to break the news in person and reopen the investigation.

'Lord and Lady Leysham will want answers, Huxley. I want answers, and I want those responsible for Tabitha Leysham's disappearance brought to book. Do I make myself clear?'

'Absolutely, sir,' said Jemima.

CHAPTER 2

It was exciting to get her teeth into a case that had baffled the Gloucestershire police for eight years. Jemima recalled how Tabitha Leysham's disappearance had been headline news for many months.

Thousands of people went missing in Great Britain every year. Some disappeared by choice — some of these returned when they were good and ready, having overcome whatever personal crisis they were trying to come to terms with. Others never returned. No matter the reason behind any disappearance, those who had been left behind had their lives brutally upended and would never be able to relax or take anything for granted again.

Tabitha Leysham, unconscious, malnourished, obviously ill-treated, would not be able to give them any answers in her present state. It was far too soon to know whether she had the capacity to recover sufficiently to tell them what had happened to her.

As Olsen filled them in on the previous day's events, Jemima quickly formulated a plan. And even as the superintendent was marching out of the room without a backward glance, she began to allocate tasks. There was no doubt in her mind that once Tabitha's reappearance emerged, the press would be all over the story like a rash.

'I don't need to tell you all that we need to adopt a methodical approach. Dan and I will go and break the news to Tabitha's parents — so we'll be out for much of the day.'

'Right you are, Guv,' said Dan.

'Gareth, I want you to take the lead on reviewing the original case file. Levi and Mack will help you. I'd like to think that the original investigating officers did a thorough job. But we need to look at the evidence for ourselves.'

'You've only got to think back to the superficial enquiries on those teenage deaths in the Rhymney Valley to know how lazy and incompetent some officers are,' said Levi. The incidents he was referring to were numerous deaths where local officers had failed to spot that they were linked. Indeed it was possible that, had they done their job properly, they could have prevented the deaths of some of the teenagers. It was yet another shocking example of ineptitude among serving officers. A level of incompetence which went right up the ranks.

'Precisely, Levi. It was a damning indictment. So, once again, we assume nothing, and approach the events of eight years ago with fresh eyes.

'That said, I want you to start by putting a timeline together for the days leading up to Tabitha's disappearance. Compile a list of witnesses. Examine their statements. I don't need to spell it out for you; you're more than capable of doing what's necessary.'

'I take it you want me to concentrate on the child?' asked Nancy.

'Absolutely. Identify reports of boys between the ages of five and eight who've gone missing. We know they've got his DNA on file, as Olsen's just told us they've established that Tabitha's not his mother. So run it through the databases and see if any familial link pops up. It's unlikely, but you never know. It's possible that, for once, luck could be on our side.'

'Why such a wide age range?' asked Nancy.

'Well, talk to the hospital team and see if they can advise you, but I suspect if he's not talking we can't really narrow it at this stage. All we know is that the boy's small and malnourished, and it sounds as though he's traumatized; given his appearance, that would seem to fit. He hasn't said anything that makes sense. Whether that's because he's scared or doesn't have the necessary verbal skills we don't know at this stage. So, for the time being I want us to keep the age parameters wide.'

* * *

Fortisham Grange was a grand old property on a sprawling estate in the Cotswolds, which no doubt took considerable resources to maintain. Jemima and Dan drove through a set of large gates, down a driveway lined on either side by ancient trees. Apart from a few small patches here and there, foliage almost entirely blocked out the sun. It was a sinister and unappealing approach.

'Wouldn't want to take this route if there were any strong winds,' said Dan. 'Hope they've got strong roots.'

'You and me both,' agreed Jemima.

The building might once have been elegant and imposing, but those days were long gone. It was evident, even from a cursory glance, that the masonry needed repair.

'What a disappointment,' Dan said. 'Must be freezing in winter, with all those cracks.'

'It's probably listed,' Jemima told him. 'Special historic interest or something. Means they can't fix anything quickly or on the cheap — all the work needs to be signed off by the authorities. And the workmen have to be skilled enough to carry out sympathetic repairs.'

'Sounds expensive.'

It seemed that someone had spotted their approach as, when they eventually pulled up outside the main entrance, they barely had time to get out of the car before one of the main doors of the property opened. It was of such grand proportions that even if Dan had stood on Jemima's shoulders and stretched his arms up to their full extent, he would not have been able to reach the top of the opening.

The woman who approached them was of medium build with shoulder length wavy auburn hair. She was dressed in a grey business suit with a pristine white blouse, buttoned up to the collar. 'I take it you're the police officers?'

'That's correct, and you are?' asked Jemima.

'Abigail Morten, I'm Lady Leysham's PA. She is expecting you, but she's on a call. Some sort of kerfuffle at the Paris branch. Shouldn't be long.'

'Is Lord Leysham at home too?' Ideally Jemima wanted to speak to both of them together.

'He's just winding up a business meeting, and in about an hour he's got a planning meeting.'

'Planning meeting?' Jemima was curious.

'Yes. He's on a tight schedule this morning. I doubt it's escaped your notice that this fine old house is in need of repair. For the last four years, his Lordship has opened the East Wing to visitors. They're allowed access four days a week. For a fee, of course. The funds are being used to pay for repairs. Ah, his business meeting must have ended.'

'Charlotte.' Abigail nodded curtly at a woman who had just come out of one of the nearby rooms. She was dressed in an off-the-peg business suit, the colour and style of which did little to enhance her appearance. She gave only a cursory glance towards Jemima and Dan, nodded at Abigail, but said nothing as she walked briskly towards the door and exited the building without a backward glance.

'Don't mind her. She was here for the business meeting with Lord Leysham.'

'I guess a place like this is a money pit,' said Dan. He was fascinated by grand old buildings.

Abigail didn't deny it. 'Lady Leysham's asked me to take you through to the drawing room. I've arranged for tea. Or there's coffee, if you prefer?'

It seemed that the Leyshams had decided to face them together, as Jemima and Dan were just finishing their coffee when the drawing room door opened, and Tabitha's parents walked in. It was soon apparent to Jemima that it was taking a great deal of effort for the Leyshams to appear calm and composed. Though, apart from the obvious strain in their voices, as they struggled to keep their emotions in check, there were other telltale signs too. From the wobble of Lydia Leysham's chin, almost instantly brought under control by the clamping together of her lips, until they formed a narrow white line, and a noticeable tick to one of Edgar Leysham's eyes.

Introductions were quickly dispensed with. Jemima was keen to begin, as she wanted to put the couple out of their misery. 'It's good news,' she said.

Upon hearing that Tabitha had been found, Lydia sobbed unashamedly. Her husband swallowed hard, but his demeanour barely changed as he adeptly retained the so-called British stiff upper lip.

Being the more composed of the two, he was the first to speak. 'Where did you find her?'

'Tabitha was found early yesterday morning at a nature reserve in Newport, South Wales.' There was no way of sugarcoating the information. 'I'm afraid the signs are that she was held captive somewhere, and was escaping when she was found. She wasn't alone. There was a young boy with her.'

'We have a grandson?' interjected Edgar.

'No, DNA tests have shown the boy is not Tabitha's child.'

'So, what was she doing with this child?' Lydia looked and sounded bewildered.

'At this early stage of the investigation I'm unable to speculate. Other than to say that, from the report I've received, it appears that your daughter and this child were both malnourished and clad only in the most basic of underwear. Neither of them had shoes.'

'Malnourished? Hardly any clothes? You're telling me that my daughter's been abused?' Lydia's sense of relief was short-lived, as she began to make sense of the implications of what she'd just learned.

However, Edgar was more pragmatic. 'You said that Tabitha was found more than twenty-four hours ago. Why have you waited until now to inform us?' His words were clipped with annoyance.

'We only learned of your daughter's identity shortly before we set off to tell you.'

'She didn't tell you who she was?'

'Tabitha collapsed at the scene and has not yet regained consciousness. She is being treated at the University Hospital in Cardiff—'

'We must go to the hospital. We have to be with her,' cried Lydia. She reached across and gripped her husband's hands tightly.

'I understand your urgency—' began Jemima.

'You understand nothing!' interjected Lydia. 'Until you've had a child taken from you, you understand nothing.'

'I apologize if I offended you,' said Jemima. 'It's perfectly understandable that you want to be with your daughter, but first we need to ask you both some questions.'

'Can't it wait?' snapped Edgar. 'You can see that my wife's distressed.'

'I'm afraid not. It's highly likely that your daughter was abducted and held against her will. Which means that whoever took her is still out there.'

'Oh, do shut up, Edgar!' His wife shot him a withering look, before turning her attention to the police officers. 'Are you saying that my daughter's still in danger?' She leaned forward, eager to learn everything they knew.

'It's possible. It's doubtful she's been kept somewhere for eight years, without learning something about her captor. If he, or she, finds out where Tabitha is, they won't want her to talk.'

'Have you arranged security for her?' Lydia's strength of character came to the fore in her determination to ensure that everything that needed to be done to keep Tabitha safe, was indeed being done.

'Yes. Look, you'll undoubtedly have many questions, but as things stand, I don't have any answers. When Tabitha disappeared eight years ago, the investigation was undertaken by officers from this area.'

'And a poor job they made of it too,' said Edgar.

'That's not helpful, Edgar,' admonished his wife.

Having no intention of being drawn into commenting on the original case, Jemima continued. 'Since learning about the case this morning, I've set up a squad to review the original case files. It's my intention to establish where your daughter was held captive and by whom. We're approaching this with fresh eyes, and I assure you that every piece of evidence will be looked at. We'll leave no stone unturned. It's in everyone's interests that Tabitha's captor is identified and arrested as soon as possible.'

'And why should we have any faith in you?' asked Lord Leysham. His tone was sharp enough to cut a diamond. His eyebrows arched to emphasize scepticism that Jemima was any better than those ineffectual officers eight years ago.

If Jemima was taken aback by the man's lack of trust, she did not show it, and certainly didn't hold it against him. She had every reason to believe that she might have acted in a similar way had the tables been turned. Instead of going on the defensive, she informed him of how she was taking things forward.

'Given the lack of progress over the years, you have every reason to doubt my words. But let me assure you both, my squad and I have an excellent track record, and I guarantee we will do everything we can to get answers about what happened to your daughter,' said Jemima.

'Edgar, these are different officers from a different police force. They're not responsible for any mistakes in the original investigation. Right now, as far as I'm concerned, Tabby's been found. I've not seen her for eight years. I'd convinced myself I'd never see her again. But I've been given a second chance and I have to be there when she wakes up. I need to make things right with her. Have her back in my life.' Lydia placed a hand on her husband's arm.

'Umm. You're right, as always, my dear.' Edgar gently squeezed her hand. 'Just ask your questions,' he said, as he turned his attention back to Jemima.

'I'd like you to talk me through the week or so leading up to Tabitha's disappearance. You must have analysed conversations you had with her or had retrospective thoughts about things she might have done during that time. Particularly anything you thought was out of character,' said Jemima.

'Since we lost Tabs, the events leading up to her disappearance have played through my mind repeatedly. I've spent every waking moment searching for answers. All I can say is that everything seemed normal. Well, as normal as things could have been with Tabs going through that awful teenage rebellious stage. When she was young, she was such a sweet little thing. Then, as hormones kicked in, she developed a mind of her own.'

Reading between the lines, Jemima realized that Tabitha had been a handful. Then again, which teenager wasn't? They all wanted to test the water. Try new things. Claim their independence. It was the age-old rite of passage.

'What my wife's trying to say is that Tabitha was challenging,' interjected Edgar. His tone was very matter of fact.

'All teenagers are challenging, Edgar. It's the manner in which parents deal with those challenges that makes a difference to the eventual outcome.' Lydia didn't look at her husband as she rebuked him. But both officers noticed a change in her attitude as she stood up, under the guise of plumping the cushion on which she'd been leaning. When she sat back down, it was noticeable that she had moved further away from him.

'As I was saying, my daughter disappeared without warning. All I had left were memories. I kept wondering if I'd missed something obvious. Something I should have picked up on at the time, because as usual I was so preoccupied with my business. I should have been much more alert to what was going on with my daughter.

'Tabs was exceptionally secretive in those last few months,' continued Lydia. 'I always thought we had a reasonably good mother–daughter relationship. Naturally, we had a few arguments. Though, nothing serious.'

'You should remove those rose-tinted spectacles, dearest,' chided Edgar. He snorted and shook his head. 'I loved . . . love Tabitha, but in the months leading up to her disappearance, our daughter was hard work. And I don't think it does any good putting a positive spin on what was truthfully a difficult time. Our daughter was a wastrel who threw away every opportunity that landed in her lap. Most people would have given their eye-teeth for the advantages she had showered upon her. She attended one of the best schools in the country. Yet she was disruptive, underperformed, and had no intention of working for a living. She point-blank refused to look for gainful employment.'

'That's unfair, Edgar. Tabitha was merely considering her options. You're casting her in a bad light and it's not fair. These officers need facts not feelings. I'm right, am I not?' She raised her eyebrows questioningly as she glanced fleetingly in Jemima's general direction, without making eye-contact. Lady Leysham continued to speak without waiting for a response.

'I recall that throughout those last few months Tabs was less engaged with us. When she was at home, she spent a significant amount of time in her bedroom. Shut herself away. Listening to music. Honestly, she was hard work. It was such a change. I remember wondering if she was taking drugs. I even searched her room when she was out. But she came back and caught me in the act. She was absolutely furious.'

'Did you find any drugs?' asked Jemima.

'Drugs? No. I'd got it wrong. There weren't any, but it destroyed our relationship. She distanced herself even more.'

'Were there any men on the scene?' asked Jemima.

'Not as far as I knew. Over the years she'd had the odd beau here and there. Nothing serious. Sons of friends of the family. That sort of thing. Though I suppose we don't know what went on at that school of hers. She boarded. It had an excellent reputation. Though she didn't achieve the grades she was predicted to get. It came as a shock to her. Knocked her confidence. Especially as some of her contemporaries did so well. But I assure you, she was starting to bounce back.'

'Those school fees were a complete waste of money, if you ask me,' muttered Edgar.

'My money, Edgar. Not yours. And Tabs would have eventually come around. She was starting to make plans. Think about her future.'

'What about you, Lord Leysham?'

'What do you mean?' he asked.

'Did you notice any change in your daughter in the weeks preceding her disappearance?'

'I can't say that I did. In hindsight she'd been quite secretive. But aren't most young people? I certainly was. So, in answer to your question, no I didn't. As far as I knew, there was nothing amiss, apart from her not putting any meaningful effort into her studies. Though I've ruminated on things throughout the years, and I've regretted not taking a proactive approach with her. Tabitha was a bright girl. She could have achieved so much.' Edgar shook his head and sighed.

'The truth is that Lydia and I are both on treadmills. Our time is not our own, as people rely on us. We have responsibilities. My time's taken up with dealing with this estate and running a business. Then of course there's debates at the House. Must hold the government to account. Can't let the country down. I sometimes think there's not enough of me to go around. You can't begin to imagine what it's like juggling three full-time jobs. Leaves little time for domesticity.'

Jemima realized that she wasn't going to learn anything useful from Tabitha's parents. She didn't get the impression that they were trying to be evasive or unhelpful. Like most parents, they only knew what their daughter had been up to in the vaguest of terms.

CHAPTER 3

Having broken the news to Lord and Lady Leysham and learning nothing of importance about those days leading up to Tabitha's disappearance, they left them to make arrangements to visit their daughter at the hospital.

'Where next?' asked Dan.

As usual, Jemima was driving. 'As we haven't heard from the others, it's safe to say they're still hard at it.'

'Yeah, they'd have let us know if there'd been any major breakthroughs,' said Dan.

'Exactly, so we'll swing by the hospital. Find out how Tabitha and the boy are doing. It'd be useful to see them for ourselves. There's only so much you can learn second-hand. You never know, she might have woken up by now. And if she has, we might have some solid facts to work with.'

When they arrived at the hospital it was immediately apparent that Jemima's initial optimism was misplaced. Tabitha remained in a coma, and the nursing staff confirmed that she was in a bad way. She was in a room of her own, with an officer standing guard outside.

A quick glance at the young woman told Jemima everything she needed to know. Her face was preternaturally pale, suggesting she had spent a sustained period lacking sunlight. And without the DNA test confirming her identity, it was possible that even her parents might not have recognized her, as over the years she had lost so much weight, and her youthful glow had long since disappeared.

'Let's see how the boy's doing,' said Jemima. She was already heading in the direction of the children's ward, and Dan had to pick up his pace to catch up with her.

'Her parents will be shocked when they see the state of her,' he said. 'There's no doubt she's been mistreated over the years. She could pass for decades older than her actual age.' He shook his head despairingly.

'It's confirmation that she's been held captive for a significant amount of time. It's inconceivable to think that she would have chosen to live in such a way, that would result in her looking like that.'

'Is it possible she could have had some sort of breakdown? Lost her memory even?'

'I doubt it, Dan. She's been gone for eight years. Even if she'd been living on the streets surely someone would have spotted how ill she is. She's nothing but skin and bones. She'd have been hospitalized and offered help. By the look of her she's been held against her will. And don't forget, she was miscarrying when she collapsed. The report said that she was only dressed in underwear and wasn't wearing any shoes. She must have been in agony.'

'Fleeing for her life,' said Dan.

'Absolutely. I'm positive that's what she was doing.'

The children's hospital was a unit within the main hospital, an addition made in recent times but accessed via the original building. A decision had already been made about security: an officer stood guard at the start of the corridor, out of sight of the children's wards, so as not to alarm the young patients. For the time being visitor access to the unit was to be restricted to named individuals only, to minimize the risk of anyone coming to harm should the boy's anonymous captor try to gain entry under the guise of visiting another child.

The colour scheme and general ambience of the children's wards were a welcome relief from the utilitarian feel of the remainder of the hospital. Bright artwork adorned the walls, bedding and curtains displayed popular cartoon characters. Toys, games and puzzles were available for those who wanted to participate in such activities. It was a well thought out example of everything being done to distract the youngsters from the reason they'd been admitted to the hospital in the first place.

Jemima's breath caught in her throat the moment she got her first glimpse of the unnamed boy. He was small, painfully thin, and his head appeared to be too big for his body. His hair was long, as though it had never been cut. Which added to Jemima's certainty that he too had been kept in enforced captivity. Possibly even born into that life.

She swallowed hard, as a burning sense of anger ignited somewhere deep inside. Over the years she and her team had worked some horrendous cases. They'd seen sights which would make people of a nervous disposition reluctant to leave the safety of their homes. Yet sadly, when she thought that she'd encountered such varied and extreme levels of depravity that nothing could ever surprise her again, here she was facing two survivors who had overcome God knows what at the hands of at least one, if not more, monsters. Brutes who must have operated in plain sight and passed as normal people. Eight years was a long time to maintain a public-facing facade, which enabled whoever was behind this not to raise suspicion.

Before approaching the boy, Jemima and Dan headed for the nurses' station. 'How's he doing?' she asked.

'Improving. Though there's a long road ahead of him. They had him on a drip when he first arrived. Little mite was severely dehydrated, but they removed that a few hours ago. He's on a course of antibiotics, and he'll be with us a while. It's obvious that his injuries aren't just physical. He was very distressed when they brought him in. I wasn't on shift at the time, but I know that they had to sedate him. He was terrified of something.'

'More likely someone,' interjected Jemima.

'Exactly.' The nurse shivered at the thought of it and rubbed her arms as if chilled. 'Dearie me, it doesn't bear thinking about. Poor little mite. I can't begin to imagine what he's been through in his short life.'

'Has he said anything?'

'Nothing we've been able to make sense of. He's generally quiet as a mouse, but you can see his lips moving and when you get close to him, he appears to be muttering something. We haven't been able to figure out if he's trying to tell us something. Could be he's just making some sounds which in some way provide comfort. You'll see what I mean if you spend any time with him.'

Jemima appreciated that the nurse's revelations suggested that the boy was traumatized by his ordeal, though what exactly he had been subjected to was anyone's guess. 'Any idea how old he is?'

'It's a finger in the air guess. They examined him thoroughly when he was out for the count. Some of his adult teeth have erupted. Which makes him at least six. Possibly a few years older. Though his teeth are badly decayed, and there's evidence some were snapped off.'

'So, poor dental hygiene?' asked Dan. It was apparent from his shocked tone, that it was a seemingly unthinkable concept for him. Anyone who knew the sergeant was aware of his fastidious nature. He disliked mess of any kind, had a phobia of blood and did his best to avoid anything unhygienic. Given the nature of his job, and the scenes they frequently encountered, it regularly tested his resolve.

'I'm not a dental expert, but I'd be surprised if he'd ever had his teeth cleaned.'

Shocked by this revelation, Dan whistled and shook his head in despair.

'I'm afraid that's not the worst of it. He was filthy when he arrived, so things weren't so obvious. But when they had the chance to clean him up, they discovered that his body was covered in bruises and scar tissue. Also, when I mentioned that some of his teeth might have been snapped off, it's likely he was hit in the face, as his nose had been broken and subsequently healed. There's no doubt that the boy's been subjected to sustained physical abuse.'

Jemima momentarily turned away, as she surreptitiously wiped away a tear. This was not the time to allow emotion to come to the fore. She coughed loudly to cover her distress. It was safe to presume that the boy was somewhere between the ages of her two sons. And the thought of anyone treating either Finlay or James in such a manner didn't bear thinking about. At that moment she knew without a shadow of a doubt that if she ever got hold of the bastard who had done this, they'd have to hold her back. Because right now, she'd happily rip his head off with her bare hands.

What's more, since the DNA test had proved that Tabitha and the boy were not related, did that mean there was another woman out there somewhere, being held against her will?

Jemima sensed that if there was, this boy's mother could be suffering even more, when her captor realized that two of his captives had escaped. Even without knowing who he was, it was safe to presume that he would view their escape as a threat. And just like a cornered animal, a threatened person became unpredictable and dangerous. There was a very real possibility that any tried and tested methods a captive may have employed to try to make life easier for themselves would no longer apply. Whoever was behind this was not averse to doling out punishments, as evidenced by the signs of abuse clearly visible on the bodies of these two escapees. The best-case scenario was that physical punishments could become more severe. The worst case was that he could feel compelled to cut and run — which could result in him killing the boy's mother.

'Has he eaten anything since he's arrived?'

'Yes, his appetite's all right,' said the nurse. 'But he doesn't appear to know what cutlery is for. He had cereal this morning and used a hand to scoop it out. There was milk slopping everywhere, and he drank the remainder from the bowl. You can imagine the reaction from the other kids. We had to tell them not to stare or make fun of him. Then at lunchtime he ignored the knife and fork and used his hands again. He eats so quickly. It's almost animal-like. You know, like a dog. Swallowing, not chewing. Afraid someone will take the food away before he has time to finish.'

These revelations were heartbreaking to hear. They confirmed Jemima's fears that throughout his short life the boy had been treated as sub-human. More than likely denied basic things most people took for granted. She was about to ask if she could speak to the boy, when a casually dressed young man entered the ward. He had a thick mop of ginger hair and a beard.

'This is Patrick. He's our resident child psychologist,' said the nurse by way of introduction. 'He's here to assess the boy you're asking about. Patrick, this is DCI Huxley.'

'I'd like to sit in on your assessment,' Jemima said to Patrick.

'Not possible, I'm afraid.'

'I have a background in psychology,' said Jemima. 'It won't be the first time I've done this sort of thing.'

Patrick crossed his arms and cocked his head to one side, as he weighed up the idea of allowing Jemima to participate. 'Sure. That's fine, but I don't want you trying to force the pace.' To emphasize the point, he raised his eyebrows, and stared at her and then Dan over the top of his thick-rimmed spectacles. 'And just one of you.'

Dan laughed. 'I won't disturb you. I'm off to make a couple of calls.' And he disappeared out of the ward.

'Naturally, I wouldn't dream of interfering,' Jemima assured Patrick. 'This is your gig. I'll just be there as an observer. It's clear he's been through enough and doesn't need any undue pressure placed upon him. Though, if possible, it'd be good if you could get him to open up about what happened, as I've a feeling his life could be in danger.'

'How so?' asked Patrick.

Jemima explained her theory and he listened with interest. 'OK, but no promises. I'll see how it goes. As far as I'm concerned, that little lad there will be the one to dictate the pace, because I assure you, if I try to push him, it'll be counterproductive. We'll begin by interacting with him on the ward,' said Patrick. 'As we've no idea what trauma he's experienced, it's best if we engage with him in a location where he feels comfortable.'

'We're on the same page, Patrick,' she assured him.

From the short time she'd spent on the ward, Jemima hadn't noticed the boy engage with anyone, or anything. Even from a distance, and without being aware of his medical prognosis, she could tell that he was undoubtedly weak and ill. But his ailments didn't fully explain his lack of movement. Especially as he was surrounded by other youngsters.

Some of the children were playing with toys or reading books, either alone or together. Yet the boy remained in his bed. Propped up by pillows. Withdrawn, yet alert. It was apparent from the way his eyes darted about that he was watching everyone, and there was nothing to prevent him from getting off the bed and joining the others.

Jemima noticed that he was using a section of a blanket as a comfort aid, holding the material to his face as he fervently sucked a thumb. Such an act was normally associated with far younger children and was something a child of his age would normally have grown out of. Though, given the circumstances in which he had been found, it was safe to assume that this flimsy material was a coping mechanism. Waking up in unfamiliar surroundings, surrounded by strangers would be stressful for an adult. Let alone a young child. And given his injuries which suggested he had endured a sustained period of abuse; it would take a great deal of time and patience to allow him to accept that he was safe.

The boy's attention was focused on a group of younger children who were listening to a story being read by a young woman. As Jemima and Patrick approached his bed, the boy glanced in their direction. The change in his body language was unmistakeable as he clearly perceived them as a threat. Desperate to put him at ease she smiled and waved. 'Hello there,' she said in a sing-song tone. Determined to keep things light and put him at ease.

Jemima's efforts went unnoticed, as it quickly became apparent that the boy wasn't paying attention to her. Instead, he was entirely fixated upon Patrick. In a matter of seconds, he'd kicked off the sheets, let go of the blanket and jumped off the bed, emitting the most awful piercing scream.

Everyone's attention was suddenly on the boy. His eyes widened, as a genuine sense of panic took hold. He looked around frantically, as if searching for an escape route. Jemima's stomach lurched at the sight of him and was horrified to see a dark stain spreading over his pyjama leggings. Though no sooner had she registered the fact that he was so terrified that he had wet himself, the boy ducked down and scrambled beneath the bed.

Jemima reached out for Patrick's arm and dragged him away. Despite specializing in assessing childhood trauma the psychologist was so shocked that he had stopped in his tracks and remained rooted to the spot. 'He's terrified of you,' she said. Her words got Patrick's attention.

'What the hell has that poor child been subjected to?' he muttered, as he allowed himself to be led away. 'In all the years I've been doing this job, I've never had a child react to me in such an extreme way.'

CHAPTER 4

'What's going on?' Every cell in Dan's body was on high alert as he raced on to the ward, on the lookout for potential danger.

'There's no threat, Dan! We're over here!' Jemima had to shout to make herself heard as the boy's screams showed no sign of abating. She and Patrick had retreated out of the boy's line of sight. Though it was doubtful that the young lad would have seen them even if they'd remained close by, as nursing staff were doing their best to calm him down.

Over the years, Jemima had encountered people of all ages who were fearful for their lives, and there was no doubt in her mind that this little lad was genuinely terrified. The moment he set eyes upon the psychologist the screaming had begun, and his bladder had emptied. What's more, his extreme reaction was upsetting some of the other children too as hysteria spread.

'He's terrified of Patrick,' said Jemima.

Patrick looked bewildered. 'Not of me, surely. That's the first time I've clapped eyes on that lad. Whatever's happened to him, it's nothing to do with me.'

'Take a deep breath, Patrick. You've had a shock.'

'Y-yeah,' he replied. His shoulders sagged, and he looked as though he was about to cry. 'But I haven't done anything.'

'I'm sure that's the case.' Jemima gave his arm a reassuring squeeze. 'We all know that his reaction could have been caused by any number of things. For instance, you could remind him of whoever it is that's treated him so badly. That said, I'm sure you'll understand that we'll have to check you out. It would be remiss of us not to do so.'

'I get it. I'll ask another consultant to assess this child. I do this job to make kids' lives better. Not to make them scared.'

Jemima left Dan with Patrick, as she went in search of the nurse they had recently spoken to. 'Has the boy freaked out when he's seen anyone else on the ward?'

'No.' She shook her head. 'He's not really engaged with anyone, but he's not reacted like that.'

'And he's seen other men on the ward?'

'Yes. We've one male nurse and a couple of male doctors who've been in and out of the ward since he's been conscious.'

'Did any of the male staff have ginger hair, a beard, wear glasses, or have any of those characteristics?'

The nurse thought for a moment. 'One of them wears glasses. Two have beards. All of them have dark hair.'

'What about visitors? Do any of them have ginger hair?'

The nurse thought for a moment then shook her head. 'No, I don't recall seeing anyone on this ward with ginger hair.'

'Thanks, that's interesting,' said Jemima. From what she'd just learned it was apparent that the boy wasn't specifically afraid of men. Or even of men wearing spectacles. But what made Patrick stand out was the colour of his hair. Which could mean that the man they were after had ginger hair.

Jemima headed back towards Dan, who was still talking to Patrick. The young psychologist appeared to have recovered his composure. 'I'll need you to give your details to one of the officers,' instructed Jemima. 'A member of my team will carry out a background check on you.'

'I passed the DBS checks,' said Patrick.

Noting the desperation in his voice, Jemima continued. 'I'm sure you have, but you must understand that given the boy's reaction to you, we have no choice but to follow through on this. We'll be thorough, but it must be done. This isn't the first time a deeply troubled child has had such a reaction to someone in authority and it won't be the last. There are procedures in place for these events.'

The only way the boy could be calmed was by administering a mild sedative, which took effect relatively quickly, though the dose was insufficient to send him to sleep. It was even more apparent how malnourished the child was as a nurse lifted him back on the bed. As tension left his body, his limbs flopped and swayed with the motion of being relocated. He was nothing but skin and bones. In his semi-conscious state, he could be heard repeatedly muttering something, though his lips barely moved.

Jemima listened hard, determined to hear what the boy was trying to say, and to her it sounded very much like he was saying, *'Beat the brave man'*, the same phrase Olsen had mentioned. Though what it meant, she had no idea. What she did know was that this was the most damaged child she had ever seen. It was a certainty that within a few weeks his cuts would heal, and bruises disappear. Over time his scars would fade too. As yet the professionals couldn't even begin to assess the extent of his emotional damage, and even after years of therapy it was possible that it might never be repaired.

'I'd hate to be that psychologist right now,' said Dan as they made their way out of the hospital. 'He looked shellshocked.'

'I think it was a first for him to be faced with something like that. He didn't look old enough to have been in the job more than a couple of years. Let's face it, we've been doing our jobs for God knows how many years, and this is the first time we've encountered something as extreme as this.'

'I took the chance to get an update from the team, before it all kicked off in there,' said Dan.

'Anything to report?'

'Not yet; mostly waiting for people to get back to them.'

'In that case, let's pay a visit to the wetland centre and take a look at the area where Tabitha and the boy were discovered.' It was one thing having a second-hand report, and quite another seeing things for yourself and getting a feel for the place. 'You ever been there?'

'Course I have. Go there quite often on my days off. Great place to take Harry. Get him interested in wildlife. Caroline enjoys it too. It's a cheap trip out. Pack a flask and a few sarnies. Most of the trails are buggy friendly. When Harry was really little we'd stick him in there and he'd fall asleep a treat. Allowed us to get some exercise and fresh air, and it's usually fairly quiet there.'

'You know the area well, then?'

'Some parts better than others. There're so many different trails. I doubt that me and Caro have explored all of it.'

Jemima wasn't surprised by Dan's response. Over the years she had listened on many occasions as he surprised her with obscure facts about nature. She recalled being shocked at his knowledge of peacocks which he'd relayed to her when they'd been startled by one at a previous crime scene. Until that moment, she hadn't appreciated that there was more than one species of the bird. But Dan had soon put her right on that.

'Since you're familiar with the wetland area, have you any idea where Tabitha and the boy might have walked from before they were spotted by the birdwatchers?'

'Not really. Once we get there, you'll see for yourself how large an area it is. It's a huge expanse, bordered to the south by the Severn Estuary and to the west by the River Usk, but there're so many ways you can access it by land. We'll reach it via a lane. Well, it's a road really, but narrow in places and twisty. So promise me you won't drive too fast.'

Jemima could hear the anxiety in Dan's voice. They had been partners for years, and she knew that he hated the fact that she had a tendency to drive fast. Not that she was ever reckless behind the wheel. They'd only ever had one collision when she'd been driving and that had not been her fault. They'd both come out of it with minor injuries, but it had resulted in catastrophic consequences for the case they'd been working. With Dan trapped in the front passenger seat and Jemima momentarily losing consciousness, a prisoner they were transporting to the station managed to escape from the vehicle and went on to do monstrous things to a family. When Jemima and Dan had eventually tracked him down, the confrontation had resulted in Dan almost losing his life, and Jemima being seriously injured.

'Chill your beans, Dan.' It was an expression Jemima had picked up from her other half, Mason. 'I'm more zen these days. I'm not the speed freak I used to be. Got far too much to lose now, what with the kids and Mason.'

'Umm.' Dan fixed his seat belt in place and said a silent prayer. He had to admit that since returning from maternity leave, she'd taken less chances behind the wheel. But he knew from personal experience that the roads leading to the wetlands weren't the easiest to navigate.

'Tell me more about the wetlands,' said Jemima as they set off from the hospital car park.

'Not much to tell. It was set up in 2000, to mitigate the effects of the Cardiff Bay barrage. It's a relatively remote area. Understandably so, as it's a nature reserve. The main visitor access is via the car park. There are purpose-built tracks that criss-cross the marshland. But apart from that you can access the area across fields and lanes. If you continued down the road from the car park you'd get to an industrial area. Right ugly place.'

'The report said that Tabitha and the boy collapsed near a bird hide. Do you know where that is?'

Dan laughed at her lack of understanding. 'Not without asking. There are quite a few of them.' He'd learned over the years that despite her obvious intelligence, Jemima had little understanding of the natural world. It wasn't that she disliked animals. It was more that her time was taken up with problems and situations of a human nature.

'Never mind. We've got a presence there, so I guess they'll point us in the right direction.'

They eventually reached the car park without any mishaps. Yet despite having driven carefully, Jemima still noticed her sergeant breathe a sigh of relief. She shook her head in despair. It seemed that no amount of reassurance would ever convince Dan that she was a safe driver.

They had passed various information signs stating that for an indeterminate period, the nature reserve was closed to members of the public. Though, with no reason specified, it was apparent that members of the RSPB and other people who just fancied a day out were taking little notice. Having spoken to the uniformed officer posted at the entrance to the car park, it seemed that he was fed up with having to listen to people complain as he turned them away. Not that there was much available space for visitors to park, as the area was full of police and the forensic service vehicles.

'Word is they're fighting a losing battle to keep a lid on things,' said the officer. 'It's quietened down a bit now. But earlier on you had more chance of spotting a drone hovering up there than any birds. There are too many potential access points to cover, and everyone from the press to the public has a drone these days.'

'Should ban the things. They're an absolute menace. They had better not have harmed any birds with those bloody devices,' said Dan.

The officer gave a quick explanation of where Tabitha and the child had been found. Though, as this was her first visit to the site, it meant nothing to Jemima. But Dan seemed to know where the location was and set off at a quick march. It was the most invigorated she'd seen him in weeks.

Leaving the car park behind them they took a right. They passed the visitor centre and children's playground on their left and headed up a short slope, gravel crunching under their feet. Moments later they'd reached the true nature reserve where paths headed in all directions.

'Where now?' asked Jemima.

'Off to the left.'

The path was flat, and Jemima soon spotted an information board, set sufficiently low to enable both adults and children to read it. Being familiar with the reserve, Dan paid no attention to the board and continued along the path. Jemima slowed and quickly glanced at it. It displayed a few pictures of insects and birds, together with textual descriptions of what they were in both English and Welsh. Determined not to allow herself to become distracted again, she sped up until she walked alongside Dan.

'Nice place for you to bring the kids,' he said.

'Not when there's a bloody sadist on the loose in the area, kidnapping women and children.'

'Fair point,' said Dan. 'Better tell Caro not to bring Harry over this way until we've got the bastard locked up.'

'Is that a lighthouse over there?' asked Jemima. She pointed to the right.

'Yeah. It's only small. It's located in the reserve. One of the paths takes you right up to it.

'Look Jem, I don't know what you think we're going to find out here, but believe me, this really is a needle in the haystack environment. If you ask me the forensics team will be on a hiding to nothing. So don't go getting your hopes up.'

'I know we're unlikely to find anything. But you're familiar with the place and I'm not. Terrain like this is out of my comfort zone, so I just want to get some sort of feel for the area. Walk the path in the direction they came from. You never know, as unlikely as it is, something we see might just break this case open.'

'Fair enough.'

'I hope you've been taking note of the route we've taken, because I'll never remember the way back to the car. And I've no intention of being stuck out in the wilds overnight.'

Dan laughed. 'It's not difficult to navigate your way around here.'

'I'll take your word for it,' said Jemima, as they set off along another path, which led them into an area of trees.

'Not far to go now,' said Dan.

Moments later a purpose-built wooden structure became visible, and beyond that the low murmur of voices could be heard. 'This is the place,' said Dan.

Up ahead were a group of forensics officers, recognizable by their white coveralls and overshoes.

'Jem, Dan! We meet again. It's good to see you.' The woman who greeted them was Jeanne Ennersley, who they had worked with on many of their cases. Jeanne was an experienced forensics scientist, and Jemima was confident in both her ability and professionalism.

'Wasn't expecting to see you here,' said Jemima.

'Not my usual area, but given the size of the place, and the fact that I'm one of the most experienced officers in this part of the country, they called me in. Makes quite a change, working out in the open like this, and not a dead body in sight. Have to say, I'm making the most of working out in the fresh air. Plus, it helps that it's not raining.' Jeanne smiled.

They chatted for a few minutes, and with the pleasantries out of the way it was back to business. 'Found anything so far?' asked Jemima.

'No, and I don't think we will. This is where the woman collapsed. The twitchers were in that hide,' she indicated the structure they had just passed. 'We know they followed the path but given the fact that we're out in the wilds and, as I understand it, both victims were wearing next to nothing, and neither of them had shoes, there's little for us to go on.'

'Just as I thought,' said Dan, nodding his head. His expression was smug.

'But the woman was miscarrying,' said Jemima.

'So I was told. All I can say is that there was evidence of it for about ten yards, but nothing before that. As far as I can ascertain, she didn't start miscarrying until a few minutes before she collapsed. And the blood trail was only visible on this path, and then very sparse. It's a natural surface, so it would have soaked into the ground,' said Jeanne. 'I'd say we're on a hiding to nothing. It's not as though any clothes would have got snagged on bushes, and given the size of this place, and the fact that they could have come from any direction, we're unlikely to turn up anything of significance. Best I can say is that we'll give it until the light fades. After that, there's no point in us being here.'

Jemima went to protest, but Jeanne interjected before the words had a chance to form. 'Sorry Jem. It's my call, and my decision's final. I refuse to spend any more time out here, when there are places where I know we can add value and make a real difference.'

Common sense told Jemima that Jeanne's assessment of the situation was an accurate one. Dan had more or less said the same thing earlier on. Blind optimism had encouraged Jemima to think that they might just come across an elusive piece of evidence which would break the case open, and they would head quickly towards a successful resolution. Yet, realistically, she had known that was never about to happen.

'We'd better get ourselves back to the station,' Jemima said, as she turned to leave.

CHAPTER 5

As Jemima drove home that evening, she could feel the weight of responsibility lift from her shoulders with each passing mile. She was grateful to put some physical distance between herself and work. Eager to spend some quality time with her boys and Mason. Having finally reached a stage in her personal life where she had everything she wanted and more, she found it a wrench to have to leave it all behind whenever she went on shift. And witnessing first-hand the damage done to the young boy, whose name they were yet to ascertain, made her long to sweep her own boys up into her arms and hold them both tightly.

In addition to being blessed with two wonderful boys, Jemima had finally found a man she was happy to spend her life with. On the face of it, Mason and Jemima were an unlikely pairing: a vicar and an atheist detective. Their paths had first crossed a couple of years ago when the body of a young woman was found inside St Agnes' church, Leighton Meadow. Jemima and her son James had recently moved to the village to live with Jemima's sister, Lucy. She'd found Father Mason Roy something of an enigma; his mysterious past, dashing good looks and Canadian accent set him apart from those who had lived in the Vale of Glamorgan all their lives.

Selecting Mason's number on the handsfree setting, Jemima briefly heard the ringtone before her call was answered.

'Hi there. How's it going?' Mason's accent never ceased to relax her.

'Just letting you know I'm on my way home. Should be with you in about twenty minutes.'

'Great timing. Dinner's cooking. The boys have already eaten at your sister's. I've invited Lucy and Ellis around for dinner, so they'll bring the boys with them.'

Jemima and Mason had started out as friends, long before their relationship developed into something deeper, though village gossipmongers would insist that this was not the case. But when Jemima and the boys moved into the vicarage, it had been a purely practical arrangement. Lucy's husband Ellis, who was a cameraman, was away for much of the time. However, when a work-related accident put him out of action, he had returned home, and despite nothing being said, Jemima felt as though they had outstayed their welcome.

It had not been an option to return to the house she and her estranged husband Nick had bought together so many years ago. After Nick had his meltdown and abandoned them, she had continued to live there with James — the son Nick had once believed to be his flesh and blood, the child she had adopted with that understanding. It had been a logistical nightmare being a single parent in a job with unpredictable hours — Jemima's sister and father had had to pick up the slack. Lucy had Eloise to rely upon, but it was problematic for their father, Donald Goodman; Celia, Jemima's mother, a narcissist, was openly hostile to any family member helping her daughter.

Things had come to a head after Jemima was raped and found herself pregnant with Finlay. As her mother, it was reasonable to expect Celia to have been supportive. But it quickly became apparent that Celia had treated and continued to treat Jemima badly. It was insidious emotional abuse which had gone on from the time Jemima was small, but which Celia had explained away as having to discipline a naughty child.

Jemima, who had a degree in psychology, had undergone months of counselling, as she had regularly resorted to self-harming, which had almost cost her her job. She had once thought that her self-loathing was a result of her apparent inability to become pregnant. She was shocked when she finally began to understand that her mother was a narcissist who had made Jemima's entire life a living hell.

Donald Goodman's eyes had finally been opened to the awful reality that his wife was not the woman he had believed her to be. Celia's attitude disgusted him, and as far as he was concerned there was no coming back from this. He could no longer look at his wife in the same way, as her actions suggested that the woman was a monster. He was determined to be there to support Jemima, and could only do that without having Celia in his life. The decision was made, and he had filed for divorce.

The temporary move to Lucy's home in Leighton Meadow had continued for longer than Jemima had first anticipated. The sisters got on well with each other, and James enjoyed being part of a large family unit, bigging it up with his younger cousins who doted on him. Having a support network around her had helped Jemima cope with what had happened. And though Lucy and Donald had both thought Jemima's decision to keep a baby conceived under such awful circumstances to be strange, they had kept those thoughts to themselves and had supported her every step of the way.

In the meantime, Jemima had rented out her former home. She had no idea where Nick was. His actions in those final days they had spent together had been shockingly out of character. Or perhaps, as she had reflected, over the coming months, and years, she had not known her husband's true character at all. But as the house was in both of their names, and there was still a mortgage to be paid, the only viable option appeared to be for her to rent it out. Jemima set up a savings account into which she paid half the monthly profit after all expenses had been taken care of. If Nick were to ever return, she didn't want him to accuse her of taking money which was rightfully his.

Whenever she cast her mind back to her first encounter with Mason, Jemima found it surprising that they went on to become such firm friends, and latterly so much more. It wasn't that he had ever been objectionable. It was entirely because Jemima was so wary of the concept of religion. Though with the passage of time, it became apparent that despite their obvious differences, they got on like a house on fire. They bonded over a discovery that they liked the same music and shared a similar sense of humour. Indeed, it wasn't unusual in private for the pair of them to act like a couple of teenagers when they were away from prying eyes. Most likely a kickback from the pressures of demanding careers. But it was friendship, first and foremost, which made their relationship special. They were yin and yang. Two sides of the same coin.

* * *

As Jemima opened the door her nostrils filled with a mouth-watering aroma. In recent months Mason and Ellis had discovered a shared passion for Asian food, which had soon morphed into a friendly rivalry. As such, they took it in turns to cook dinner once a week and were always trying to outdo each other's culinary skills. But despite their competitive natures, they got along like a house on fire. Which was good, considering they were practically family.

'What's for dinner?' asked Jemima, as she walked into the kitchen and wrapped her arms around Mason.

'Chicken jalfrezi.'

'Smells delicious.'

Vehicle headlights panned the glass panel inset in the front door.

'That'll be your sister and the others,' said Mason. 'She messaged me about five minutes ago to say they were on their way.'

The evening was a welcome respite to the troubles of the day. Before they sat down to eat, Jemima got to read Finlay a bedtime story until he fell asleep. It saddened her that she didn't get to spend as much time as she would like with him. It was the curse of every working parent.

James was allowed to join the adults as he claimed that he was still hungry. He sat next to Mason, whom he adored, and chatted with everyone as they ate their food. Once dinner was over, he headed upstairs to bed, leaving the adults to it.

'Dad's divorce has come through,' said Lucy.

'About time. He's better off without her. We all are,' said Jemima.

'Absolutely. Hey, have you filed for divorce yet?'

'Keep meaning to. But I've no idea where Nick is. I haven't seen or heard from him in years.'

'I could help you locate him if you like,' said Mason.

'You'd do that?' Jemima raised her eyebrows, surprised at her partner's offer.

'Of course I would. I haven't mentioned it before as I didn't want to push you into anything you weren't ready for. But it seems to me that your marriage was over a long time ago.'

'James asked me the other day why you hadn't divorced his dad yet,' said Ellis.

'He did?' Both Jemima and Lucy uttered this in unison.

'Yeah. He knew your parents were getting divorced and said that he thought it was time you did the same. From what he told me, I think he's keen for you to get on with it, so that there's no chance of Nick returning to try to wheedle his way back into your lives.'

'I had no idea James felt that way,' said Jemima. 'Guess I should have spoken to him about it before now.'

'You're just protective of him,' said Lucy. 'But he's growing up fast, and he's settled now. He's happy.'

'I'll give Mason a hand with tracking him down,' said Ellis. 'Never liked Nick as a brother-in-law. James is right. It's time to get rid.'

CHAPTER 6

When she eventually went to bed, Jemima found it difficult to fall asleep. It seemed that however hard she tried, she couldn't get the image of that terrified little boy out of her mind. And when, after hours of tossing and turning, she eventually managed to fall asleep, her dreams were haunted by his screams, though his facial features morphed to become her beloved boys James and Finlay.

Over the years, Jemima had learned that it was counterproductive to become personally involved with any victim of a crime she was investigating; she had to harden her heart to do her job. Her chosen career often forced her to confront things most people would wish not to encounter, and she knew that if she was going to get to the bottom of what had happened to Tabitha and the boy, she would have to dig deep to keep her emotions at bay. But she also appreciated that she needed to establish that he had calmed down and was improving, if she were to stand any chance of putting those upsetting images aside and get on with doing her job.

That morning, as she pulled off the drive, she headed for the hospital instead of the police station. The first stop was to check on Tabitha, where Jemima immediately spotted the officer charged with guarding her asleep in a chair outside the

43

single room. The corridor was empty apart from this sleeping numpty, who was as much use as a cardboard cut-out. She appreciated that being tasked to guard a door in a hospital was boring. But it was essential to overcome that feeling and take the job seriously. After all, it was possible that a person's life depended on the vigilance of whoever was assigned to protect them. This uniformed officer was on shift and was certainly not being paid to sleep when he was on duty.

Jemima homed in on her target like an Exocet missile. Her rapid steps sounded loud in the quiet corridor — that should have alerted the officer of a potential threat. Yet his legs were stretched out, crossed at the ankles. Arms folded, and head tilted to the side. As Jemima was about to make her presence known, he snorted loudly. It was the final straw. This useless excuse for an officer wouldn't make the same mistake again. She'd have his guts for garters.

Bending down so that her mouth was inches from his ear she readied herself for his inevitable reaction. 'Wake up!' As she barked the order, she shoved his shoulder hard.

A snort of surprise strangulated with a squeal. The constable's eyes opened wide. Clearly discombobulated, he struggled to remain seated. There was a real danger he was about to fall off the chair. 'What the hell?' As he came to his senses he stared at her in surprise.

Jemima had taken a step backwards, and stood there, hands on hips, her eyes like laser beams.

The officer struggled to his feet. 'Lady, you're in so much trouble. You've just assaulted a police officer. I'll have you up in court for that.'

'I'll have your badge first, sunshine. Sleeping on duty! How dare you! You're an absolute disgrace to the force.'

'You can't,' interjected the officer, who suddenly looked wide awake. His complexion had reddened, and with feet now firmly on the floor he squared his shoulders, ready for an altercation.

'Shut it, you muppet!' growled Jemima. She shoved her warrant card in his face, so that there would be no doubt in this moron's mind that he should just back down and take what was coming to him. 'I'm SIO on this case. Chief Inspector Huxley to you. You've been tasked with guarding a victim and from what I've just witnessed, you've really messed up. Falling asleep on the job? Seriously?'

'Sorry, ma'am, but believe me I hadn't long dropped off. You've no idea how hard it is to stay awake in a place like this. It's so hot, and apart from the nurses coming around every so often there's nothing to focus on. The combination of boredom and heat's a killer.'

'Save it, Constable. I'm not interested in excuses. Tabitha Leysham . . .' As she said the name, Jemima saw no recognition in the officer's eyes. 'For God's sake, man, Tabitha Leysham's the person you're supposed to be guarding. The woman lying helpless in that room. I hope for your sake that nothing's happened to her while you've been snoring your head off!'

The officer had no defence to offer. He'd been caught bang to rights. Hanging his head in shame he resentfully muttered an apology. Being antagonistic wouldn't get him anywhere. He tried his best to sound contrite, but it was all he could do to keep the surliness from his voice. 'Sorry ma'am. Not my finest moment. It won't happen again.'

Jemima knew that the apology wasn't sincere, but it would have to do. With a busy day ahead of her, she needed to check on Tabitha and the boy before pushing the investigation forward. Every wasted second was an opportunity for whoever was behind Tabitha's abduction, and the subsequent mistreatment of both her and the boy, to find his former captives and make them pay for their daring escape. 'I've got my eye on you, Constable. Don't mess up again.'

As she uttered this warning, a nurse appeared in the corridor and headed towards Tabitha's room. Jemima waited for the constable to challenge her, but when he didn't, she stepped directly in front of the door, blocking the woman's path. 'I need to check your identification.' The nurse's eyebrows raised, surprised she'd been asked.

'Constable, your list of nursing staff in attendance, please.' Jemima held out her hand, sighing heavily as the young man fumbled with the paperwork he'd been given at the start of his shift. Jemima checked the nurse's photo ID against the list. The photograph matched the person standing in front of her, the name was on the list of hospital personnel, and the pass looked to be the genuine article.

'After you,' said Jemima, as she stood aside to allow the nurse to enter the room.' Turning momentarily to face the constable she uttered her final warning. 'Are you on work experience? Because you don't seem to know the basics. From what I've seen, you're as much use as a chocolate teapot.

'Sorry about that,' said Jemima, as she stepped inside the room, which seemed even smaller given the amount of equipment surrounding the head of the bed.

'It's fine. Reassuring, I suppose. If I was in that bed, I'd want someone to look out for me,' said the nurse.

'How's she doing?'

'Took a turn for the worse in the early hours. She developed an infection. Her temperature spiked. Caused her to convulse. We've got her on a strong course of antibiotics. We'll know more in the next twenty-four hours. But she's young and obviously a fighter, so fingers crossed.'

'Did her parents come to see her?'

'Her mother did. Not that she would have known about it. She was out cold, and her mother was very upset. Wanted to stay the night. We had quite the battle, insisting that she had to leave. Told her to come back after lunch.'

'So she hasn't said anything?' Jemima knew it was wishful thinking.

'No. She's been out of it since they brought her in.'

Jemima gave Tabitha Leysham a final glance before leaving the room. She swallowed hard as her breath caught in her throat. The young woman, who was nothing but skin and bones, had undoubtedly faced sustained abuse. It was heartbreaking to see her so vulnerable and sickening to know that the force had seen fit to task a useless dimwit to stand guard over her, when there was a very real possibility that someone out there posed a threat to her life.

'When's your replacement due?' asked Jemima, as she stepped back out into the corridor.

The constable cleared his throat. His tone was sheepish when he replied. 'Five minutes, ma'am.'

'Good. I'll wait. What's your name?'

'Kyle Acres.' The sense of alarm was immediately apparent in his voice. 'I've learned my lesson, ma'am.'

'Save it, Acres, I'm not interested.'

PC Acres stood there helplessly as Jemima called the station and reported him to his shift commander. She didn't mince her words as she explained that she wanted him as far away from the hospital as possible, and that whoever was sent to replace him had better be someone who carried out their duties with professionalism.

When she finished the call, her attention returned to PC Acres. 'Get yourself home, Acres. I'll remain here until your relief arrives. When I find the time later today, I'll be filing an official complaint about you. In the meantime, it might be wise to contact your union rep, because I've no intention of letting this matter drop. As far as I'm concerned there's no place on any force for such incompetence and downright dereliction of duty.'

Jemima kept the list of authorized hospital personnel to enable her to hand over to the replacement protection officer. It was worryingly frustrating that so many serving officers lacked basic skills, motivation and commitment. Police forces up and down the land were mired in controversy. So much so that it was no longer an unusual occurrence to hear reports of thuggish, even criminal behaviour, carried out by people who were employed to uphold standards, protect the public, and ensure that the geographical area for which they had responsibility, was a safer place.

It didn't bode well.

CHAPTER 7

Despite leaving early for work, Jemima arrived at the incident room almost half an hour later than she'd anticipated. It was fortunate that the replacement officer sent to guard Tabitha had seemed far more clued up than Acres, but Jemima still had doubts that if push came to shove, he'd be up to the job. She'd spoken at length to him, explaining how vital a role he was playing, and just hoped that he'd taken her warning seriously.

The unanticipated delay meant that she had no time to spend with the boy. Instead, she had a quick word with the ward staff, who assured her that he was calm, though still reluctant to engage with the other children on the ward. He'd shown no inclination to speak to the nursing staff, but he was happy enough to eat all the food that was placed in front of him.

* * *

Upon reaching the station, Jemima raced up the stairs to find her team hard at it. 'Sorry I'm late. Called in at the hospital. Tabitha took a turn for the worse overnight, but she's improving now. How are things going here?'

'First off, we drew a blank with the drone search of the wetlands,' said Gareth.

'So we're certain that the boy's mother isn't out there?' asked Jemima.

'As certain as we can be. There's always the chance that a body could have gone into the water and become tangled up with the reeds. Though as far as we could tell there was nothing obvious out there. Oh, and we have the case file from the original investigation into Tabitha's disappearance,' said Gareth.

'Anything useful?'

'Just started going through it. Though my initial assessment is that I'm surprised that given the fact she has a high-profile father, the case notes are pretty thin on the ground.'

'Anything we can immediately run with?'

'There's a statement from' — Gareth glanced at the notes he'd made — 'Audrina Fleishman. She was Tabitha's best friend.'

'Funny that the Leyshams didn't mention her yesterday,' said Jemima.

'Ah, I've done a bit of digging this morning,' said Dan. 'Seems Audrina isn't so squeaky clean. Had a caution for shoplifting, and there's two counts of possession. Got caught puffing a spliff. On one of those occasions, she was at a party-cum-orgy, half-naked with a group of other youngsters, including Tabitha. Blood tests showed they were all under the influence, plus pissed as farts. Neighbours called the cops when the music kept playing in the early hours.'

'I'm sure the background check on Tabitha didn't show up any caution or minor convictions,' said Jemima.

'Well, she was definitely mentioned along with her friends in the police report. Not a huge leap to presume Daddy's got clout. A few backhanders and nods to the right people. Keep the family honour intact and give some higher-ups on the force a gong,' said Gareth.

'It's the way this country works,' sighed Mack.

'You're not wrong there, mate,' said Dan.

'Less of the politics. We need to focus. Did you find anything useful in Audrina's statement?' pressed Jemima.

'Not really. Apart from a brief mention that Tabitha was infatuated with Didier Fontaine, the chat show host, apparently.'

'That's not unusual; he's quite a looker,' said Jemima.

Everyone stared at Jemima in surprise. It was the first time she'd ever made such a comment about anyone. Seeing their collective surprise, she thought she'd better clarify her comment.

'I've not seen Fontaine. Chat shows aren't my thing. My sister had a thing for him. Said he was drop dead gorgeous with a voice that made her want to . . .' Suddenly embarrassed at betraying Lucy's confidence, Jemima cleared her throat. 'Well, I don't need to spell it out.'

'Okaaay, now where was I?' continued Gareth. 'What I meant, Guv, was that the girls knew him personally — they met him at a charity fundraiser, held at Tabitha's family home. According to Audrina, Tabitha was head over heels. Case file shows that Fontaine was interviewed at the time of her disappearance but discounted as a suspect. It's all a bit sketchy. No real details.'

'In that case, Dan and I need to speak to Audrina and Fontaine. Do we have contact details for them?'

'Yeah, I'll give them a call and make the arrangements,' said Gareth.

'Great work, guys.' Jemima smiled as she complimented her team. She knew how fortunate she was to have such capable officers on her side. They had a varied skillset and a similar mindset to her. Each one was prepared to put in the effort to get the job done.

'Nancy, did you establish whether any young boys went missing in the area in the last year or so?'

'As far as I can tell there were three, but we can discount two. Isaac Abimbola lived locally. Disappeared without trace. He's the right sort of age for our child, but of Nigerian heritage so the wrong ethnicity. Oliver Jones was six when he disappeared, but he had Down's syndrome, so not our boy. But Caleb Porter's a contender. Went missing eighteen months ago, just shy of his seventh birthday. Walking home from school with an older sibling, who got distracted by some friends. In a matter of minutes there was no sign of Caleb. It was a high-profile case at the time. They pulled out all the stops. More than a hundred interviews. All sorts of media coverage and appeals for witnesses to come forward. Even had a so-called psychic trying to cash in, claiming that the boy had been killed and dumped in the lake at a local beauty spot. Her claim came to nothing. Police divers were there for a few days, but they found nothing except a couple of dead dogs and some submerged vehicles.'

'Might be our boy,' said Jemima. It was something that could be ruled in or out with a DNA test. Something which if the result went their way could make the Porter family very happy. 'Have you contacted the family yet?'

'Not yet. Neighbours confirmed they're on holiday. Due back tomorrow, so it's on the backburner until then, but I'll be on it as soon as.'

'Guv, just arranged for you and Dan to interview Audrina Fleishman. When I told her it was about Tabitha she was very keen to speak to you. She's renting a place in the Forest of Dean and will be there all morning.'

* * *

It took less than an hour to reach Audrina Fleishman's bedsit in Newent,

which was in a less salubrious part of town, where some rooms were rented out above a fish and chip shop. There was a separate entrance for the living quarters, with a buzzer system for the three tenants.

'Bit of a comedown for someone who was privately educated,' said Dan, as he pressed the buzzer.

'Understatement of the year,' said Jemima.

The intercom crackled, as Audrina answered. As Gareth had already given her their names, she informed them that she'd come straight down.

Audrina Fleishman was tall and willowy, with flowing auburn wavy hair and delicate features. Her accent marked her out as privileged, though the tattoo visible above her inner wrist together with the stud embedded in her tongue signalled a rebellious streak.

'You can buy me a double-shot caramel macchiato. Costa's a five-minute walk away, and I think more clearly when I've had my caffeine fix.' She stepped on to the pavement and shut the door behind her. 'Believe me, you don't want to spend any time at my place. It's too small for one person, let alone three, and it smells of fish and fat.' It seemed like the best option as the stale smell of the previous night's endeavours still hung in the air.

Jemima fell into step with Audrina, while Dan walked behind.

'Bit of a comedown for someone with my start in life,' said Audrina.

'I guess it must be.'

'I've blown it with my folks. They don't want to know. Come to think of it, I seem to have made a hash of every relationship I've had. But hey, at least I've got my independence. So I can still be me, even if I have to work two jobs to keep my head above water.'

Jemima said nothing. As they approached Costa, she fished out a twenty-pound note and handed it to Dan. 'Get the coffees out of this. Mine's a latte.'

Audrina was the first through the coffee shop door. She quickly scanned the room and selected a vacant table near the window. 'This all right?' she asked. She pulled out a chair and sat down without waiting for an answer.

Updating Audrina in the vaguest of terms about Tabitha's reappearance, Jemima got down to the reason they were there. 'Tabitha's in a bad way. As things stand, we're unable to question her, and have real concerns that whoever was responsible for her disappearance and presumably held her captive for all these years might still pose a threat to her should he discover her whereabouts.'

'So you've no idea who abducted Tabs?'

'None. That's why we need your help.'

'You've got it. Anything. She was my best friend.'

'Tell us about Tabitha in the weeks leading up to her disappearance.'

'I gave a statement at the time, but on reflection perhaps I wasn't clear enough. Tabs was acting cagey in those last few days. I've thought about it a lot over the years. Wondering if I'd missed some vital clue which could have led to you lot finding her.

'Back then, we were wild. Wanted to live life to the full. Experience things while we had the chance. Nothing was off limits, and I mean nothing. Drink, drugs, wild sex. We did the lot. Pissed off our parents, big time. Happy days.'

'Not so happy for Tabitha, given what happened to her,' muttered Dan. It was obvious from his tone that he disapproved of Audrina's previously feckless lifestyle.

Jemima shot her sergeant a warning look. They had come there to get Audrina to open up. Reveal things about Tabitha which until now she might have kept quiet about. There was a real possibility that Dan allowing his mouth to run away with itself could make Audrina clam up altogether. She needed to keep the young woman onside. 'Would you like another cup, Audrina?'

'No, haven't got time. I'll have to get going soon. My shift starts in twenty-five minutes, and I mustn't be late. Need the job to pay the bills.'

'Dan, go check on the car, and while you're at it, call Gareth for an update,' ordered Jemima. She wanted him out of the way. With only a few minutes left before Audrina set off for work, she was determined to make the time count.

Dan stood up and stretched. As he did so his shirt moved upwards revealing a section of his hairy paunch. Retrieving his jacket from the back of the chair he muttered goodbye and went on his way.

'Men, eh?' Jemima rolled her eyes in mock despair.

'Can't live with them. Can't live without them,' said Audrina.

'Do you recall any special man in Tabitha's life around the time of her disappearance?'

'She was soft on that Didier Fontaine. We met him at her parents' house. At one of their parties. He was at least fifteen years older than us. Charming. Sophisticated. Famous and drop dead gorgeous. Tabs was all over him, made it obvious she was up for it. He was polite, but awkward about it — clearly didn't want to offend her. Or her parents. But he was uncomfortable. I felt sorry for the guy. He was trying to work the room, with Tabs following him around like a love-struck puppy.'

'So he wasn't interested in her?' pressed Jemima.

'Tabs thought she was in with a chance, but she was deluded. I got the impression he was getting annoyed with her but knew better than to draw attention to it. He posed for a photograph with her. Whispered something in her ear, and she backed off. Gave him some space. She kept showing that photograph off for the next few weeks. Making out that they were going to meet up. Like that was ever going to happen. It was sad really. All in her head. She didn't want Didier for Didier. Knew nothing about him. Just wanted him for his celebrity status. A kudos thing.' Audrina sighed and shook her head. There was a wistful look in her eyes. 'If I could go back in time, I'd have made her see sense. She was a fantasist. I'd have done anything not to lose her in such a cruel manner.'

'Do you think Fontaine was responsible for Tabitha's disappearance?'

'I thought he might have been at the time. I even told the police that. After that party Tabs was all Didier this, Didier that. It was the first time she'd ever really fallen for someone, and she fell hard.'

'And there was no jealous boyfriend on the scene?'

'No. The lads we hung about with were like us. Out for a laugh. No commitments.'

Jemima thanked Audrina for her time and promised to keep her informed about Tabitha's progress. She sighed as she watched the young woman weave her way out of the coffee shop. Was it just wishful thinking that their investigation could uncover anything new? *Wake up, Tabitha*, she thought. *You're the only witness who can help us now.*

CHAPTER 8

As Jemima rounded the corner, she spotted Dan leaning against the car, staring up at the sky. She glanced upwards to see what had caught his attention and spotted a couple of large birds, the smaller of which appeared to be playing tag with the larger one.

'Why are you watching seagulls?' she asked.

'Seriously? They're not seagulls. They're kestrels. It's a mother and her young. An early outing. She's giving it a lesson. Making sure it comes to no harm.'

'If you say so,' said Jemima. She had never understood Dan's fascination with birds.

'Sorry about earlier. Should've kept my mouth shut,' he said.

'You're going to have to work on that if you want to move up the ranks. It's not wise to show your true feelings. It's all about putting on a performance. Adapting to circumstances to get the information you need. Being overtly judgemental will inevitably be counterproductive.'

'I know. It's just sometimes I can't help myself. I mean, how can someone with all those advantages throw it all away and end up on a race to the bottom?'

'Takes all sorts, Dan. And you have to admire the fact that she appears to be doing her best to turn her life around now. After all, she's working two jobs.'

'I suppose. But I'm telling you, I'll be damned if I allow Harry to become a waste of space.'

'I'm sure most parents set out with the best of intentions. But never say never. As the saying goes, "*You can lead a horse to water, but you can't make him drink.*" None of us can foretell the future, and kids have minds of their own.'

'Yeah. I don't want to think about that,' sighed Dan. 'Changing the subject, I've spoken to Gareth. He's been in contact with Fontaine. Arranged for us to see him and given me the address. Mind if I drive? I want to calm down before we come face-to-face with a jumped-up self-entitled celebrity.'

Jemima smiled and handed him the keys. She knew that Dan invariably got uptight whenever she was behind the wheel. It would also allow her time to think.

Didier Fontaine's property was set in extensive grounds on the English side of the River Severn. It was immediately apparent that the man valued privacy as the house was hidden from sight behind a high wall. A set of solid electrically operated gates prevented any passer-by from seeing what lay beyond. And when the two officers announced their arrival via an intercom and held their warrant cards up for inspection, a security camera inset into a panel, whirred as it zoomed in to focus on the documentation. Eventually the gates trundled along their respective tracks allowing them to proceed.

As the vehicle came to a halt on the colossal driveway, Dan's attention was focused on the impressive house. However, Jemima's eyes were drawn to a large barn. The outbuilding was at least thirty feet away, and the doors were open. The dark interior was a marked contrast to the daylight. But as she squinted, she realized there were at least five classic cars in view. It was possible there were more and it was obvious that these were expensive vehicles. With all the trappings of a privileged lifestyle on display, it was safe to presume that Fontaine was a man of means. And if he had abducted Tabitha, there were numerous vehicles he could have used. It was something they would need to check out.

Jemima had one leg out of the car when the front door of the property opened and a tall, immaculately dressed man came down the three stone steps to meet them.

'Hello there. I'm Blake Masters, Didier's personal assistant.' His smile was both genuine and dazzling, as he held out his hand to shake hers.

'DCI Huxley and DS Broadbent,' said Jemima.

'Come on inside. Didier's on the phone, but he shouldn't be long. Can I get you both a drink? Tea, breakfast or herbal? Coffee? Or perhaps a juice of some kind?' Blake showed them into a sitting room at the far end of the hallway. They sat at opposite ends of a sofa sufficiently large enough to accommodate at least five people. 'Back in a sec,' he said, then turned and walked swiftly out of the room to get the drinks.

They sat in silence, both gazing out of the bi-fold doors which opened on to an expansive lawn, where a young woman was sitting on a mower, systematically steering it to ensure the grass was cut to perfection. 'That's Julie,' said Blake, as he returned with a tray containing two jugs of juice and four crystal tumblers. 'She's our gardener. Does a fantastic job, and it's not easy given the size of the place. Shall I pour? Or would you prefer to help yourselves?'

Jemima was about to answer when the door opened, and Didier entered the room.

'Hello there, I'm Didier.' His voice was as smooth as chocolate. He, too, offered a hand in greeting. 'Sorry to have kept you waiting. Just trying to calm my sister down. Apparently, she discovered our niece smoking and World War Three broke out when she confronted her. Teenagers, eh?'

With the introductions out of the way, Blake spoke. 'Would you like me to stay?'

'Naturally. We've no secrets,' said Didier. He patted the cushion next to him, on a smaller sofa, and smiled.

Turning his attention back to Jemima and Dan, he continued. 'Now, how can I help you?'

'We're re-examining the Tabitha Ley—'

'Didier was cleared of suspicion at the time,' Blake snapped, sounding upset. 'There was—'

'Blake,' Didier touched his arm. 'Let the officer speak. You don't need to protect me.'

'But it's not—'

'It's fine,' Didier's tone was firm. Placing an arm around Blake's shoulder he turned to Jemima and continued. 'Please forgive my husband, he's very protective of me. So has there been a development in the case?'

'Yes. Tabitha has recently been found,' said Jemima.

'Safe and well, I hope?' said Didier. 'It will be a relief for her parents. So why do you want to speak to me? Surely Tabitha must've told you why she disappeared and where she's been all this time?'

'I wish it was that simple,' said Jemima. 'Tabitha's in a coma. From what we've been able to ascertain it seems likely that she was being held against her will. All we know is that she was found in South Wales, which is quite a distance from where we were led to believe that she disappeared. Given the time that's elapsed and our unfamiliarity with the case, we've very little to go on, which is why we're re-examining the original investigation. Speaking to everyone interviewed at the time. Looking for something which might have been missed.'

'Makes sense.' Didier nodded his understanding. 'But, as I said at the time, I wasn't even in the country when she went missing. It was our wedding three days earlier. We were in Martinique making the most of our extended honeymoon, in a friend's luxurious villa.'

'And this was checked out at the time?'

'I assure you it was. Though, there might not be a record of it on the general file.'

'How so?' asked Dan.

'Let's just say that I called in a personal favour. Even high-profile celebrities such as I have a right to privacy,

Sergeant. But I understand that you will not be able to take my word for it. You'll have to check it out.

'Blake will look out the contact details for the investigating officer who interviewed me at the time. He'll also provide you with the relevant details for our dear friend whose home we stayed at. Give him your email address and he'll start the ball rolling. I'm afraid it's so long ago that I don't recall the officer's name. All I remember is that she was female. Once you speak to her I'm sure she'll be able to verify what I've just said and will undoubtedly let you see the relevant documentation from the time. Though I ask you to be discreet, as there is no reason this information should find its way into the public domain.'

Jemima appreciated that the celebrity world was far-removed from everyday life. High-profile people had expensive lawyers on speed dial. And she could think of no better person to methodically check out Fontaine's claims. Gareth was the soul of discretion. Nothing would get past him, but equally so, she trusted him not to let slip any juicy titbits which could inevitably come back to bite them with a potential lawsuit.

'One last thing, Mr Fontaine: how well did you know Tabitha?'

'I met her only once, and we spoke for less than five minutes. I was a guest at a charity fundraiser at her parent's house. It was one of those dreadful work occasions I'm regularly forced to attend. The truth is I hadn't met the Leyshams before that evening, and I haven't had cause to have any dealings with them since. I'm afraid I couldn't even tell you which charity was being represented.

'My agent at the time would have arranged it; the kind of thing they called a "win–win event".'

'I don't follow,' said Jemima.

'Putting it simply, the hosts benefit by having a celebrity draw. It attracts the right sort of people, that is, those with deep pockets; gives them a photo opportunity. It's an experience. You know, the misnomer "things that money can't buy". Whereas their money absolutely bought the experience as they've paid handsomely to attend.'

'What's the win for you?' asked Dan.

'Apparently it keeps me in vogue. Makes me relevant. Shows that I have a philanthropic nature. It's not enough that I donate a substantial proportion of my income to various charities of my choosing, which I have done for many years and do willingly. You see, it doesn't cut the mustard for someone like me to do good things if no one knows about it. Publicity is everything. So that's the trade-off. I attend an obligatory number of these insufferable events at the behest of my agent. I scrub up, dress up, smile and make nice with a roomful of insufferable bores. Which for some reason seems to keep everyone happy. Apart from me, that is. But apparently that doesn't matter, as it's what the job requires.'

Jemima let Dan drive again while she mulled over their conversation with Didier Fontaine. As a seasoned officer, she believed that she was a good judge of character. Fontaine had had a long and successful career in the entertainment business, and throughout that time details of his private life had remained just that. Private. Which meant that he was good at playing a role. Hiding certain things while making people believe that his professional persona was him in his entirety.

There was no doubt in Jemima's mind that this celebrity was more than capable of pulling off a convincing lie, yet she was inclined to believe that he had told them the truth. After all, he would know that they would check out every detail of the alibi he had given them. And the original investigating officer would have no doubt done the same. By reinvestigating Tabitha Leysham's disappearance, any holes in the original case would be exposed. It was pointless, and even detrimental, for Fontaine to lie to them. For if it came out during their enquiries that he had lied, it could ultimately harm, if not end his lucrative career.

Jemima's phone rang when they had less than a mile to go to reach the station. After finishing the call, she hung up and turned to Dan. 'When we reach the station, you get back to the squad room and find out how things are progressing. I'm

61

off to the hospital. There's been some worrying developments with the boy.'

'He's not taken a turn for the worse?' asked Dan.

Jemima noted the concern in her sergeant's voice. An ill child was every parent's worst nightmare. 'No. At least, not exactly. Apparently, he's started to display some worrying behaviour when he was encouraged to join in a play session with other children.'

'Are you sure you don't want me to come with you?'

'It's best you don't. There's plenty for you to follow up on and we need to keep up the momentum. I just want to go there to observe things for myself. See if I can understand what's going on in his head. He's so obviously traumatized. But perhaps in his own way he's trying to tell us something. Quite possibly something important. Something which, if we can understand what it is he's trying to communicate, could help us identify the monster who's done this to him.'

The member of staff who had phoned Jemima hadn't gone into any detail about what had occurred during the play session. Saying instead that she'd prefer to explain it to Jemima in person. And for the entire journey to the hospital, Jemima's imagination was running wild.

There was sweat glistening on Jemima's brow as she entered the children's ward. In her eagerness to know what had occurred for her to warrant such a call, she had all but jogged along the maze of overly hot corridors.

'Chief Inspector. You made it here exceptionally quickly,' said the nurse. 'We had to take him out of the play area. He's back on his bed for now. Having a sandwich and a carton of milk.'

'You said there was an incident when he was playing with the other children?'

'That's right. Though I wouldn't go as far as to say that he was playing with the other children. More watching them from the sidelines when they were playing board games. We've introduced him to some of the others. He's obviously seen them from a distance when they're all in bed. But I've not come across a child like him. He's very withdrawn. I don't think it's an exaggeration to say that he doesn't seem to know how to play. He hasn't interacted with any of the staff. Other than when he had that extreme reaction when he saw that poor young psychologist. But more worryingly in my opinion, the little mite hasn't made any attempt to join in with the other kids.'

'What exactly was it that caused concern?' asked Jemima, ensuring the frustration she was feeling was conveyed in her voice.

The nurse picked up on the silent reprimand. 'Sorry, I'm waffling. Well, as I said, there were six or seven of them all sat around playing board games. They're very friendly kids. Just happy to spend a bit of time doing normal things, instead of being poked and prodded by the likes of us. Our mystery boy was sitting on the floor, back against the wall, alone. Just watching everything that was going on.

'But everything changed when Jeremiah walked in. He's from the next room along. So, our boy wouldn't have seen him before. Anyway, Jeremiah's about the same sort of age as the others but he's a lot taller than them. At first sight he could easily pass for someone at least three or four years older than he is.'

Jemima sighed and made a show of looking at her watch. 'I'm sorry but could you get to the point?'

'When our lad spots Jeremiah he jumps up, runs over and grabs him. Poor Jerry was scared out of his wits, because our newest arrival was shaking him, screaming the same awful words over and over again. *"Big boys die! Big boys die!"* Jerry's being treated for leukaemia. We put a significant amount of effort into his mental well-being. The last thing he needed was for someone to scare him into believing he's about to die.'

'I imagine Jerry was traumatized.' Jemima shivered at the thought of it. It was easy to picture the chilling scene playing out. Though she could only begin to imagine the confusion and terror the boy must have felt to have a stranger proclaim your death in such a forceful manner.

From the moment Tabitha Leysham and the boy had been discovered, it had been obvious that they had both suffered greatly. And it was becoming clearer by the minute that this so far unidentified child had not only been the victim of physical abuse but was psychologically damaged too.

'Too right he was. Poor little soldier has been so brave. He's suffered so much in his short life, and I've never once heard him complain. We had to prise your lad off him. Left bruises on Jerry's arms, he was gripping him so tight. I dread to think what he's gone through.'

'Can I see him?' asked Jemima. It was one thing being told about the disturbing incident that had taken place. But she wanted to see the boy for herself. Perhaps if she could get him to understand that she was no threat to him, she could win his trust. After all, from what the nurse had just told her, he could clearly talk. 'Big boys die' was both a coherent and worrying statement. Something he'd either heard before or had learned to say. Though whether it was because he had known some older child who had died, or whether it had a far more sinister meaning she had yet to discover. It was easy in Jemima's line of work to always presume the worst. But even a layperson could see that this child was psychologically damaged, and she was determined to find out what was behind this sinister statement.

'Absolutely. It'd be good if someone could get through to him. Understand what's going on inside that head of his. We've tried, but the poor little mite is so withdrawn. It's quite the balancing act with his recovery. We're equipped to deal with his physical injuries. They're the easy ones to diagnose and treat. But as no one knows his background and he's not very communicative, we're out of our depth on that. The bottom line is he's going to need more specialist care to deal with his psychological issues.'

Jemima glanced around as she headed on to the ward. It was apparent that the atmosphere was subdued. For one thing, there was no laughter and very little chatter. Most of the young patients had taken to their beds. Two of the older children lounged on bean bags, each with a book, as they were supposedly reading. Yet it was obvious even to a casual observer that they were using the books as cover, as they were deep in conversation. They spoke in low voices, and on occasion glanced furtively towards the boy's bed.

The boy was sitting up on top of the covers, using pillows to prop him up. His legs were bent. Hands clasped across his shins, to keep them in place as he rested his chin on his knees. Jemima noticed that despite being still, the child wasn't relaxed. His eyes kept darting about as he watched everything that was going on in the room. It was as though he sensed danger and was waiting for the moment when something bad would happen.

As she headed towards him, the boy stiffened. Jemima smiled and stopped, appreciating that he might consider her to be a threat. 'Hello,' she said. Her voice was soft and gentle. It was her *mummy voice*. The way she spoke to Finlay. 'My name's Jemima, but you can call me Jem.' She held out a small chocolate bar, having bought a Cadbury Freddo at the hospital shop. The chocolate was Fin's favourite. 'I got you this. Would you like it?'

The boy stared quizzically at what she was holding, and Jemima sensed that he had no idea what it was. Still standing a few feet away from him, she opened the wrapper to reveal the chocolate. From his continued blank expression it was clear that he still had no idea what it was. Jemima broke off a small piece. 'Tastes good,' she crooned, as she showed it to the child, then placed it in her mouth. 'Yum.' She stuck out her tongue, to show him the melted chocolate. 'Would you like to try some?' she offered the remainder of the bar.

The boy nodded and held out his hand. Jemima stepped forward and handed him the remainder of the bar. He snatched it, cramming the remainder of the chocolate into his mouth as he munched and swallowed it quickly.

'Tastes good?' she asked, as she smiled and nodded.

The boy nodded his approval but made no attempt to speak.

'Is it all right if I sit down?' she asked as she pointed first to herself and then at the chair located at the side of the bed.

The boy nodded once more.

This was progress. He was starting to trust her.

'Jem,' she said, as she placed a hand on her chest. The boy stared at her and she repeated it. As she was about to say it for the third time, there was the sound of footsteps as a visitor entered the ward.

Distracted by the sound the boy turned his attention towards the entrance.

'Mum!' shouted another boy.

'Hello, my darling!' The woman smiled and made a bee-line for her child's bed. Her attention was entirely focused on her son, and as she pulled out a chair, her body turned, so that Jemima and the boy could clearly see that she was heavily pregnant. The unborn child must have kicked at that moment as the woman winced and touched her abdomen.

Without warning, the boy sprang from the bed and rushed towards the pregnant woman. He held out an arm and pointed at her. 'Three strikes, you're out! Three strikes, you're out! Three strikes, you're out!' His voice was shrill. Filled with fear. As urine ran down his leg and splashed on the floor, he kept repeating the phrase over and over until he was completely hysterical and screamed the words.

Jemima watched, aghast at the scene playing out in front of her. She wondered what the hell this poor child had been subjected to before he had been discovered in the wetlands. She had no idea what it was but was convinced that the boy must have witnessed some unimaginable horrors for him to behave in such an extreme manner.

This time there was no calming him down, and for his own good, the boy had to be sedated.

CHAPTER 9

When she returned home that evening, Jemima hugged her boys long and hard. Burying her head in the nape of their necks, she breathed in their innocence. Not wanting to let them go. She was determined to keep them safe, away from harm. Which is what ninety-nine per cent of parents wanted to do. Were the parents of the unnamed boy in the remaining one per cent?

Jemima was so troubled by what she had seen at the hospital that she was compelled to tell Mason about it. Though all he could do was hold her close and offer words of comfort.

That night, Jemima spent hours tossing and turning in bed as she tried to block out thoughts of the unnamed boy. Whichever way she lay, she just couldn't get comfortable. It was a devastating experience to see a child so obviously disturbed and know that there was nothing she could do to prevent or even ease his distress.

With her mind in overdrive, her imagination conjured up all sorts of horrendous scenarios as she tried to explain his worrying behaviour. *'Three strikes, you're out,'* rang in her head. This unnamed boy must have escaped a situation where he had seen things no child should ever witness.

* * *

It had gone midnight when Jemima's thoughts gave way to exhaustion, and she eventually succumbed to sleep. Shortly before 3 a.m. she became vaguely aware of an annoying sound. As she turned over and grabbed the pillow, forcing it against both ears, she discovered that the noise hadn't stopped. It was then that she appreciated that the sound was coming from her phone.

She reached out blindly, patting the surface of the bedside cabinet to locate her mobile. 'Yeah?' Her lips barely moved as she uttered the word. It was all she could manage to say. It was Dan Broadbent.

'Guv? About time. You need to get to the hospital.'

Hearing the urgency in her sergeant's voice was as effective as having a bucket of icy water thrown over her. She was wide awake and searching for her clothes as he spoke.

'What's happened?'

'The duty sergeant's been trying to call you. Someone tried to kill Tabitha but was stopped by a nurse. The officer guarding her is nowhere to be seen.'

'Shit! I'm on my way. I'll see you there.' Jemima tucked her shirt in as she ran across the landing. As she reached the top of the stairs the door to Mason's bedroom opened and he looked out, hair sticking up at odd angles.

'What's up? Everything OK?' He could barely open his eyes.

'I've gotta go. Work emergency. Could you see to the kids for me in the morning? Or let me know if not and I'll call Lucy to see if Eloise will do it. Can't stop.' She was out of the door before he had the chance to reply.

Jemima had the side window down, allowing cool night air to flood the car's interior. The freshness helped her focus as she drove at speed. She felt guilty that she had been too tired to hear her phone ring when the duty sergeant had tried to contact her. As the SIO she was the one that the rest of the team looked to. She was the one who set the standards. And if Superintendent Torsten bloody Olsen got to hear that she had been uncontactable he'd without a doubt make a song and dance about it. Make her feel like she wasn't up to the job.

Jemima pulled up outside the hospital just as a vanload of uniformed officers arrived, ready to help secure the building. Given the serious nature of the incident, the building had been locked down. At the front entrance, a lone hospital security guard stood behind the locked glass door. He was doing his best to exude authority though his voice gave away the fact that he was clearly out of his depth, and wished he was anywhere other than there.

Once she was inside, Jemima raced along the corridors, with the six uniformed officers following her. Two of their number had relieved the security guard of his duty, and the man had eagerly allowed them to take his place.

Jemima reached the ward to discover that she was the last member of her team to arrive. The others were busily taking statements.

When Dan spotted Jemima, he headed in her direction, and asked to speak to her alone. 'Don't worry, I told the others you were in the middle of something and would get here as soon as you were able.' They'd been partners for years and were very protective of each other.

'Thanks, Dan. I owe you.'

Not wanting to waste any time Jemima turned and called for everyone's attention. As her team and the uniformed officers gathered around, she made a start. 'Has anyone checked on the boy? If this man's come after Tabitha, then he could view the kid as being a threat too.'

'It was my first port of call, Guv,' said Gareth. 'They're aware of the seriousness of the threat, and they've got the children's ward locked down. He won't get through those doors. No one is going in or out of that ward without our say-so.'

'Good, but I don't want to take any chances. I want two of you lot outside that ward.' She indicated the uniformed officers. 'If that bastard's still inside this building, he'll think twice about trying to get to the boy. I don't care which two of you go. Sort it out between yourselves but do it quickly.' Not having worked with any of those officers in the past she had to take it on trust that they would be up to the task.

After a few low mutterings, two officers stepped forward. 'Thank you,' said Jemima. 'And keep your wits about you. This isn't a soft option. This man is violent, and I don't want anything to happen to either of you.'

'You can trust us, ma'am,' said one of the officers. 'We won't let you down.' They headed off in the direction of the children's unit.

'Right, what've we got?' This was addressed to her team.

'First off, Tabitha's still alive,' said Dan.

'That's a relief.'

'Yeah, they'd seen an improvement in her condition. She's wired up to various machines, which monitor her vitals, administer fluids and drugs. A nurse checked on her every thirty minutes.'

'OK, sounds reasonable I guess, but how the hell did an intruder get past our guy if he was standing guard outside the room?'

'No idea.'

'Has anyone spoken to him yet?'

'No one knows where he is. Seems to have disappeared off the face of the earth.'

'That doesn't sound good. I hope he's not injured or worse.'

'All we know for sure is that the nurse tasked with undertaking the checks on Tabitha arrived about five minutes early. She noticed that our officer wasn't at his post, thought it strange, but it occurred to her that perhaps he might have needed a comfort break.'

'So why did she arrive early?' asked Jemima.

'Part of the care routine. Additional things to be done every so often, and that was the case for that particular check. She was so focused on what she was doing that she didn't think of looking through the door's glass panel. She walked in to find the intruder holding a pillow over Tabitha's face.

To be honest, if she hadn't turned up when she did, Tabitha would have been done for.'

'Is the nurse badly injured?'

'She'll be OK. Got a broken nose and will have a couple of black eyes. More shaken than anything else. I've spoken to her briefly — she says the attacker was male. She was unconscious for a short while, as he punched her face so hard that her head hit the wall. Her colleagues found her within minutes. The intruder must have appreciated he'd run out of time. As a last resort he ripped out a handful of cables connecting Tabitha to the machines.'

'Sounds like an improvised attempt at killing her, while giving himself a better chance of escaping,' said Mack.

'Sure does,' said Nancy.

'When the connections were broken it set off all sorts of alarms, which alerted staff that something was wrong. Their immediate priority was to stabilize Tabitha, which they managed to do. Then someone called it in.'

'Did you take a statement from the nurse?'

'No, I only spoke to her informally. She was in a right state. About to be treated. I was told to come back after they'd seen to her.'

'Fair enough. So, what do we know about the officer who was guarding Tabitha?' asked Jemima.

'His name's Len Graham. He's from our station. Eleven years' service. There's no way he'd just walk away from his post,' said one of the uniformed officers.

'So, you all know what he looks like?' asked Jemima. Everyone nodded. Jemima had a bad feeling about this. They needed to find Graham as soon as possible. But first, she needed to ensure that she covered all the bases. 'Levi, take one of the uniforms and guard Tabitha. Stay alert. For all we know the intruder could still be on the premises.'

'Sure thing, Guv,' said Levi. He nodded at one of the constables, who joined him.

'Gareth, get yourself off to the security room. They've probably made a start on going through the footage, but I want you to head things up. We don't have a description yet, but we've got a timeframe, and you might just spot someone acting furtively.'

'On it, Guv,' said Gareth, as he headed off to speak to the hospital security staff.

'Nancy, go and speak to the nurse. See if she's up to giving us a description of the attacker and get her to make a statement. She's the best chance we have of getting a detailed description of this man, and we sure as hell need to know what he looks like.'

'As for the rest of us, we'll pair up. My team will take the lead in each case. We're primarily looking for Len Graham. We have to presume he's incapacitated. Until we know otherwise, every second counts to get him the help he needs. Keep your wits about you, and your emotions out of it. Your colleague's life could very well depend on your swift actions and clear thoughts. And once again I'll remind everyone that the intruder could still be inside this building. He's already tried and failed to kill Tabitha. He took a hell of a risk coming here. Which makes him desperate and unpredictable. I don't need to tell you how dangerous he is.'

Jemima elected to search the entire floor on which Tabitha Leysham had been attacked. She had a bad feeling about the fate of PC Graham and was sure that if he had been attacked or worse, she would find him somewhere in the vicinity of Tabitha's room. She couldn't discount the possibility that he had wandered off and left his charge unguarded, but she thought it unlikely. If the constable's disappearance was down to the assailant, he would have wanted to subdue and hide him as quickly as possible. After all, his priorities would have been to kill Tabitha and quite possibly go after the boy. Len Graham would merely have been a hurdle to overcome to enable him to achieve his goal.

She paired up with PC Anne Rowlands and they set off together. Ten minutes later, Jemima came across a partially filled laundry hamper inside a room where cleaning products were stored. It seemed innocuous enough at first, but as she reached in to disturb the linen her hand encountered what was obviously a body.

Anne Rowlands confirmed it was that of Len Graham. The constable's neck had been broken.

CHAPTER 10

The day had got off to the worst possible start. It wasn't even 5 a.m. and the case had gone from a potential abduction and abuse to now include murder. What's more, it was the murder of one of their own. An officer whose life had been snuffed out in the line of duty. What was clear was that the man responsible was brutal, ruthless, and quite prepared to take risks. In other words, they were hunting a psychopath.

It was distressing to leave PC Len Graham in the linen basket, but it was important that nothing was disturbed. It was an undignified end to a good man's life, to be bundled into a container of soiled linen. As upsetting as it was, the last thing any of the officers wanted was for the crime scene to be compromised. The intruder had been forced to improvise to disguise the fact that he had killed a man. And as he would have needed to act quickly, there was every chance that he might have slipped up and left some DNA or other evidence at the scene, which might enable them to discover his identity.

Jeanne Ennersley and her team arrived to process the scene. After undertaking a thorough search of the hospital and finding no evidence of the intruder on site, Jemima arranged for the six uniformed officers to remain to guard Tabitha and the boy.

Jemima and her team headed off to find Gareth, who was watching the hospital security tapes. 'Any progress?'

'It's slow. They're working with a skeleton staff and haven't got spare capacity to help.'

'But you know precisely where the attack took place and you've got a reasonably short timeframe in which it took place.' Jemima's voice failed to mask the frustration they were all experiencing.

'It's not that straightforward, Guv. The security footage only covers communal areas and corridors. The wards and staffing areas are not covered,' said Gareth.

'In that case, Mack and Nancy will give you a hand. I'll get Levi up here as soon as I can too. We've a murdered officer and nothing to go on. The security footage is our only chance of finding the person responsible. If we can find him on those screens, we can try to trace him. There's no sign of him in the building, so he's scarpered. So split your resources. Two of you study the internal footage. Two of you take the externals. As I've said, we've got a rough timeline, which should enable you to find him.'

'Unless he was familiar with the layout of the hospital and knows where the cameras are located,' said Gareth.

'I think there's only a very small chance of that being the case. Everything suggests that Tabitha and the boy escaped from captivity. Which means, this guy is on the back foot. He's panicking about Tabitha revealing his identity and telling everyone what he's done. That's why he tried to silence her once and for all. To do it in such a public place when any number of people could have seen or stopped him, highlights just how desperate he is. He's had to improvise and killed one of us to save his own skin. He's desperate, dangerous and unpredictable.'

After arranging for Levi to join the others, Jemima and Dan returned to the station. They were about to walk into the incident room when her phone rang.

'Detective Chief Inspector Huxley?' It was an unfamiliar voice.

'Yes.'

'I've some news for you. Results have come through on your unknown boy's DNA. We have a match to one Giselle Braverman. She's on the system because she was reported missing seven years ago from the city of Bath. I'll email you our findings.'

'The boy's mother's been identified,' Jemima told Dan as she accessed the Police National Computer files. 'Giselle Braverman.'

'Let's hope she'll be able to tell us what happened to her son,' said Dan.

'Don't get your hopes up. I've a feeling it's not going to be that simple. She's on the database because she went missing from Bath, seven years ago.'

'Another missing woman? And Bath's not far from the Cotswolds where Tabitha went missing. He's abducted them in England and has been holding them somewhere near the Newport Wetlands.' Dan sat down heavily as he mulled over this latest piece of information. 'Seven years ago. How old do you think the boy is?'

'He could be seven, or a bit older, or even younger. It's impossible to say. First off, we need to establish whether Giselle has turned up in the meantime. And if she hasn't, we need to speak to her next of kin and inform the family that she has a child.'

'Shit! I've just realized that ever since he was found the poor little mite's been trying to tell everyone who he is.'

'He has?' asked Dan.

'Yes. He kept repeatedly mumbling what everyone presumed were four words. *"Beat the brave man."* But what he must have been saying was, *"Peter Braverman"*. He was trying to tell us that his name's Peter Braverman!'

'Let's hope that he's got a family who'll take care of him.'

Jemima soon established that Giselle remained missing, and a call to the investigating officer revealed that she had been eighteen years old at the time of her disappearance. It was confirmed that her mother, Mary Braverman still lived at the family home in Bath, and arrangements were made for the two officers to visit her later that morning.

It was barely nine o'clock when they knocked on the woman's door. It was an impressive property in a desirable part of the city. The door was opened by a slim woman whose shabby but good quality clothes were too big for her. She had messy grey hair, a heavily lined face, and a haunted expression. A stranger could be forgiven for presuming she was in her seventies, but Mary Braverman had recently had her fiftieth birthday. Though the milestone had passed by unnoticed.

'Are you the police officers? Oh, what's happened? Have you found Giselle? Where is she? Is she all right?' Mary barely drew breath as the questions tumbled out of her mouth. Her expression was a blend of fear and hope, and her fingers were white as she wrung her hands. It was apparent that even after the passage of seven years, her daughter's disappearance still affected Mary greatly.

Mary led them into the living room, which was clean, with a minimal amount of furniture, and smelled of polish. A crumpled duster lay discarded on a coffee table. 'Have to keep busy,' she said, by way of explanation.

Jemima nodded supportively. All the while trying not to stare at the hundreds of framed photographs lining the walls. 'First off, you need to know that Giselle is still missing.'

Mary's shoulders sagged, as the morning's glimmer of hope deserted her. She gulped loudly as she tried to control her emotions, and turned her head as she wiped away tears.

'It's not all bad news, Mary,' reassured Jemima. 'There's been a development and we're investigating.'

'What's happened? What have you found?'

'There's a child, Mary. A young boy. We believe he's Giselle's son.'

'A boy? You mean I have a grandchild?' Mary began to shake and sobbed uncontrollably.

Dan suddenly felt awkward and wanted to do something useful. He went to the kitchen to make a cup of tea.

'Giselle's boy? A grandchild?'

'Yes,' said Jemima. Seeing her distress, she moved to sit next to Mary, and reached out to squeeze the woman's hands. 'We believe his name might be Peter.'

Mary gasped. 'Peter? That was my husband's name. I lost him four years ago. My wonderful man, my rock. He died of a broken heart. Giselle was his world. The light of his life. He never . . . *we* never got over not knowing what happened to her. It's a terrible thing. The uncertainty eats away at you bit by bit. If you haven't experienced it, you can't begin to understand. People say things like, "*no news is good news*", and "*there's always hope*". They don't know what they're talking about. It's the hope that makes it worse. You build yourself up only to have your heart shattered all over again, and there's only so many times you can stick the pieces back together.'

'I'm so sorry,' said Jemima.

'No, don't be sorry. You've just told me I have a grandson. That's wonderful news. The only good news I've had in seven years. So where is he? What's he like? Can I see him?'

'You can absolutely see him, but not today. He's currently in hospital in Cardiff.'

'Hospital? What's wrong with him? Oh, don't tell me he's going to die. I can't lose him too.'

'I believe he'll be fine. He's had a traumatic experience and is malnourished, very scared and withdrawn. I appreciate that you'll be desperate to see him, but Peter's needs will have to take priority.'

'Of course. I understand and agree.'

Jemima proceeded to fill Mary in on what happened.

'Is there a realistic chance of you finding Giselle?'

'My team and I are doing everything we can. We're following some lines of enquiry, but I would say that it's best for you not to get your hopes up. I don't wish to overstep the mark, but perhaps it's best to concentrate on Peter for now. I'll arrange for you to see him soon, but you'll need to take things slowly with him. He's suffered a lot. Both physically and mentally.'

'I wouldn't do anything to hurt or upset him. Believe me, even though I've only just learned of his existence, that little boy is the most precious of children. Would it be possible for him to be transferred to a hospital here? That way, I could regularly spend time with him. Get to know him. Tell him about his mother.'

Jemima thought it was a great idea. It would remove Peter from the immediate threat his captor posed. Though she knew that her opinion would ultimately count for little as to what would eventually happen to the boy. The fact that she was his maternal grandmother might tip the scales in favour of this course of action. But knowing how much this woman had already suffered, she didn't want to give her false hope. It was better to err on the side of caution.

'Mary, it's not my decision, but I promise to have a word with the hospital staff and children's services. I'll establish some contacts for you, so that you can liaise directly with them. This is my direct line.' She handed the woman her card. 'You can call me at any time, and I'll ring you as soon as I have any updates.'

'Thank you.' Mary took the card, then grasped Jemima's hand. 'I appreciate it. Could you perhaps give Peter a photograph of Giselle? It'd be good for him to see his mother's face. It might help him.'

'That's an excellent idea,' said Jemima. 'First, though, tell me about Giselle. Specifically, everything you can remember in the weeks leading up to her disappearance, along with any ideas you might have about what happened to her.'

Dan returned with a tray containing three cups of tea. He sat down and joined the others.

'Giselle was always a good girl. Worked hard at school. Bright as a button. I suppose it was in the genes. Peter was a GP. Believe it or not, before Giselle disappeared, I was a child psychologist.'

'Your professional knowledge will be useful,' interjected Jemima. 'You should be the perfect person to help Peter.'

'I hope so. I really hope so,' said Mary. 'Giselle wasn't one to go out every night. She had her head screwed on. Wanted to do well. Make something of herself. We got her A-level results three weeks after she disappeared. Four As. Physics. Chemistry. Biology. Mathematics.' Mary's voice was filled with pride. 'She'd been accepted at Bristol to study medicine. Wanted to follow in her father's footsteps.'

'Did anything out of character happen in the weeks leading up to her disappearance?' asked Jemima.

'No, not really — I mean, she was a bit stressed out waiting for her A-level results, but she was enjoying being free from exams. She'd become a bit of a cooking show fan while she was revising. In fact, she was somewhat infatuated with Valentino Bianchi.'

'The celebrity chef?' asked Dan.

'That's right. Giselle and a few of her friends had tickets to see him when the BBC were recording one of his shows. It was touring Britain for some reason. She was absolutely smitten with him. Kept saying how wonderful he was. Had some photographs taken with him at an event they all attended. There was even one of them dancing together, arms around each other. She looked so happy.'

'Did anything happen between Giselle and Bianchi?' asked Dan. 'He's a fair bit older than her.'

'I'm not sure. I didn't think anything about it at the time, because her friends had photographs taken with him too. I would have thought it's part and parcel of being a celebrity. It's all an act. Not the real person. I recall telling her as much. I know she followed him on social media. Then again, I think she followed a lot of people. Well, they do at that age, don't they?' said Mary.

Mary selected a photograph of her daughter for Jemima to show Peter, and they said their goodbyes.

CHAPTER 11

As there had been no mention of Valentino Bianchi in the original investigation, Jemima dropped Dan at the station for him to undertake some background checks on the man. She headed to the hospital to firstly check on Tabitha and Peter, and then meet up with Gareth and the rest of the team to review their progress.

Jemima's first stop was the children's unit, where she was pleased to find officers standing guard outside. 'Any problems?' she asked.

'None whatsoever,' came the reply.

Jemima found Peter sitting up in bed, watching everyone else as usual. When he saw her approach, she spotted a flicker of recognition in his eyes. She waved, and watched as his lips twitched, though didn't quite form a smile. 'Hello, Peter,' she said, when she was a few feet away from him.

'Beat the brave man,' he muttered.

'Your name is Peter Braverman,' said Jemima.

Peter's eyes sparkled as he nodded.

'Can I sit down, Peter?' Jemima pointed at the chair.

The boy nodded.

'I'd like to show you something.' Jemima took the framed photograph of Giselle out of her bag and held it up for him to look at.

The response was instantaneous. 'Mummeee! Mummeee!' There was now no doubt that Giselle Braverman was Peter's mother. It was as though a cloud had been lifted, as Peter kissed his mother's photograph then hugged it tightly.

Two of the nurses heard the boy's shouts and ran over to find out what had happened. Jemima told them that the boy's name was Peter Braverman. She left Peter hugging the photograph of his mother and gestured to the nurses to follow her. When they were out of earshot, she told them that she had also learned the identity of Peter's mother, but that Giselle was still a missing person. She also explained that they had found Peter's grandmother.

Having agreed to return later to spend some time with Peter, her next stop was to check on Tabitha Leysham. Armed officers guarded the door and Lady Leysham was at her daughter's bedside, reading aloud from *The Secret Garden*. She stopped when Jemima entered the room.

'They told me that she might be able to hear us, so I brought her favourite book. I've lost count of the number of times I read it to her when she was a child.'

'Any improvement in her condition?' asked Jemima.

'They've been reducing the medication throughout the day and are thinking about trying to bring her out of the coma. She's off the ventilator now. Amazing really, when you think what happened last night, when that monster tried to kill her. How did he know she was here?'

'I've no idea, but he obviously made a determined effort to find her. This hospital is in a different health authority from where she was found. We kept it under wraps about bringing Tabitha here.'

'Edgar's up in arms about it. I spoke to him earlier. He wants your head on a plate. I've told him you're all doing your best for her, as are the hospital staff.'

'I assure you we're taking every precaution to ensure Tabitha's safety. I thought your husband would have wanted to be here?' said Jemima.

'Unfortunately, there were other matters which had to take precedence. Edgar's time is not his own.'

'Even when it comes to Tabitha being found?'

'Apparently even then. Of course I'm keeping him updated, and it's not as though there's anything he could actually do were he here. He's assured me that once he's sorted out whatever he's dealing with, he'll come to the hospital.'

'Tell me, did Tabitha ever mention having contact with any celebrities, other than Didier Fontaine?'

Lydia placed the book on the bed and thought for a while. 'No. The only one she spoke about was that Fontaine chap, but that was because she'd met him at one of our fund-raising events. But I don't recall her speaking about anyone else who was a household name. Why?'

'No reason. I just thought I'd ask. Look, I'm sorry to have intruded. I'll let you get back to the book,' said Jemima. She headed out of the room before Lydia had a chance to say anything further.

Jemima's next stop was the hospital's security suite, and she arrived to find that the team had made a breakthrough. Everyone was huddled around a monitor, and they were eagerly watching something. Levi was the first to notice her enter the room.

'Just in time, Guv. We think we've finally got him on camera.'

Jemima headed over to watch the footage.

'We think that's our man,' said Gareth. 'We've footage of him entering the hospital a couple of hours before the attack took place. He didn't interact with anyone and walked the corridors, clearly scoping the place as he searched for Tabitha.'

'Any clear facial shots?' Jemima knew the answer even before asking the question. If they had captured his face, they'd be doing something about it.

'No. He's disguised himself well. Wearing a hoodie and a baseball cap. Even has gloves. Kept his head down for the entire time.'

'So, we don't even know the colour of his skin,' said Nancy.

'I'm surprised that no one challenged him,' said Jemima. 'Let's face it, during the day, hundreds, if not thousands of people enter this building and wander about the corridors. No one would raise an eyebrow. But in the middle of the night? Surely someone must have seen him?'

'Doesn't say much for security,' said Levi.

'Get the impression it's a soft option. There's not that many of them on shift, and they probably sleep through most of it. There'd be no one to check up on them. Certain corridors and wards have locked access. But once someone's opened a door it'd be easy enough to follow on behind, and if no one's watching there's nothing to stop you. It's how our man got to Tabitha's room. We've watched him wandering the corridors, waiting for locked doors to open. I think he couldn't have known for sure that she was even in the hospital,' said Gareth.

Jemima sighed and shook her head. Despite the hospital management being made aware of a potential threat to both Tabitha and Peter, a threat evidenced by the fact that police officers had been stationed outside the children's unit and Tabitha's room, they had not seen fit to remind all staff about ensuring that no unauthorized personnel or visitors should be allowed into restricted areas. This complacency had ultimately resulted in the death of a police officer, a murder attempt on a patient and the assault on a nurse who was carrying out her duties.

'It seems we know next to nothing about him, but there must be things we've learned,' said Jemima. 'For instance, you said you know he'd been searching the hospital for hours?'

'Yes.'

'Have you established which entrance he used to access the building?'

'It was this one,' said Gareth, as he showed Jemima a plan of the hospital.

'Did he leave the hospital that way?'

'That's what we're trying to establish.'

'Would it speed things up if I looked at some of the security footage?' asked Jemima.

'Definitely. The more people searching, the quicker we'll get through it,' said Gareth.

Twenty minutes later Jemima was beginning to wish she hadn't volunteered. But she knew it was the most useful thing she could be doing so kept on watching the screen, fast-forwarding, until the timeframe made it unlikely that their man had exited that way. She was about to switch to a camera covering a different door, when she did a double-take. 'I think I've got him. Is that our man?'

Everyone stopped what they were doing and headed to her screen. 'Yeah, I'm sure that's him,' said Mack.

'It's definitely him,' confirmed Gareth.

'Where's that door on the building plan?' asked Jemima.

'It's there,' said Nancy, as she pointed to the exit.

It was the breakthrough which allowed them to trace the intruder's route through the hospital grounds.

'He's exited the building by a different door, but once outside it looks as though he's going to retrace his steps through the grounds,' said Gareth.

'Towards one of the onsite car parks?' asked Nancy.

'One of you check the footage, but my money is on somewhere else. It'd be too risky to park a vehicle onsite. He'd know there'd be every chance we'd be able to establish make, model and number plate,' said Jemima. 'But he must have parked his vehicle close to the hospital grounds.

'There are houses along that route. Get out there, bang on doors, and see if anyone has doorbell cameras or CCTV where we can trace him. Even if we don't get a clear view of his face, we might be able to see what vehicle he gets into. Once we do that, there's a chance we can track him with traffic cameras. This could be our opportunity to establish where he's heading. We could find out where he kept Tabitha and Peter, and hopefully find Giselle Braverman.'

Jemima checked her watch. It wasn't too late for her to head back to the children's ward to see how Peter was getting on.

In such a short space of time, the change in Peter was remarkable. Instead of sitting alone on his bed, the boy had ventured into the play area where he and another child were drawing pictures with crayons.

'Hello, Peter,' said Jemima. The boy looked up and smiled then continued drawing his picture. 'That's a lovely picture, Peter. What's that you're drawing?' It was a crude drawing of what appeared to be women and children. One of the women and a child stood apart from the others. She pulled up a chair and sat next to him.

'Family,' he replied.

'So, what are their names?'

'Tab. Beter.' He pointed to the two figures standing away from the others. 'Mummy.' He pointed to a taller figure with a round stomach.

'Is mummy having a baby?' she asked.

Peter nodded.

'And who are these?' She pointed at two other adult women, two small girls and a baby.

'Jolie.' He pointed at another adult. 'Anna. Bea.' He pointed at two small girls. Though one appeared to be far bigger than the other.

'And who are these?' Jemima gestured to the other woman in the drawing along with a baby.

'Summer.' Another adult. 'Baby Freya.'

'And did you all live together?'

Peter nodded. 'Family.'

'And what about your daddy?'

Peter jumped up and grabbed Jemima's arms. Her stomach lurched as she saw his expression change to one of pure terror. Urine soaked his pyjama trousers and dripped on to the floor as hysteria took hold.

Jemima's blood ran cold as she held Peter close and did her best to reassure him that he was safe. As tension eventually dissolved, the boy's muscles relaxed, and he melted into her arms. Still sobbing uncontrollably, he eventually took comfort from her closeness and the sense of security she provided.

As she comforted the boy, Jemima's mind raced through the implications of what she'd just learned. It wasn't just Giselle who remained captive. There were two other women, and three children too. What's more, Peter had called them his family. Was this monster abducting young women to create his own 'family'?

The scope of the case was spreading like an oil slick. They were no further forward with identifying the man. Yet the number of victims kept increasing.

Having established the perpetrator's exit point from the hospital grounds, Gareth had trawled through council CCTV footage of the area, while the others, along with uniformed officers drafted in for the task, had walked the streets, knocking on doors to establish if any households in the vicinity had doorbell cameras or other CCTV cameras facing the street.

In the meantime, Jemima returned to the station to find out how Dan Broadbent was getting on with his fact-finding mission about the celebrity chef, Valentino Bianchi.

'There's so much speculation about the guy in both mainstream and social media. As far as I've been able to establish, he's engaged to the TV weather presenter, Layla Kenyon. I've got an address for them. Do you want to head over there now?' Dan glanced at his watch.

'Where do they live?'

'Just outside Cheltenham.'

'No. It's too late in the day. We've all been up since silly o'clock and we're running on empty. Get Bianchi's local force to contact him and tell him we'll be at his house at nine o'clock tomorrow, and he needs to be there to answer some questions.

'I'll ring Gareth and ask him to tell the rest of them to call it a day. It's time to get ourselves home. We'll meet back here in the morning, seven o'clock sharp. Pool our findings and take it from there.'

* * *

On the way home, Jemima called in at Lucy's to collect the boys. James was busy doing his homework, while Finlay was playing with one of his cousins. Her own children along with Lucy's brood looked so content. They were well-nourished, loved and grounded in a loving family environment. It was so far removed from everything Peter and those other children would have known.

Back at home, Jemima walked into the kitchen to discover that Mason had had the foresight to prepare dinner in the slow cooker. He had left a note to say that he should be back in about an hour's time, which allowed her time to bathe Finlay and read to him as he fell asleep. During which time, James had finished his homework.

Kicking off her shoes she sat on the sofa with her eldest son, as he gave her a blow-by-blow account of everything that had happened that day.

Mason returned home slightly later than he'd thought, and James had already gone to bed. When she heard the door open, Jemima headed into the hallway to greet him.

'Thanks for preparing dinner. You're the best,' she said as she nestled her head against his shoulder.

'Not a problem. I know you're up against it. You and the boys are my family now.'

'And we're very lucky to have you.' Jemima tilted her head and they kissed. 'I love you, Mason.'

'Love you too, Jemmy.'

Spending time with her boys and the remainder of the evening with Mason, was the perfect antidote to the awfulness of the day. It was wonderful to know that her feelings were reciprocated. She felt so fortunate to have found love again. She knew that some people spent their entire lives without ever experiencing it.

CHAPTER 12

Jemima awoke refreshed. For once, her sleep had been deep and dreamless. Before setting off for work, she checked in with the hospital to find out how their two victims were doing. She was informed that Peter had had a good night and seemed much calmer since waking. Tabitha's vital signs were strong, and the doctors had every reason to think that she would recover consciousness, though no one was prepared to commit to a timescale as it seemed that every case was different.

The entire team was assembled in the briefing room ten minutes earlier than their agreed start time. It was evident that everyone was keen to get started, and so Jemima kicked off the briefing session by pinning Peter's drawing on the board.

'Are you sure Peter was telling the truth?' asked Levi.

'He's a disturbed child who has clearly been subjected to mental and physical abuse, but I haven't seen any evidence to suggest that he's lied to us. His eyes lit up when I showed him the photograph of his mother, and it was shortly after that that he drew the picture. Children do have a very different approach to reality and fantasy, so we can't be sure on the basis of a single conversation and picture. Though I'd like to take it as a starting point.

'My conversation with Peter suggests that Giselle is alive and pregnant; if that picture's anything to go by, the pregnancy's advanced. What's more, we can guess from the state Tabitha and Peter were in that she doesn't have access to medical treatment.

'He's also given us the first names of the two other women. Jolie is the mother of Anna and Bea. Summer is the mother of the baby, Freya. Including Giselle's unborn child, we can assume there are seven lives in imminent danger. Our top priority is to establish where he's keeping them. Even if we catch a break and manage to arrest him, I can't imagine he would easily give up the location. This man is all about control. He's successfully operated out of sight for years. As far as he's concerned, they're his family and I'm convinced he'd allow them to die rather than risk them turning against him.'

'He must be holding them somewhere close to the wetlands,' said Gareth. 'Until Tabitha and Peter escaped, he had nine captives. So, it has to be a large remote property.'

'I agree. He could coerce the women into keeping quiet by threatening to harm the kids. But it's impossible to control children like that, and if they're that small there'd be plenty of temper tantrums. I know from experience, it's hard enough to keep one child quiet, let alone four,' said Dan.

'Right, tasks for this morning,' said Jemima. 'Gareth, I want you to continue taking the lead on trying to track his movements when he left the hospital grounds. Levi, Mack, you'll assist him.

'Nancy, I want you to search for any records of missing women named Jolie and Summer. We don't have any other information to go on, but at least they're not very common names. If we can establish who they are and when they went missing, we might be able to find a common thread with Tabitha Leysham and Giselle Braverman.

'Dan and I are off to speak to Valentino Bianchi. I know we're clutching at straws,' she said, seeing the looks on her team's faces, 'but it's the only new point of interest on

Giselle's disappearance. Let me know immediately about any developments. Other than that, we'll catch up later.'

* * *

'Fill me in on your findings about Bianchi,' said Jemima, as they headed towards Cheltenham.

'I know you should take a lot of what's said on social media with a pinch of salt, but the guy's got quite the following. Women seem to love him, and reading between the lines I get the impression that he encourages it. I found numerous accounts of him bedding various women. Most if not all of them seemed to be one-night stands. I got the impression the man's a serial philanderer.'

'What sort of timescale are you talking about?'

'Years. Ever since he got his first daytime TV slot. I even found a magazine article where he talks about being addicted to sex. Claims he has an exceptionally high libido. Says he has to have it at least six times a day.'

'If that's the case it's a wonder he can find any time for his so-called career,' muttered Jemima. 'Perhaps if he had a proper job, he'd be too busy and knackered to think about sex all the time. I can't imagine how he's managed to maintain a long-term relationship with anyone. That weather presenter must be a right sap to tolerate behaviour like that.'

They pulled up at Bianchi's house to hear a huge argument going on inside.

'I can't take it anymore! Do you understand? No more, Val! I've had it with you and those whores!' screamed Layla.

Bianchi's voice was low and measured, making it impossible for them to hear what he said.

'Welcome to celebrity life,' said Dan as they headed towards the front door.

The argument was in full swing, expletive-laden and ferocious. They were within five paces of the front door when a nearby window shattered as a vase was propelled through it and smashed on the ground at their feet.

'We're not paid enough to deal with this shit,' said Dan. He pressed the doorbell but there was no answer. The shouting had stopped, replaced by an eerie silence.

'Try the door,' ordered Jemima.

Dan pressed the handle and the door swung inwards.

'Police!' shouted Jemima. 'Mr Bianchi, Miss Kenyon, it's the police. We're coming in.'

As they stepped inside the property, Jemima heard a woman crying. Making for the sound, she stepped through an open doorway into a lounge, though in its current state it looked more like a war zone: chairs toppled, television smashed, broken ornaments and other debris littering the floor. At the far side of the room was a gaping hole in what was once a picture window.

Layla Kenyon was hunched on the sofa, hugging herself as she continued to sob. The woman sounded bereft. Valentino was hovering over her. He turned in their direction when he realized they were there. His lip was split, and blood flowed from his busted nose.

Jemima and Dan held out their warrant cards as she introduced them. 'I believe someone from your local police station informed you that we were coming to speak to you this morning.'

Valentino's expression was momentarily one of confusion, but it soon passed. 'Ah, y-yes. Sorry. I forgot all about it. Afraid you caught us in the middle of one of our domestics.'

'Happens regularly, does it?' asked Dan. He raised an eyebrow questioningly.

'Far too often,' sobbed Layla. 'The cheating bastard. I thought he'd change when he put a ring on my finger. Turns out he still can't help himself. If anyone with a pretty face flutters their eyelashes at him, he can't help himself. He's nothing but a cheating, lying, scumbag.'

'I swear on my life, honey, those days are behind me. I know I've been an absolute shit in the past. But from the moment I asked you to marry me, there's only ever been you, Lay. Only you.'

'Stop lying to me, Val! I'm not stupid. So don't treat me as though I am. Why are the police here? Have you been having it away with an underage girl?' Layla hardly stopped to draw breath. 'Is that it? I'm right, aren't I?'

'God, no! I wouldn't do anything like that. How can you think such a thing?' Valentino stepped backwards, his body rigid with shock: clearly horrified at what his fiancée had just accused him of. He then turned his attention to Jemima and Dan. 'Tell her I haven't done anything. Please!'

'We're not here about any of Mr Bianchi's recent infidelities,' said Jemima. It was not an absolute exoneration, and she knew it. She was not prepared to be centre stage in their messed-up relationship.

'So why are you here?' asked Layla.

'Are you happy for your fiancée to be present while we speak to you?' Jemima asked Valentino.

Before he had the opportunity to reply, Layla jumped in. 'I'm staying. From now on there are no dirty little secrets, Val. I get to hear everything they ask you, or you can get the hell out of my life for good. That's the deal.' She stared at him defiantly.

'That's fine, honey. I've got nothing to hide. Really, I haven't.'

'In that case, we'll get started,' said Jemima. 'We're here to ask you about Giselle Braverman.'

'Who?' Valentino appeared genuinely confused. 'I don't recall having met anyone with that name.'

'Perhaps this will jog your memory,' said Dan. He showed Valentino the photographs posted on Giselle's Instagram.

Valentino stared at them, long and hard, turning back to the one of him dancing with Giselle. Finally, he spoke. 'No . . . no, I don't remember her. Though I don't deny it's me in the photographs. Looks like it's from a meet-and-greet event? I know it might seem odd not to remember someone I danced with so closely, but it's the sort of thing I did a lot back then. It's an old photograph — I remember that jacket, but I got rid of it years ago, and I haven't had my hair like that for a very long time. When did she say she was with me?'

'She hasn't said anything, Mr Bianchi. She disappeared seven years ago. We believe she was abducted.'

Valentino's jaw dropped. 'And you believe I took her? Are you crazy? There are cameras on me wherever I go. I've got a very recognizable face. That's why there were always stories in the press about me. When you're the centre of media attention, it's virtually impossible to do anything without the paparazzi trying to make a quick buck out of you.

'And I couldn't count the number of people approaching me for a photo and hoping for something more. If you're a celebrity, people throw themselves at you. It doesn't even matter if you're a looker or not. Or even if you want the attention. You're on their screens and they want part of that. It's ridiculous. But that's the way it is.'

'Val's right. It's like that for me, and I only have five-minute slots presenting the weather,' said Layla. 'The trouble is Val's an addict. Instead of booze, drugs, or gambling, he's addicted to sex.'

'I'm in therapy,' Val said. 'I'm trying my best because I want to make our relationship work. Since I got together with Layla, I've been doing my best to stay at arm's length with my fans, hired a PA to deal with all the approaches. Though some of my PAs have got fed up with having to fend off young women who want to sleep with me.'

'How long have you and Layla been together?' asked Dan.

'Eight years, off and on. We moved in together five years ago.'

'Would you agree to us taking a DNA sample?' asked Jemima.

'Sure, why not. Like I said, I've nothing to hide.'

'I'll get the kit from the car,' said Dan.

As Jemima waited for Dan to return, she decided to have a last throw of the dice. 'Have you ever had any dealings with Didier Fontaine?'

'The chat show host? No, can't say I have. Still waiting for an invite to his show.'

'Wasn't one of your PAs his PA at some stage? I seem to recall seeing that on a CV,' said Layla.

Jemima suddenly had a glimmer of hope. It was nothing to get too excited about at the moment, but if Layla was correct, it was a connection between the two men. 'Male or female?' she asked.

'Definitely male,' said Layla. 'I remember him because he made me feel very uncomfortable, and I asked Val to let him go.'

'Oh, him? That was years ago. Yeah, there was something unpleasant about him. Couldn't put my finger on it, but there was something, all right.'

'Do you recall his name?'

'Began with a D. Derek?' said Layla. 'Dermot? Dougall?'

Valentino shook his head. 'But I can find out. It'll be on file somewhere. I have to keep records. I'll most likely have a photograph too.'

'I'll make sure he does it. You'll have it later today,' assured Layla.

Jemima and Dan headed back to the station. Though their first stop would be to deposit Valentino's DNA sample. As they already had Peter's DNA, it would be a quick and easy way to rule him in or out of the investigation.

CHAPTER 13

Nancy was the only one in the incident room when Jemima and Dan returned. She was perusing case records held on the PNC database.

'You managed to find anything?' asked Jemima.

'A number of possibilities so far. There are seventeen Jolies and ten Summers. So it's now a case of reading through the information on the files to try to narrow down the list. That's easier said than done as apart from knowing that both women are of childbearing age, we don't have anything else to go on.'

'Print off the headshots and I'll show them to Peter. There's every chance he'll be able to tell us which, if any, of those women are the ones who were captive with him,' said Jemima.

'I'll give you a hand,' said Dan.

'Where are Gareth and the others?'

'They're in the surveillance suite. Been there for hours. I haven't heard a peep out of them.'

Jemima opened the door of the surveillance suite to see a wall of screens, each displaying footage from cameras sited around the city. No one turned to see who had entered the room, as the three officers were focused on their screens.

'Think I've picked him up on this one,' said Levi. He pointed at one of the screens.

Gareth looked from one to the other. 'Yeah, that's him, all right.'

'He's a canny one, and cool with it,' said Mack. 'He's got his hood up and head down the entire time. Not to mention keeping his hands in his pockets.'

'If that is our man, he's had years of practise at staying out of sight,' said Jemima. 'It takes skill and balls to walk into a hospital, kill a police officer and almost get away with another murder. He even had the self-control not to panic as he made his getaway. He's confident, and able to improvise when necessary.'

'Is he heading for that car?' said Levi.

'He bloody is,' said Mack.

Moments later they watched as their target stopped beside the driver's door, removed the key from his pocket and got inside. Suddenly the tension in the room was palpable. This was a real step forward. They had a chance of tracking his journey.

'Anyone know the make and model of that car? What about the number plate, does the camera pick it up?'

They all stared at the screen. Determined to find something which might help them identify their suspect. Being night-time footage, they were unable to see the colour of the vehicle, but they soon discovered that the number plate was indecipherable as it was obscured by thick layers of dirt.

'Keep on it,' said Jemima. 'We need to know where he went. In the meantime, Mack, email Kate Franklin the best images you can get of that car. If anyone knows what type of vehicle that is, it'll be her.'

DS Kate Franklin was a friend and kickboxing sparring partner of Jemima's. Both women were accomplished at their chosen sport and had trained together for many years. Through sheer commitment and willpower, they inspired each other to become the best they could possibly be. Pushing each other to train harder, longer, and work through physical and mental barriers.

Kate was also an expert on cars. Having been the youngest child in a large family of petrolheads, from an early age she'd taken an interest in cars. There were many years when her brothers and classmates ridiculed her fascination with the machines. Though Kate took no notice and was now a competent mechanic, much to the annoyance of her brothers she spotted and fixed problems far quicker than them. In addition to her mechanical skills, she had amassed a phenomenal amount of information about the vehicles. She was the go-to person on the force, often able to recognize the make and model of a vehicle from the grainiest of images.

Jemima's phone rang and she stepped away from the others, mindful of not breaking their concentration.

'Chief Inspector? It's Valentino. I've found the information you asked for. The PA we were talking about was a man named Douglas Taylor. If I could have your email address, I'll send a copy of the documentation over to you. I have a photograph of him too if that would be of use?'

'Absolutely. I'm messaging my email to you now. Thank you for getting back to me so quickly,' said Jemima.

'You should receive it in the next few minutes,' said Valentino, before he ended the call.

Leaving Gareth and the others to their task, Jemima headed back to the incident room. She sat at her desk and logged on to find that Valentino had indeed sent her an email with attachments. She opened the message, hoping that this man would be the one responsible for the abductions. Douglas Taylor didn't look particularly remarkable from his photograph, but he did have ginger hair. If he was the man they were after, it would explain why Peter had reacted so badly when the ginger-haired child psychologist had approached him. As she read the attached document completed for his employment by Valentino, she noted that his home address seven years ago had been in Stroud.

'Dan, I'd like you to follow up on this,' she said. 'Valentino has sent through the details of the PA who creeped Layla out — from the dates, he must have been working for Valentino around the time Giselle disappeared. I'll send you the file. Establish whether he worked for Didier Fontaine, and when. If he did, then find out what Fontaine thought of him. If there were any problems with his behaviour. How he reacted around women, and if there were any complaints made against him.

'Check out Taylor's address too. He lived in Stroud when he worked for Valentino, but that was a while ago and could easily be out of date now. There's nothing that obviously points to him being our man, but you never know. Quite frankly, I'll grasp at any straw at this point.'

Even as she spoke, her phone rang again. This time it was the hospital. It was the news they'd all been waiting for. Tabitha Leysham had regained consciousness.

* * *

Jemima arrived at the hospital to find Tabitha asleep. Lydia Leysham was at the bedside, holding her daughter's hand.

'How's she doing?' asked Jemima.

Lost in thought, Lydia jumped in surprise and involuntarily squeezed her daughter's hand. Tabitha moaned. As Lydia turned her head, Jemima saw that she was crying.

'Don't worry. These are happy tears. The doctors are optimistic she's going to make a full recovery. I was here when Tabs opened her eyes. She recognized me but she's still very weak. They said she'll most likely drift in and out for a while yet.'

Tabitha's eyelids fluttered as she regained consciousness. 'Don't worry, my darling. Mummy's here,' crooned Lydia. She stood up and stroked her daughter's cheek, placing her face directly in front of Tabitha's to enable her to see it without turning her head.

'Drink,' croaked Tabitha.

Lydia reached for a glass of water and manoeuvred the straw into her daughter's mouth.

Tabitha sipped the liquid eagerly. 'Enough,' she eventually said. The water seemed to invigorate her, and her eyes eventually focused upon Jemima. 'Who are you?' she asked.

Before Jemima had a chance to speak, Lydia jumped in to reassure her daughter that Jemima was not a threat. 'There's no need to worry, my darling. This is Detective Chief Inspector Huxley. She's the police officer trying to find out what happened to you.'

Confusion played across Tabitha's face as the young woman tried to organize her thoughts. It was apparent that she was struggling to think coherently. 'Peter. Where's Peter?' she eventually asked.

'Peter's doing well. He's on the children's ward,' said Jemima.

'Had to . . . get him out. Would've died,' said Tabitha.

'What do you mean by that?' asked Jemima. Suddenly her heart was thudding.

'Father hates boys . . . Sees them as . . . threat. Kills them before they get . . . big. Murdered Marcus. My beautiful boy. Used to say, "*Big boys die.*" Said it to Marcus, and to Peter.'

Jemima shivered. It was as though the temperature in the room had dropped significantly. Suddenly feeling the need to sit down, she pulled a chair up to Tabitha's bedside. The phrase was one which Peter had shouted at one of the other patients. It was apparent now that he'd been trying to warn the child that he was in danger. A danger Peter knew would have resulted in his own death had he not managed to get away from the monster who had played God with all their lives.

Lydia, who was unaware of these other events, paled and did her best to stifle a gasp, clearly shocked to the core. To learn that her grandchild had been murdered before she'd even known of his existence was unimaginably cruel. And despite her determination to be supportive of her daughter, this unanticipated revelation was too much to bear. 'P-please excuse me,' Lydia muttered, scraping her chair back abruptly and making a hurried exit.

Jemima glanced back as she went. The older woman was crying; Jemima guessed that she was determined not to allow her daughter to witness her distress. She needn't have worried, as Tabitha was still groggy. It was taking a lot out of her to think and speak coherently. As such, she was oblivious to much going on around her.

Tabitha was clearly struggling to concentrate, with even a basic level of communication sapping what little energy she had. Her eyelids drooped until she went silent.

Jemima knew better than to try to force the pace. The young woman was clearly in no fit state to say more. Instead, she sat in silence and her thoughts turned to her two boys. She loved them fiercely. It was heartbreaking to hear that Tabitha's son was murdered by the monster who had most likely fathered him.

It seemed an age before Tabitha's eyes opened once more. Though in reality it was probably no more than a matter of minutes.

'Water,' said Tabitha.

Jemima picked up the glass and manoeuvred the straw to Tabitha's lips, allowing her to drink as much as she needed.

Eventually Jemima pushed for more information. 'Are you able to tell me what happened to you?' she asked. It seemed harsh, but as one attempt had already been made on her life, and with the distinct possibility that other people were in danger from a man who clearly had no scruples, it was necessary to establish as many facts as she could, as quickly as possible.

Tabitha nodded. She spoke more coherently, though her voice remained croaky. 'I was abducted by a man who worked for Didier Fontaine. It was my fault. I was stupid.'

'Is this him?' Jemima showed Tabitha the photograph of Douglas Taylor.

'Yes. That's Father.'

'When you and Peter escaped, did you leave anyone behind?'

'Three women. Giselle Braverman, she's Peter's mother. Jolie Perkins, and Summer Abberton. There are other kids too. You've got to get them out of there.'

Jemima scribbled down their names in her notebook. 'Where are they, Tabitha? Where's he holding them?'

'I don't know. It was dark.'

'How far did you walk?'

'No idea. We walked all night. But not fast. It was so dark and neither of us had the strength to go fast.'

'Did you see anyone or anything along the way?'

'We walked along a lane until we reached a stile and headed into a field. It was safer to stay away from the road until we had some idea of where we were.'

'So, you didn't come across another lane or surfaced road once you crossed the stile?'

'No.'

Tabitha's descriptions were of little help in pinpointing the property in which they had been held. It had to be somewhere close to the nature reserve as, given their weakened state, it seemed a reasonable assumption that they could not have walked more than a few miles.

'I know about Giselle, and I've contacted her mother.'

'She's pregnant again. Heavily pregnant. That's why she couldn't come with us.'

'But you were pregnant too,' said Jemima.

'I'd not been right for a few days. I had no choice but to leave.'

'To save the baby? Didn't he allow you to see a doctor or a midwife?'

'No. We had to look after each other. He'd never allow us to have any contact with outsiders.

'But I didn't escape because I wanted to save the baby. I knew I was losing it. I was trying to save Peter and myself. Otherwise, he'd have killed both of us.'

'Why would he do that?'

'Because of his rules. He murdered my son, Marcus on his seventh birthd—' Her voice broke, and for some minutes she couldn't continue. Jemima waited, until eventually she started speaking again in a low tone. 'Said it was for the good of the family. He said any other boy would have to be killed on their seventh birthday — Peter's the only one. I think he was afraid of any future threat they might pose. Scared that as they got older, they'd turn against him.'

'So he didn't see the girls as a threat?' asked Jemima.

'No. They were his gold dust. An opportunity with no risk to himself as it meant he didn't have to abduct other girls. His daughters would ultimately replace us. Once they'd reached puberty, they could give him more children. It was all about family. His sick, twisted vision of family life, with him ruling over us. Setting the rules. Punishing us if we disobeyed. He was Father. We were his slaves. His playthings. His women. There to amuse him and satisfy his needs.'

Tabitha's speech was becoming laboured. The woman was weak, and Jemima sensed that she wouldn't be able to get much more information out of her during this encounter. 'Where were you being held? If we're to find the others I need to know where to look.'

'Don't know. House.' The effort proved too much for Tabitha, and she drifted off again.

CHAPTER 14

Jemima wished that she had been able to get more information from Tabitha but knew that at this stage of her recovery she was fortunate to have learned the identity of the man they were after, and to know the names of the other women he had abducted.

Tabitha needed to regain her strength. Jemima felt guilty for having pushed her so hard. It had been necessary, but she hoped it didn't have a detrimental effect on the young woman's recovery. Officers were still stationed outside Tabitha's room and the children's ward, and Jemima showed each of them the photograph of Douglas Taylor. They needed to know that he was the primary person who posed a threat to the victims. But she also informed them that it was possible that there could be other, unidentified perpetrators too.

As she headed out of the hospital, Jemima rang Dan and informed him that Douglas Taylor had been identified as the abductor. 'Have you made any progress with your search?' she asked.

'Not as such. I contacted the local nick for that area, and they sent someone out. Turned out to be for a house of multiple occupancy, but there was no sign of Taylor. No one seemed to know him. So either it was a false address, or he moved on long ago,' said Dan.

'Any vehicle registered to him?'

'Still searching.'

'Check to see if Kate Franklin's identified the make and model of the vehicle Gareth's team are tracking. It should help you narrow things down.'

'Will do.'

'I'm on my way back in. Should be there within half an hour. Tell Nancy that the other two women he's abducted are Jolie Perkins and Summer Abberton. I hope that's enough for her to go on. Abberton's not a common surname, but we could be unlucky and find that there's more than one Jolie Perkins reported missing. She needs to read through their case files to see if there's anything useful. We've got to find out where Taylor's holed up, before it's too late for those other three women and kids.'

Back at the station, Gareth, Levi and Mack were still following the vehicle on the CCTV footage.

'How's it going?' asked Jemima.

'It's slow. We've managed to track him to the far side of Newport, but he's avoided major roads wherever possible, which makes him harder to follow. He didn't panic. Looks as though he knows the location of the traffic cameras and planned his route accordingly,' said Gareth.

'Did Kate come up with anything?'

'She's confident of the make and model of the vehicle,' said Mack. 'Dan told us you've identified the scumbag, and I've told him what we know about the vehicle.'

* * *

Nancy was reading through the information on the original case files of Jolie Perkins and Summer Abberton's disappearances, making notes as she went.

'Come across anything useful?' asked Jemima.

'Pretty standard stuff. Jolie went missing four years ago after a night out in Chepstow with two female friends. It was a regular weekly event. Same pub every week. Neither of them recalled anything out of the ordinary. They left the venue shortly after ten, and as they all lived in different parts of the town, they each headed off alone. That was the last time anyone saw or heard from Jolie. She shared a house with her sister and didn't make it back there.'

'What age was she when she went missing?'

Nancy scanned the notes she'd made before answering. 'Twenty.'

'Figures. Plenty of years for her to be able to have his kids,' said Jemima. 'Does it look as though her disappearance was investigated thoroughly?'

'I'd say so. They went door-to-door along the route she would have taken. Did a televised reconstruction of her walking that route to try to jog people's memories. Expanded the search area in case for some unknown reason she went a different way. Got footage from doorbell cameras, and other security cameras, but there was nothing, apart from a few potential leads which quickly fizzled out. It was as though Jolie disappeared into thin air.'

'What about Summer Abberton?' asked Jemima.

'She was nineteen. Lived at home with her parents in the Forest of Dean. Went missing eighteen months ago, when she cycled to the Forest of Dean Sculpture Trail to meet up with a friend. She knew it well; it was less than two miles from her home. That morning, her friend got delayed. When she arrived, she spotted Summer's bicycle locked up in its regular place, but Summer was nowhere to be found. She looked around. Asked other visitors if they had seen her. Called her phone, which went straight to voicemail. It was later found discarded in an area of long grass. The only prints found on it were Summer's. There was an extensive search of the area, but there was no sign of her.'

'It's a bold move, abducting someone from a tourist attraction during a busy time of the day. Fits with the profile we're building of him. He's confident. Knows what he wants and plans how he's going to achieve his goals. He's also prepared to take risks and kill anyone who gets in his way,' said Jemima. 'And yet it's so different to Jolie's abduction, where he snatched her in the evening when very few people would have been around. Thinks on his feet, maybe.'

'It's scary to think that you could just be going about things as normal, and someone like Taylor could upend your life,' said Nancy.

'Sure is. Tabitha told me he's abducted women to create a pseudo-family. But from what I've learned he doesn't seem to value any of them. It's like he's got a shopping list, and when he sees what he likes he takes it. Just like you or me picking a tin of beans off a supermarket shelf. And when they no longer fit into his ideal vision of a family, he'll get rid.' Jemima shivered at the thought of it. 'Does Summer's file contain any data about vehicles in the car park at the time of her abduction?'

'There's a list of registration numbers. Pretty standard in pay and display car parks, so that people don't gift their ticket to someone else. Helps maintain a revenue stream,' said Nancy.

'In that case, compare what's in the file with the list of vehicles Dan's compiling from the DVLA database. Hopefully we'll get a hit and learn where and to whom the vehicle's registered.'

Jemima's phone rang. This time it was the officer guarding Tabitha. 'Ma'am, the witness has come around again, and she insists on talking to you. Says it's urgent.'

'Tell her I'm on my way.' She seemed to spend half her time going back and forth to the hospital on this case. It was especially problematic as Tabitha and Peter had been placed in the hospital in Cardiff to put some distance between them and their captor. Though even then, he'd been determined enough to track them down. Even with blues and twos alerting other motorists along the way, it might still take about half an hour to get there. She just hoped that Tabitha was still awake and able to speak coherently when she arrived.

CHAPTER 15

From the moment she walked into Tabitha's room, Jemima could tell that she was far more alert than when they had spoken a few hours earlier. A mound of pillows had been arranged to prop her up in the bed, though she looked positively skeletal against them. The glazed look in her eyes had gone, emphasizing the dark smudges beneath. Overall, her complexion was exceptionally pale, most likely from a lack of natural sunlight.

The young woman took birdlike bites from a sandwich. 'The nurse insisted I must eat. Reckons I'm underweight. Don't know what could have given them that idea.' Her lips curled in the faintest of smiles, though the humour didn't reach her eyes. It was apparent that she was feeling much improved, though there was no doubt it would be a long journey until physically she was fully recovered. As for the inevitable mental scars, she might very well carry them for the rest of her life.

'Little and often, my darling,' said Lydia. She squeezed her daughter's arm in a supportive manner. 'Remember what we said?'

Tabitha looked at her mother blankly, as she tried to work out what Lydia meant. In the end she gave up and shook her head.

'Baby steps, my darling. You've not eaten much for quite a while. Your stomach's shrunk. You need to build yourself up. Regain your strength. Slowly and steadily, but you'll get there. I'll see to that.'

'Could you give us a moment?' Jemima's question was directed at Lydia.

The woman was about to protest when Tabitha interjected. 'Mum, please. The detective and I have things to discuss. Go take a break. I can't talk with you here.'

They waited in silence as Lydia gathered her things and headed out of the room, huffing and puffing as she went.

'I couldn't speak freely in front of her,' said Tabitha. 'It's all too raw. I'm sorry I couldn't tell you more, earlier on today. I'm just exhausted and everything's so muddled.'

'I understand,' said Jemima.

'But there are things you need to know. Father is ruthless. I told you that he was going to kill Peter soon. Well, he was going to kill me too. He has what he calls a "three strikes rule".'

'Three strikes, you're out,' muttered Jemima, as Peter's words came back to her.

'That's right. From your expression you seem to know what I'm going to say.'

'Not at all. It was a phrase Peter used. A heavily pregnant woman came to visit another child on his ward. The baby must've kicked. She winced and touched her stomach. Peter went to pieces. He pointed at her and kept repeating the phrase. Quietly at first, but then faster and louder until he was hysterical.'

'The poor little mite,' said Tabitha. Tears rolled down her cheeks. 'No child should see or hear the things he's been exposed to.'

'What does the phrase refer to?' asked Jemima. She needed to know, but dreaded hearing the response.

'It was one of the sick rules for us, his so-called wives. He wanted a large family. Had sex with us all the time and refused to use any birth control. We were a means to an end in every way. None of us wanted to have sex with him, but we had no choice. He beat Summer unconscious when she tried to say no, and he raped her anyway.'

'Explain the strikes to me.'

'If any of us had a miscarriage it counted as a strike. If we gave birth to a boy, that counted as a strike too. If any combination of those things happened three times, he said he'd kill us.'

Jemima listened in horror. Douglas Taylor was indeed a monster. She suddenly realized that her jaw had dropped and closed her mouth.

'Marcus was my first strike. I miscarried a baby three years ago, strike two, and I knew that I was about to miscarry again. I had no choice. If I'd stayed, he'd have killed me. And Peter only had a matter of weeks until he reached his seventh birthday. Time had run out for both of us.'

'What about Giselle? Why didn't she come too?' asked Jemima.

'Giselle's baby's due any day. Her ankles are swollen, and she tires easily. She wasn't capable of getting Peter out of there. There was no way she could leave without compromising him, and he was her priority. She would just have slowed things down, and if Father caught us, he would've killed us all.

'Peter and I were living on borrowed time. Giselle begged me to take him. The other kids will be safe for now. They're all girls. Jolie had Anna and Bea. They're three and one. Summer had Freya, who's six months. Peter was Giselle's only strike, so she'll be safe for now. They'll all be safe for now.'

'Unless he decides to punish all of them or figures out that the net is closing in on him and decides to cut and run. As things stand, he doesn't realize that we know who he is, and we want to keep it that way,' said Jemima.

'But you and Peter are still at risk. This hospital's in a different health authority from where you were found, yet he still found you. He's already taken a huge risk by coming here to try to kill you, and in all honesty, there's nothing to suggest that he won't try to do it again. If it wasn't for the others that are still captive, we'd consider putting his name out there. As things stand, you'll appreciate it's not an option. But now that your condition's improved so that you're no longer connected to the machines it would be possible to move you to a more secure location.'

'You could do that?'

'Yes.'

'What about Peter?'

'Giselle's mother is on the case. She's hoping to get him transferred to a hospital near to her home.'

'That's great. At least he won't be on his own. Giselle often spoke about her parents. They sounded like lovely people. I'm sure Peter will be safe with them for the time being.'

Jemima wasn't inclined to tell Tabitha that Giselle's father was no longer alive. It had no bearing on what would happen to Peter and was irrelevant to Tabitha's situation.

'In your case, there might be two options. Firstly, we could arrange for you to be taken to another hospital. It might buy us some time, but as it's a large public space we'd still have the same fundamental security issues. There'd be a police presence, but staff and visitors would see them, and people talk.'

'What's the other option?'

'That would be far more secure, but it would be a private security firm and it would cost you.'

'I'm sure Mother would pay.'

'You'll need to talk it over with her first, and I'd need to make some enquiries to establish if they are able to take you on as clients. I'm not in regular contact with them and it's possible they might have other commitments which would rule them out of this. But I can vouch for them. My old boss almost died and there were numerous influential people who would have happily seen him dead. This group saved his life. They provided qualified medical assistance, and having seen how effective they were, I trust them implicitly.'

'If you were me, would you go for that option?'

'I would, but don't let me influence you. I'll just be putting you in touch with them. The decision ultimately lies with you and your mother.'

'In that case I'll ask her when she comes back.'

'You asked to see me, so are you able to tell me anything else which might help us establish where Taylor kept you?' Jemima was conscious of time ticking by, and every second which elapsed gave Douglas Taylor the opportunity to harm or even kill the others.

'There's not much I can tell you, other than the fact that we were held in a large house with a long driveway and no neighbours that I could see. Whenever he went out, and during the night, he chained us women up. The restraints were long enough to allow us to see to the children. Thankfully the little ones were never chained.

'He's obsessed with security. It's like a fortress. He keeps the outer doors bolted and padlocked, except for one, because if there was an emergency, he wanted to ensure he'd be able to make a quick exit.'

'How certain are you about the security measures he has in place?'

'Believe me, between us we've made it our mission to know everything about him and the inside of that property. We've spent years being his prisoners and sex slaves. The only thing that's kept us going is the thought that one day at least one of us would be able to make it out of there undetected and get help for the others. We'd pool our information. Discreetly, of course. We couldn't risk letting him know that we were plotting against him.'

'Sounds as though he's paranoid,' muttered Jemima.

'He is. There were bars on the windows too, and security cameras on the outside of the property. He'll know you're coming before you reach the house.'

'In all the time you were there, did he ever allow you to go outside?'

'No. Even the kids were kept inside.'

'So how do you know about the security cameras?'

'He used to come and collect whichever one of us he'd decided to take to his room. His room was downstairs, ours was upstairs. One time, he'd left a door open down there and I saw inside: it was full of screens with different views of what I thought must be the grounds of the house.'

'It sounds as though he'd kitted the place out like a high-security prison,' said Jemima. 'What did you see?'

'It was too far away to see properly what was on the screens.'

'What about when you left the house — could you tell me anything about the outside of it, or the direction you walked in?'

She shook her head. 'I'm sorry, my thoughts are all jumbled, and it was dark when we left the house — too dark to see much more than outlines. I know it was . . . big. I was terrified of getting caught. I'd been in pain for a few hours. Hiding it whenever he was around. Luckily for me there were no outward signs of the miscarriage at that stage. But it was all I could do to put one foot in front of the other. Looking for clues as to where we were wasn't a priority, but I'm trying my best to remember things which might help you.'

'I know you are, and I'm sorry to push you like this.' Jemima paused. 'But this is important. Can you tell me anything about the property that will help us identify it? Could you tell me what you could see out of the windows, perhaps?'

'Yes. There was a sort of concrete yard in front of the house, and a driveway.' Tabitha squeezed her eyes shut as she tried to recall the exact details. 'And a large metal gate.'

Jemima's heart rate increased. This was new and potentially useful information. She just needed Tabitha to recall more details. Provide her with information which could help them identify the property. Eager to find out more, she offered some prompts. 'A gate you could see through, or a solid gate?'

'Solid. With spikes across the top, and I think there were coils of barbed wire across the top too.'

This was good. 'What colour was it?'

'Umm . . .' Tabitha's gaze slid away. She was tiring rapidly.

Jemima masked her impatience. After everything she had been through, and in such an early stage of her recovery, of course Tabitha was going to struggle to give her the right details.

'Possibly green. Though it might have been blue . . . Or perhaps it was brown.'

Jemima's heart sank. Tabitha's uncertainty made her question the reliability of the young woman's memories. Which was hardly surprising, given the horrendous level of sustained abuse she'd been subjected to for much of her adult life. 'You don't remember, do you?'

'No, I'm trying to, but it's too difficult. I seem to recall some things clearly. While other things are still a blur.'

'Don't worry about it, Tabitha. You've given us something to go on.' Jemima squeezed her hand and smiled. 'So was the gate open or shut when you escaped?'

'Open. On the few occasions the power went down during the day, it opened. So, I knew that we'd be able to get out that way.'

Jemima nodded. This was something which might come in useful when they eventually managed to locate the property.

Tabitha continued, 'I was the first of us to be abducted and spent a long time on my own with that creep. I'm sure he planned to take me.'

'What made you think that?'

It was as though the recollection of the gate had buoyed her up and Tabitha sounded more confident as she spoke. 'It didn't occur to me at first, but after a while I realized that the security measures were already in place. It was as though he'd set it up for that purpose. He'd thought of everything, even down to having changes of clothes for me.'

'And they fitted you?' asked Jemima.

'Yes. Weirdly, they did.'

Jemima raised her eyebrows in surprise. 'Yet when you were found, you were both dressed in underwear that were little more than rags.'

'He hardly bought us anything. Occasionally he'd hand out a few things. He'd pick up things for the little ones. I guess that wouldn't have raised any eyebrows. It's the sort of thing a father might do. But as for the adults, he must've thought it was too much of a risk. Sometimes he gave us a jumper or T-shirt he no longer wore, but we rarely got anything new.'

'Guess it might have raised suspicions if he'd regularly bought clothes of different sizes,' said Jemima.

'I suppose so. Did you know that he attended a fundraiser at my parents' home? There were so many people there that night that it would have been impossible to keep tabs on everyone. So, I guess it would have been possible for the creep to have gone into my bedroom and looked through my things. Makes me sick just thinking about it. If only one of us had spotted him we could have reported him to the police, and he'd not have had the opportunity to abduct me.'

'Can you think of anything else about the property that I need to know?'

'Not really. Like I said, there're so many security measures in place, so it won't be easy for you to rescue the others even when you know where they are.'

'If you were routinely chained up, how did you manage to escape?' asked Jemima.

'Over the years I'd learned how to pick the lock on my restraint. I was fortunate to have found a paperclip which had been dropped on the floor. Kept it hidden away. We all looked out for things we could use, but very rarely did we find anything. We were careful to hide things as he'd get aggressive if he found us doing something that was against the rules.

'I'd been trying to find the switch for that gate for years, but that night, I was in luck: there was a power cut. The only thing we could hear was Father — he was keeping us awake with his snoring. He didn't drink often, but when he did, he drank to excess. He was out for the count, and I knew that it was my one and only chance to save myself and Peter.'

'You said Giselle wasn't capable of escaping, but what about Jolie and Summer?'

'Their daughters are too small. They wouldn't have been able to get out of there without risking waking him, and they'd never have been able to keep running with the little ones. Peter and I were the only two who were immediately at risk. So, it made sense for us to be the ones to try to escape. They knew that if I made it, I'd send help. It was their best chance too.

'Peter's still young, but he's no ordinary child. He's damaged but wise beyond his years after the things he's seen and been subjected to. He's learned from experience to be quiet. To watch things play out, fade into the background and try to make himself invisible. Giselle had already told him that he should go with me, and he always does as he's told. Once I'd freed myself, I collected Peter, and we crept downstairs. We all knew where the key was kept. Father didn't consider it to be a risk, keeping it easily accessible as it hadn't occurred to him that we had any means of freeing ourselves from the restraints.'

'As Taylor was drunk, why didn't you all go into his room and overpower him? Surely that would have enabled all of you to escape?' Jemima was determined to refer to him by name, though she understood that after so many years in captivity, it was only natural for Tabitha to refer to her captor by his chosen moniker.

'If only it was that easy.' Tabitha shook her head. 'I wish we could have done that, but it wasn't an option. There was only the one paperclip to release the restraints. It would take too long to free everyone, and each time it was used, we risked snapping it.

'As for overpowering him, Father was way stronger than us. He ate well and exercised regularly, whereas we were routinely given the smallest rations to survive. He had this metal bar he used to beat us with if anyone played up. Believe me, everyone quickly learned not to mess with him. No matter what, he always came out on top.'

'That night, when you made it outside, what do you remember? You must've seen or heard things.'

'It was dark apart from the crescent moon. No street lights. We made our way over rough ground, possibly fields. Though I can't be certain. We seemed to have been going for hours. We couldn't run. Just had to walk quickly, as we couldn't risk tripping or turning our ankles. It didn't help that we were barefoot. I haven't had shoes for years, and the children have never had any. It was painful, making that journey, but the pain in my feet was the least of my concerns.

'We kept going, crossed a few surfaced roads. I guess they were lanes as they were narrow and there was no traffic. We climbed over a few stiles. I thought it was safer to stay off the roads. I didn't want to risk him waking up and coming after us in a car. It would have increased his chances of finding us if we'd stuck to the roads.'

'Were you out for more than one day?' Jemima was trying to gauge the distance they could have covered on foot.

'No. It was dark when we left the house, but I've no idea what time it was as we didn't have access to a clock. All I know is that it had been dark for a while. Father decided when we did things. When lights went on and off. When we ate. When we slept.'

'Did you come across any other houses?'

'Not that I could see. We were in the middle of nowhere. The only light was from the moon, and some stars. But we did reach the coastline, which surprised me. I had no idea that we were so near the sea. When Father took me, he placed a rag over my nose and mouth and the smell knocked me out — I was sick when I woke up.'

'Sounds like chloroform,' said Jemima.

'He did the same to the others. None of us knew where we were. I had no idea that he'd driven so far.

'I remember the sunrise. The first I'd seen in many years out in the open. The first Peter had ever seen. It would have been magical if we hadn't both been so exhausted. I was bleeding by then. The stomach cramps were bad. Peter tried to help. Forced me to keep going. That's all I remember.'

'You've done well, Tabitha. You saved Peter's life. You should be proud of yourself,' said Jemima. She stopped talking when she heard voices outside the room, and turned to see that Lydia Leysham had returned and was speaking to the officer standing guard outside the door.

'I've mentioned the possibility of moving Tabitha to a safer location,' said Jemima. 'She'd be guarded by private contractors and there would be medical assistance on hand.'

'Do it,' said Lydia. 'If you think she'd be safer, then do it. The cost doesn't matter. I'll pay whatever it takes for however long it takes.'

'In that case I'll make the call. The outfit's run by an ex-special forces man named Frank Rutherford. He also works with my former boss, Ray Kennedy. If they take you on, you can trust them. They're the people I'd go to if I needed protection.'

'That's good enough for me, Detective,' said Lydia. 'How will they contact me?'

'I'll give Ray Kennedy your phone number. This is what he looks like.' She swiped through some photographs on her phone and showed Lydia one of her former boss.

CHAPTER 16

It seemed to Jemima that she was spending most of her time
on this case driving around instead of doing anything useful.
Might as well kill two birds with one stone, she thought, dialling
Ray Kennedy's number. As the ringtone sounded, she started
the engine, checked the mirrors, and pulled away.

For many years, Ray Kennedy had been Jemima's boss,
mentor and friend. He'd had a reputation on the force for
being a no-nonsense copper, and his squad had an exceptional clear-up rate. Not because he looked the other way or
was in anyone's pocket. Kennedy was an exceptional person,
a man of principle. Someone who expected one hundred
per cent commitment from every officer on his squad and
insisted that everything be done by the book.

Jemima had always considered herself to be principled,
and she had been delighted to take up a detective sergeant's
post on his squad. Throughout the many cases they'd investigated, the entire team had been to hell and back. Losing one
of their own in the most brutal and unexpected way had been
hard for all of them. And then, on Jemima's first day back
on the job following a period of maternity leave, they almost
lost Kennedy too. That day had sent shockwaves through the
entire force, with some of the events playing out for all the

119

world to see. It had ended the working regime as they knew it and resulted in Kennedy leaving the force and Jemima being promoted to the rank of DCI. A role she easily adapted to. Though there wasn't a day that went by, when Ray Kennedy wasn't in her thoughts, and she knew that Dan and Gareth felt the same way too.

'Jemima? Is everything OK? It's not Bilko, is it?' Kennedy's voice was full of concern. When the previous year's events had ensured that Ray had to make an immediate exit from the only way of life he knew, he was forced to make some hard decisions. One of which was entrusting the care of his beloved cat to Jemima's sister.

'Hi Ray, don't worry. We're all fine, as is Bilko. He's quite the pampered puss and the kids love him to bits. This is a purely professional call.' Jemima continued to appraise him of the need for protection for Tabitha. 'Her mother, Lydia, would also like to tag along. I know it's short notice, but any chance you and Frank could do the honours?'

'It's a possibility. In fact, it's good timing on your part. As luck would have it, we've just wrapped up our latest assignment. I'll have a word with Frank and get back to you. If he agrees to take it on, I'll need to issue you with a codeword to pass on to the client. Stay safe, Jem.' The line went dead before she had the opportunity to respond.

* * *

'Any progress, Gareth?' Jemima knew, even before asking the question, that they hadn't had a breakthrough.

'It's slow going,' he replied, without taking his eyes off his screen. 'If he'd stuck to the major roads, it would've been fine, but he's kept his cool and got it all worked out. Trying to pick him up from a traffic camera on one of the major routes, further down the line, is like searching for the proverbial needle in a haystack.'

'Unless he's decided to cut and run, he has to be heading back to wherever he's holding the others in the vicinity of the wetlands. I've just come from the hospital and Tabitha's told me they were held inside a large remote property. They can't have walked more than a few hours — it was dark when they set off and not long after sunrise when they were found. Neither of them was in good enough health to go fast — so I'm going to head along to the incident room and try to find it. Keep going with those camera feeds and let me know the moment you get a breakthrough.'

As she was about to leave the room her phone rang. Glancing at the screen she saw it was Kennedy.

'I've spoken to Frank and it's a go,' said Ray.

'That's wonderful news. How soon is it likely to be?'

'Ninety minutes and counting. As you've given me Lydia's number tell her I'll call her in the next quarter of an hour. The code word I'll use will be "pterodactyl". I'll expect her to respond with the phrase, "dead as a dodo".'

Jemima forced herself to stifle a laugh, but Kennedy sensed her amusement.

'Don't blame me. I'm not the one who comes up with these codewords and phrases. This new career of mine has taken me so far out of my comfort zone. Sometimes I think I'm a fusion of bodyguard and cold-war spy.'

'I'll pass the message on. Let me know when she's safe and sound.'

'Will do, Jem. Speak to you later.'

With arrangements for the secure extraction of Tabitha in place, Jemima had one less thing to worry about. It was time to settle down in front of her screen and use technology to scour maps in the vicinity of Newport Wetlands. With so many people in imminent danger from Taylor, she was determined to use every tool available to try to find where he was holding them. A solid metal gate with barbed wire across the top wasn't much to go on, but it was more than she had an hour ago. When put together with a large remote property, it narrowed down the possibilities.

'Anything to report?' she asked as she walked into the room.

'Diddly squat,' said Dan. 'Taylor's vehicle is still registered to his old address. We've been on to Land Registry, council tax records, there's nothing so far.'

'I'm trying to track down phone records. He must have a mobile,' said Nancy. 'But I'm hitting one brick wall after another. Network providers are so pissy about data confidentiality. I've begged, threatened. You name it, I've tried it, but no one's prepared to play ball.'

'Have you spoken to Didier Fontaine about Taylor yet?'

'Yes, but he couldn't tell me much. Sounds like he wasn't there long, Guv,' Nancy said.

'Tell him to send you over Taylor's CV, along with every bit of personal information they held on him. They'd have needed things like his bank account, National Insurance number. You know the sort of things employers are required to hold. There's a chance he might not have changed his bank account, and even if his address isn't up to date, we'd still be able to find out information such as where he withdraws cash, or payments he makes. If he's ordered something online, there's a chance he might have had the item delivered. Or at least sent to a designated pick-up point. Anything could help us to narrow things down and pinpoint his location.'

'On it,' said Nancy.

'Dan, I need help with something.'

'Name it.'

Jemima told him about the solid metal gate with barbed wire coiled at the top of it. 'The only geographical point of reference we have is the point at which Tabitha and Peter were found. And the coastline helps, too, it narrows down the places they could have walked from.'

Dan nodded his agreement.

'Tabitha said that when they escaped there were no other properties nearby. They crossed a road, though there was no sign of any traffic, so it's not likely to have been a major carriageway.'

'More likely a lane,' said Dan.

'Precisely. So, I'd suggest we narrow the search area by discounting any places where there are more than a handful of properties. Which, by my reckoning leaves us with this.' She circled an area of the map with her finger. 'Let's look at satellite pictures for large, secluded houses; then we can check the street images to see which ones have solid metal gates.'

They worked in silence. Given the fact that they had so little to go on, it was a mind-numbingly boring yet necessary task. When it came down to it, most investigative work, was just that. Boring. Repetitive. Painstaking. Looking for that elusive something which once found, would make sense of many of the seemingly random pieces of information you had gathered along the way.

Jemima was concentrating so hard on the screen that she had no idea how long she had been sitting there. All she knew was that her eyes were beginning to feel the strain. She looked across as Dan stretched and yawned noisily.

Further down the room, Nancy got up from her seat and headed towards Jemima's desk. 'Guv, Didier Fontaine has sent through everything he has on Taylor. I've got bank account details. They're the same on both sets of records. The address he's given on both is the house in multiple occupation we've already checked out and know he no longer lives at.'

'Anything else of use?'

'Just a next of kin: his father, Benedict Sebastian Taylor.'

'In that case, do the necessary to enable us to have sight of activity on that account. Press home the fact that we believe there's a credible and immediate threat to life. Let me know if you need me to speak to anyone about it.

'Once you've sorted that, do a background check on Benedict. That might throw up something useful. Taylor doesn't seem to have lasted long in any of the jobs we've seen on his CV, and he certainly didn't have a lavish lifestyle if he was prepared to rent a room in a HMO. But there's nothing to say that his old man doesn't have money. Could be that he's the one who owns the property we're looking for,' said Jemima.

'On it, Guv,' said Nancy, as she headed back to her desk.

'How's it going, Dan?'

'I've come across one possibility, but I'm still scanning the area just in case there are others.'

'Let me see,' interjected Jemima. She all but jumped out of her chair in her haste to see for herself.

'Wait a mo. It'll take a while for me to return to that spot . . . Almost there.' As he continued to click his mouse the view changed.

Jemima pulled up a chair and sat down beside him. 'It's got to be the place we're looking for,' said Jemima, as the gate came into sight. 'Switch to satellite view so we can take a look at what's behind those gates.'

It was time to contact Lydia and ask her to show Tabitha the images they were about to forward of the property where they believed she had been held captive. And it was a tense few minutes as they waited in silence for their suspicions to be confirmed.

CHAPTER 17

It took the best part of an hour to make the arrangements. During which time, Jemima received a call to say that Ray Kennedy and Frank Rutherford had collected their latest clients, and that Tabitha and Lydia were on their way to a far more secure location. She had also been informed by another source that Peter had been transferred to the Children's Centre at Royal United Hospitals in Bath. Which should reduce his risk of being found by Taylor and meant that his grandmother should be able to spend time helping him recuperate.

It was a relief to know that at least they were safe. One less thing for everyone to worry about, and it also freed up the armed officers who had guarded them. Though, there would be no downtime for them, as they would be needed to assist with the breach of the property and the rescue of the three women and the children, they believed that Taylor had held in captivity for such a long time.

Jemima called a halt to the work Gareth and his team were doing. They had not made any further progress tracking Taylor's vehicle, and it was likely that he had either gone into hiding or had secretly returned to the property they were now focusing on. Either way, their top priority was to rescue the women and children, hopefully before it was too late for any of them.

Jemima asked Nancy to check the Land Registry website and establish who owned the property. She also asked Levi to contact the National Grid to get the relevant person with the authority to temporarily cut power to the property and the surrounding area when Jemima gave them the go-ahead. There was always the possibility that a remote property might have a backup generator, and if that were the case they could do nothing about it. Though it seemed unlikely; Tabitha had already told her that there had been a few occasions when they had power cuts and hadn't mentioned a generator backing up the power supply. Shutting down the conventional electricity supply might help disrupt the CCTV surveillance system and buy them time to enter the grounds unobserved.

'Guv!' called Nancy. 'Seems as though a company named L&T Holdings own the property. But I don't have any details about them.'

'Excellent work, Nancy. Now get on to Companies House. See what you can find out from there.'

Despite Jemima's team having completed firearms training and used the weapons in some of their cases, they were joined by officers from the firearms unit. With the lives of six civilians at stake, and that of an unborn child, it was essential that they took no chances. Taylor was only one man. But he was an individual who had proven that he did not value human life. He was quite prepared to kill a police officer merely for getting between himself and his target.

Jemima looked around at the group of assembled officers who were waiting for her instructions. 'This is our suspect, Douglas Taylor.' She pointed to a photograph of him displayed on the whiteboard. 'I don't need to tell you how dangerous this man is. In addition to killing one of our own, he also attempted to kill one of his former captives while she was being treated at the UHW to prevent her from identifying him. We've been led to believe that he has also killed a child. He's holding these three women against their will.'

She pointed at photographs of Giselle, Jolie and Summer. 'As a result of him repeatedly raping them, there are also children born inside that property and still living there.' She went on to tell the assembled group their names and ages. 'When Tabitha Leysham and Peter Braverman escaped from the property a few days ago, Giselle Braverman was heavily pregnant. As such, it's possible she could have already, or be about to give birth.'

'What do we know about the property?' asked Gareth.

'Very little. Apart from the satellite images.' At a signal from her the lights dimmed slightly and the satellite images were projected on a screen by the whiteboard. 'The only information we have is that Taylor has a surveillance system. There's a ground-floor room used as a surveillance centre, where he's rigged up various monitors to display images from CCTV cameras installed on site. So, it's safe to say that if he's there, he'll see us coming. We'll cut power to the site before we go in, but there's always the chance he'll have a backup generator. Though I think it's unlikely.'

'Do we know if he's got remote access to the cameras?' asked Gareth.

'We don't.'

'In that case we can't rule out the possibility of him having rigged up a device or devices to blow the structure when we breach it,' said an officer from the firearms unit.

'Correct. Though there's nothing to suggest he's familiar with the use of explosives,' said Jemima.

'That's not good enough.'

'I agree,' said Jemima. 'Operational safety is paramount. I don't want there to be any loss of life or injuries. I need suggestions and solutions to make that happen. But keep in mind that every second we delay increases the danger our suspect poses to those women and children.

'As you can see, the property's located in a remote area. Yet despite being far away from anything other than the lane upon which it's located, I've been informed that Taylor never allows any of the captives to go outside.'

'Not even the kids?' asked Dan.

'No one's allowed outside. Taylor keeps his captives on the upper floor of the building. He shackles the women with chains long enough to enable them to see to the children.'

'Don't tell me he shackles the bairns too?' said Mack. His voice was filled with anger.

'No. That's his one concession. But it's not down to any sense of compassion. I think it's because he doesn't see them as a threat. At least until the boys get older. Which is why Tabitha took Peter with her when she made her escape.'

'Are you saying that bastard would have hurt him?' asked Dan.

'According to Tabitha, he killed her son on his seventh birthday. He was threatening to do the same to Peter.' As Jemima told them this, there were a few expletives muttered and the temperature in the room seemed to rise, as every officer seemed more determined than ever to end this monster's reign of terror.

'It's only natural to be upset by what you've heard. But for everyone's sake you all need to put that out of your minds and focus on the operation. We can't afford to have anyone going in there and acting on their emotions. If that happens it increases the likelihood of someone making a mistake that could cost lives.'

'Agreed,' echoed the lead officer of the firearms unit. 'It's the way we approach everything. A tactical operation. End of.'

Jemima nodded her approval, then continued. 'First off, we don't know how recent these satellite images are, so I've arranged for drones. They'll help us establish how many cameras he's set up and pinpoint their location.'

'And hopefully we'll be able to establish if he's set up any boobytraps along the way,' interjected Gareth.

'Absolutely. We must go in there as clued up as possible. The only information we have is what Tabitha's told us about the inside of the property, and she really didn't see much while she was there, so there'll be a lot of unknowns.'

'How did the victims escape?' asked one of the firearms officers.

'It was during a power outage. Apparently, the gates opened, which allowed them to make it out of there quite easily. Which suggests that if there is a backup generator it would need to be started manually. It wasn't a problem when they escaped, as Taylor was drunk and had passed out. But with everything that's happened he'd be on high alert. He's not going to make that mistake again, so we should presume that once the power's cut we've got a maximum of a couple of minutes, possibly even less to get through those gates.'

Jemima glanced around and was pleased to see everyone nod their head in agreement.

'He must have moved on by now, Guv,' said Dan.

'Perhaps, but I don't think it's likely. Taylor would have been running about like a headless chicken when he realized they'd gone. He eventually found Tabitha, but that wouldn't have been the first hospital he would have searched. Face it, we chose that location because it was quite a distance from where they were found. It would have taken a lot of time to track her down,' said Jemima. 'Plus, he has put effort into building this "family" of his. It'd be difficult to find another secure property for such a large group.'

'Wouldn't he just leave them behind, then?'

'It's a possibility, though I don't think it fits with his psychology. I think he's still based there. But I could be wrong, and time is of the essence.'

'Do we know if he has any weapons on the premises?' asked the leader of the armed response unit.

'We've not been advised of any firearms, but that's obviously not definitive proof,' said Jemima. 'From what Tabitha's said, he occasionally used a metal bar to keep his captives under control, but most of the time he shackled them, only freeing them on an individual basis, for specific purposes and a limited amount of time. He didn't take a weapon to the hospital, but that could be because he didn't want to run the risk of getting caught with one.'

'I agree,' said Dan. 'He'd have known there'd be security in place at the hospital. If he'd been stopped and searched at any point it would have increased his risk of arrest.'

'And if he was challenged, he wouldn't have been able to talk his way out of it,' said Mack. 'By going there without a weapon, he could pretend to be an innocent member of the public. It would have increased his chances of getting to Tabitha undiscovered.'

'I suggest we go for a two-tier road restriction. Set an outer cordon to seal off access to the lane at these points.' Jemima marked them on the map. 'Put up signs about a major gas leak and have some uniform presence to prevent any idiots still determined to get through. Inside that we'll have paramedics and the fire service in attendance.

'We obviously need to get closer than that, but we mustn't alert Taylor to the fact that we intend to storm the property. With that in mind, I suggest that we position our vehicles at this passing point. It's far enough away that he won't see us. We'll deploy the drone from there and assess the external threat level. Once we've got an up-to-date picture of what's on the other side of that gate we'll proceed on foot and wait just outside the property's perimeter until we have confirmation that the power has been cut. If all goes to plan the gates should open and we rescue the captives.'

'I suggest we split into six teams,' said the leader of the armed response unit. 'That way there'll be at least one of my sharpshooters with each of your team. You should focus on locating and freeing the victims. Our focus will be on neutralizing the threat. Agreed?'

'Agreed,' said Jemima. 'But if you find yourself in a situation where you have to shoot, I expect you to do everything possible to preserve life. I want Taylor alive to answer questions and face trial.'

'We'll do our best, but if we face a situation where it's believed he poses an immediate threat to life, we'll take appropriate action to ensure that officers and the victims are kept safe.'

'Understood.' Jemima knew it made sense but hoped it didn't come to that. There were so many questions that Taylor needed to answer. Plus, the victims and their families needed to have the opportunity to see him tried in a court of law and have the satisfaction of knowing that an almost inevitable guilty verdict would mean that he would face a lengthy prison sentence without any hope of parole.

'I suggest that four of my officers cover the perimeter in case Taylor makes a run for it. That'll enable us to have four teams entering the property. Two for the upper floor where the women and children are, and two to search at ground level.'

Levi entered the room carrying a phone. 'Guv, I've got a representative from the National Grid on the line.'

'Excellent, I'll speak to them now,' said Jemima as she held out her hand. 'Get your equipment together everyone, and remember, no one leaves this station without wearing a Kevlar vest.'

CHAPTER 18

As they headed to the scene, the enormity of what they were about to do played heavily on Jemima's mind. So many things could go wrong, and mistakes could cost lives.

An operation of this size and complexity would normally have taken days of planning — time they didn't have. After a great deal of effort and some coercion it had all seemingly come together. As the vehicles pulled into the passing place, Jemima took a deep breath to centre herself. This was the moment of truth.

Everyone got out of the vehicles and gathered round. 'Let's get the drone up,' she said. 'See what we're up against.'

The device in question was sufficiently small and quiet enough not to attract attention if you weren't specifically looking out for it. In recent years the police force had used such devices on many cases where they needed to get a closer look at an area which might be hazardous. They'd also been used successfully for search and rescue purposes.

As the drone was launched, the officers gathered around the screen, noting everything in sight. Gareth was in control, deftly manoeuvring the device to get the best views.

'This is definitely the location they're being held,' said Jemima. 'There's the coiled barbed wire on top of the gate, and bars covering the windows on the upper floor. Just like Tabitha described. Wait, go back a bit.'

Gareth changed the drone's trajectory.

'Zoom in on that window, Gar.' Jemima pointed at one of the upper windows. Moments later, they were staring at a woman's face, which was contorted in pain. She was gripping the bars on the window so tightly that they could see her knuckles were white. It was as though they were close enough to reach out and touch her. Yet, as things stood, they were helpless.

Jemima shivered, as her blood turned to ice. 'That's Giselle Braverman. That bastard's either hurting her, or else she's already in labour. We need to get her medical attention. God only knows how she's managing, and she won't have any pain relief.'

Dan glanced across at Jemima. As their eyes met, she knew he was recalling the traumatic circumstances of Finlay's birth. He'd had no choice but to overcome his phobia of blood and deliver the baby himself. And although proud of his achievement under exceptionally stressful circumstances, it was an experience he did not wish to repeat again.

'It's proof they're alive,' said Levi.

'For now, and the noise she must be making will be a distraction from what we're about to do.'

'Might work to our advantage,' said Dan.

'I've counted six cameras,' said Gareth. 'As for access points, there's one door on the front of the property and another on the far side.'

'Two teams should be sufficient to cover the exit routes,' said one of the firearm officers.

'Everyone ready?' asked Jemima. She looked around, making eye contact with each of the officers in turn. Waiting for their nods of confirmation. 'Let's move.'

They set off in line formation, holding their weapons ready for the assault. As they assembled to one side of the gate a message on her phone confirmed that the power had been cut.

As the gate rolled open, she let out a sigh of relief. So far, so good.

CHAPTER 19

They had a plan and were about to follow it. Knowing this was their one and only chance of breaching the property to rescue the women and children, meant that they couldn't afford to make a mistake. If Taylor noticed the power had been cut, he would be alerted to the possibility that something was up. Then again, if Giselle was in labour it was equally possible that any disruption of the power supply might go unnoticed. Even a monster such as Taylor, would be hard pushed not to be distracted by the groans and screams of a woman in the throes of a contraction.

It seemed that as far as their rescue mission was concerned, the stars might have fortuitously aligned.

With no need to confer, they set off in formation along a poorly maintained driveway. The once asphalted surface had decayed over time, now little more than a series of cracks and potholes. It swung around to the left until the property became visible about forty yards further on.

To the sides were areas of what might have once been lawns. Though these areas had not been tended to for a long time and had been allowed to grow wild. What could have been a pleasant outdoor area was hazardous, with nettles, brambles and weeds in abundance.

It looked like a house from a horror film. Which, given the nature of the atrocities that had occurred inside the building, seemed apposite. The building was in a state of disrepair. Copious amount of greenery sprouted from cracked mortar on a blackened chimney. Roof tiles were cracked, others had slipped out of position. The wooden window frames were so rotten that it was easy to believe that they would crumble at the touch. The only signs of modernization or upkeep were the CCTV cameras, and modern windows fitted at the upper floor level.

Having already agreed teams and responsibility for individual lines of sight, they scanned the surroundings. Moving fast, everyone kept low, weapons at the ready. This part of the operation was no different to training exercises each of them had undertaken. Things would undoubtedly become hazardous the moment they encountered resistance.

As the two external teams broke away from the formation, it was down to the others to force entry to the property. Two of the internal teams, led by Gareth, headed towards the side access to establish whether they could easily gain access to the property there.

Jemima led the way for the other two teams and ascended the three stone steps which led directly to the front door. Reaching out, she grabbed the handle firmly, hoping the door would be unlocked. She applied pressure, but it didn't move. The door remained firmly shut.

There was a choice to be made. If they forced the door open, it might alert Taylor to their presence. And as there was no glass panel in the door or anywhere close, there was no way of knowing whether it would be easy to break the door down. It was entirely possible that Taylor's failed attempt to kill Tabitha could have spooked him into taking extra precautions. One of which could have been to barricade the door. If he had done that, it would have the double benefit of making it more difficult for outsiders to get in, while making it impossible for more of his captives to escape without making a hell of a racket.

They had all known that it was unlikely he would have left the door unlocked. After all, the bars on the upper windows and the CCTV cameras evidenced his preoccupation with and need for security.

A member of Gareth's team appeared from around the side of the property. He shook his head to indicate that they didn't have an easy means of access.

Jemima had a choice to make. It was either enter via a window, or she could pick the lock and hope that the door wasn't barricaded on the other side. The window panes were large enough that, once removed, the empty space would enable a person to climb through. In normal circumstances there would have been no hesitation in breaking the glass. But the noise of smashing the pane could easily alert Taylor that they were coming for him. Plus, once they'd entered whichever room it was, there was no guarantee that they'd easily be able to get to other parts of the house, as it was entirely possible the internal door to that room could also be locked or barricaded on the other side.

'Give me a chance to pick the lock,' said Jemima as she extracted the small toolkit she always carried with her. She dropped to her knees and got started immediately, oblivious to the surprised and sceptical exchange of glances from some of the others.

'It's her party piece,' whispered Dan. 'Seen her do it loads of times.' At that moment he looked and sounded like a proud parent. 'She's bloody good at it too. If she can't do it, then that lock is unpickable.' He had barely finished asserting his confidence in Jemima's ability when there was an audible click.

'Jeez, respect, Guv,' said Levi, as he nodded his approval. He, like a few others on her team, had no idea that Jemima was so accomplished at such a nefarious skill.

Jemima stood up, slipping her toolkit back into its small pouch. 'Let's go, and keep your wits about you,' she said.

The door creaked as it opened inwards. It was hardly surprising that the hinges needed to be oiled, given the shabby state of the door and the apparent disrepair of the exterior of the property. The state of the hallway mirrored Jemima's expectations. It was impossible to make out the patterns and colours of the cracked floor tiles, as they were so caked in grime. And each time someone raised a foot from the surface, the movement was accompanied by a squelching sound as the sole was pulled away from the glaze of dirty residue.

No one had spoken since setting foot inside the premises. Everyone was straining to hear something which could help them identify the location of the inhabitants. But it quickly became apparent that apart from their own breathing, there was no sound of either movement or life. It was implausible that the building was empty, as they had only just seen Giselle at a window on the upper floor, and from the pained expression on her face it didn't seem likely she'd be capable of going anywhere. There should be some sort of noise. Some sense of movement. Yet worryingly, they had heard nothing as they approached the building and it had remained absent since they had stepped inside.

Every officer was asking themselves the same question. Yet no one was prepared to voice it. Had Douglas Taylor already killed his captives?

The small corridor they were assembled in revealed four closed doors, with no sign of a staircase. They needed to find it, and soon, for Jemima and the other team to make their way to the upper level. Their only option was to open each of the doors and establish what was on the other side of them. As they'd already been assigned into teams, they split up accordingly.

Jemima reached out and turned the handle of the door in front of her. Like everything else they had encountered so far, it was grubby. She could feel the dirt on her palm and fingers and sensed a sticky residue. As the door slowly swung inwards, its hinges creaked as loudly as those on the front door. She stood aside so as not to make herself a target should Taylor be waiting on the other side. Every officer's weapon was raised in readiness, and Jemima was the first to enter the room. As she glanced around, she couldn't help but wrinkle her nose. The air was stale with the stench of sex, and heavily laden with dust motes. The room was squalid. Bare apart from a chest of drawers and a double bed with a duvet thrown back, bunched untidily towards the foot of the mattress. A fitted sheet, more stained than patterned, stretched across the mattress. The covering was old, faded, and threadbare in places, leaving nothing to the imagination about the activities that took place inside this room.

'Go through whatever's in here. If he's hidden anything, I want it found,' she said to the closest officer.

As she stepped out of the room, she saw Dan headed in her direction. 'You'll want to see this.' His voice was low and urgent. He turned and headed back towards another room without waiting for her to respond.

Jemima followed him and moments later found herself inside Taylor's monitoring hub. Against the far wall was a large desk on which there was a laptop. Fixed to the wall were twelve monitors, all of which were blank. Which made sense as the power was off. 'Given the number of monitors, it suggests he's rigged up cameras somewhere inside.'

'Tabitha and the lad were lucky to make it out when they did,' said Dan. 'I bet he's got cameras set up in their living quarters. He'd be able to keep an eye on them twenty-four-seven if he wanted to.'

'I don't think he did,' said Jemima.

'What makes you say that?'

'Tabitha said she'd found a paperclip and used it to remove the shackles. If he had cameras in the living quarters, he'd have known that she had it. I'd guess he monitored the hallway up there. He'd know they couldn't escape from the windows. The bars would make it impossible. Plus, she didn't mention any cameras in the living quarters.'

'Guv, we've found the staircase. It's on the far side of the house. You have to go through the kitchen to reach it,' said another officer.

CHAPTER 20

As Jemima led the way, two of the teams headed up the stairs. Alert to the possibility of danger, treading carefully on each of the risers, weapons ready should they be needed.

Jemima's heart rate increased with each passing moment, as her sense of unease intensified. There were so many things which didn't add up. Apart from the police presence, there should be numerous people inside the property. Which meant there should have been some noise. Yet, apart from the muted sound of the officers' boots, there was none.

It didn't make sense. It was possible that Taylor could keep two of the women quiet, but Giselle had obviously been in pain. A woman in labour couldn't possibly be kept quiet.

Then there were the three small children. They were far too young to understand any rules imposed upon them. Plus, they would surely have been scared by what was happening to Giselle. To see or hear an adult in pain would be terrifying for any child. Little ones turned to their parents for strength and comfort. And it wasn't unusual that once one child was distressed, the others would pick up on it too.

At the top of the stairs was a narrow landing and four closed doors. A quick glance around revealed no evidence of padlocks or any other locking device, and as there was still no sound coming from any direction at that level, it was potluck which door to open first.

Jemima quickly worked out the direction the drone had been flying in when they'd spotted Giselle at one of the windows. If her recollection was correct, it was likely that the young woman must have been in one of the rooms to the right of where she now stood.

Having come this far, they knew better than to speak or even whisper. Everyone was aware that the slightest sound could give the game away. Which in turn could have terrible repercussions for the captives.

The moment had arrived to put an end to Taylor's reign of terror. Jemima pointed right to indicate it was the direction her team would take. With the decision made, it was time to get those doors open, neutralize the threat, and deal with whatever they encountered on the other side.

With everyone in position, all eyes were on Jemima as she held up an arm for all to see. With three fingers aloft, she lowered the digits one at a time, until her hand formed a fist, the signal to act.

Silence gave way to a wall of sound as all hell broke loose. Doors and frames splintered and burst open. Having kicked the door in, Jemima was the first to enter her allotted room. She felt the blood drain from her face as she quickly scanned the area, established that Taylor was nowhere to be seen, and focused on the two bundles on the floor.

Giselle Braverman had collapsed. Having already given birth and lost a lot of blood, she lay in a crumpled heap, unconscious and barely breathing. The umbilical cord was still attached, and the baby, although alive, was not doing well.

'I need medics in here now!' she yelled. She had to act instinctively, appreciating that whatever she did now would decide the fate of this tiny human being. Get it wrong and this baby boy would die. Dropping to her knees she reached out and scooped the preternaturally quiet baby into her arms. For a split second it was Fin's life she was trying to save. She held him close to provide some warmth. Elsewhere in the house she was vaguely aware of shouts and cries, along with the thud of hurried footsteps. Though all this activity was taking place in the periphery, she was focused on desperately trying to save the fragile little life she held in her hands.

An officer rushed into the room. 'Medics are on their way.' He sounded breathless.

The baby was still. Silent. Placing one hand on his forehead, she tilted the head back and lifted the chin. As his tiny lips parted, she quickly looked for obstructions and swept her finger inside the mouth to ensure it was clear. Satisfied, she lowered her face to his to enable her to give the child five initial rescue breaths. There had been occasions where she had performed mouth-to-mouth, though never on a child, let alone one who had only just been born. Placing her mouth over the baby's mouth and nose she began to blow five times, each time for only one second. The rise of the little chest confirmed she was doing it correctly. Next up was performing chest compressions. Placing two fingers in the middle of the baby's chest she pressed down to one-third of the depth of the chest, with the aim of repeating this action thirty times, in far less than thirty seconds. With still no sign of life she gave another two rescue breaths and was about to repeat the chest compressions when the little one's blank facial expression altered, and he cried.

Jemima scooped him up into her arms once more; holding him close to give him warmth. The baby's cries were the most welcome sound she had heard since the start of her shift. She only appreciated that she was crying too when she opened her eyes and realized that her vision was blurred.

'They're in there.' Jemima recognized Gareth's voice. As she turned, she saw that he was accompanying four paramedics.

'Give me the baby, ma'am. You've done a good job. Now leave it to us.' A member of the medical team was addressing Jemima and held out their arms in readiness to take the little one.

141

Jemima had been so focused on holding the child, that the insistence in the woman's voice brought her back to the here and now. 'Yeah, yeah, of course.' She handed over the child then wiped her eyes on her sleeve. As she looked across to where Giselle still lay, she saw other paramedics working on her.

'I've injected oxytocin and the placenta should come away soon,' said one.

'Help me get a line in,' said another. 'She needs blood and fluids before we move her.'

Giselle moaned and moved her head slightly. Jemima spotted the woman's eyes flicker and sensed she was trying to say something.

'It's all right, Giselle. You're safe and so is your baby. They'll take you to the hospital soon. Peter's safe too. I've seen him and spoken to him. He's going to be OK.' Jemima had no idea whether the woman could hear her voice or understand what she was saying. But she hoped her words brought some comfort.

'Guv, I need a word.' It was Gareth. His tone was serious. Insistent.

'What is it, Gar?'

'There's no sign of Taylor anywhere on the premises. He's gone, and he's taken one of the women with him.'

CHAPTER 21

With Taylor's captives saved and under medical attention, Jemima and her immediate team looked over the property. They established that each of the rooms on the upper floor had been soundproofed, which explained why, even when they were downstairs, they hadn't heard any sign of life coming from above. It also explained why the windows on this level had been replaced, as Taylor hadn't wanted to risk any cries for help being heard by a passer-by.

A quick glance into the other rooms on that level confirmed everything Jemima had feared. She had entered better squats. With these windows barred, there was no opportunity for fresh air to circulate. The result was a cloying, fetid atmosphere. Which was bad enough to have to breathe for a relatively short while. But these women and children had been forced to suffer it. Accepting it as normal, for years on end.

There were various filthy mattresses strewn across the floor of the largest room suggesting that this was the communal sleeping area. A few buckets in the corner served as toilets.

Emergency service personnel were in the process of taking the three toddlers from the property. Each child was pale from lack of natural sunlight, grubby and malnourished. The older girl was naked, while the younger ones were clad in ill-fitting rags, more holes than cloth.

The fire brigade who had also been on standby, were in the process of freeing a young woman from the hefty chain which confined her to the room.

'That's Jolie Perkins,' said Gareth. 'She told me that Taylor knew we were on to him. Apparently, he took off with Summer not long before we arrived. She had no choice in the matter. Jolie saw him push her into the car and he drove off like a bat out of hell.'

'How the hell did he get wind of us tracking him down?' asked Jemima.

'No idea, Guv. But he was furious and scarpered. No doubt taking Summer as leverage in case he's cornered.'

'Does she know which direction he was heading in?'

'No,' said Gareth. 'She got distracted by the little ones. I've circulated his description and put out an APB asking for all available units to patrol the area. No one wants him to get away.'

'Good work, Gar.' Addressing the highest-ranking officer of the support team, Jemima gave him an order. 'When they're taken to hospital, I want protection teams in attendance until I say so. For Taylor to get wind of us coming for him, someone had to have tipped him off. Which means there's another unknown threat out there.

'I also want a forensic team to go over every inch of the building and the grounds. We know Tabitha's son Marcus was murdered here; I'm sure he's buried somewhere on this land. Also, if there is someone who's operating in the shadows helping Taylor, we might just get lucky. If they've visited this place, he just might have left some trace behind to help us identify him.'

'Go find the bastard, Guv. We've got this,' said the officer.

'Gar, round up the rest of our team. We're going to go after Taylor and save that poor girl. Who knows how he might react now that he's lost his bolthole and his "family"? I've no doubt he'll keep Summer alive until he's made it out of the area. Though I'd have thought that once he's got away, she'll become an albatross around his neck. He hasn't got a conscience. He's killed before and I'm sure he won't hesitate to do it again. We don't have confirmation of the direction he took, but it's safe to say that we didn't pass him on the way here, so we'll continue down the road and take it from there.'

Jemima and the rest of the team set off along the lane in their respective vehicles, with blues and twos deployed to alert other travellers of their presence and the hazard they posed. Given the remoteness of the location there was initially only one road Taylor could have taken. But according to the satnav there would soon be a choice of directions, which meant that the team would have to split up in the hope that one of them would catch up with him.

It was agreed beforehand that when they reached the junction, Jemima would head in the direction of the nearest major road. Common sense told them that Taylor would want a quick getaway. But it would be negligent to ignore the possibility that he might go to ground somewhere close to where he had holed up for so many years. His time spent in the vicinity of the wetlands would have afforded him the opportunity to scope the place out. Which meant that it was possible he could have any number of potential safe havens in mind.

The country lane was narrow, with passing places few and far between, bounded on both sides by overgrown hedgerows; it took all her skill to drive at a safe speed that would still enable them to close the distance between the vehicle they were pursuing.

As usual, Dan wished that he was anywhere other than in the car next to Jemima. He fought to keep his imagination at bay, but images of an inevitable imminent collision filled his mind. Common sense told him that they'd most likely reach whatever destination point they were headed for without encountering a catastrophe. After all, they had only ever been involved in one collision in the thousands of times they had travelled together. Jemima had been driving on that occasion, when a drunk driver had run a red light at a busy intersection.

Still, no matter how hard he tried to rationalize the odds, it didn't have the effect of making him feel more relaxed.

As they hit yet another pothole in the road, Dan cursed, but knew better than to tell her to slow down. Catastrophe almost struck as they took yet another bend at speed, sticking to the middle of the carriageway to negotiate it successfully, and came face-to-face with a cyclist heading straight for them. He was hunched forward, clad head-to-toe in Lycra sportswear, his legs pumping furiously as he propelled a top-of-the-range bicycle at a speed appropriate for a road race. But this wasn't the Tour of Britain, where roads were cleared in advance to reduce the chance of an accident occurring, and the idiot had come within a hair's breadth of serious injury, or even losing his life. Fortunately for him, Jemima reacted immediately and took evasive action. As the vehicle swerved it clipped the nearside hedgerow, but she compensated effectively and managed to continue.

'Jeez! That was too close for comfort.' Beads of sweat had erupted across Dan's brow. Glancing over his shoulder to make sure the cyclist was all right, he noticed him swing the bicycle out then turn abruptly on to a cycle path. 'A second either way and it would've been goodnight, Vienna for him.'

The hair-raising journey continued without further incident until almost five minutes later when they spotted Taylor's abandoned vehicle. Rubber imprinted on to the surface of the road showed that the car had skidded to an uncontrolled stop. With the engine still running, steam spewed from beneath the mangled bonnet, where it had impacted with a tree.

Jemima slammed on the brakes and they both raced towards the vehicle. A quick glance confirmed the reason for the collision. The front nearside tyre had blown and was completely flat. A sudden blowout at speed would have made it difficult, if not impossible, to control the vehicle's trajectory. The driver's door was open, but there was no sign of Taylor or Summer. The deployed airbag was stained with blood. The steering column and driver's door were misshapen from the impact.

Dan reached inside the vehicle, turned off the engine and pocketed the key for safekeeping.

'Where the hell is he?' shouted Jemima, as she raised her arms and tugged her hair in frustration, as she scanned the immediate area. 'And where's Summer?'

'He must've—'

'Shh!' Jemima interjected. 'What's that?' She cocked her head as she strained to hear a faint sound.

Dan looked at her blankly.

'It's coming from nearby. Get the boot open.'

As the boot swung open, Jemima got her first look at Summer Abberton. The naked young woman was huddled in the foetal position. Her nose was shattered, and her mouth bleeding. The injury was so severe it would require surgery.

'Get her a blanket, Dan,' said Jemima. Turning her attention back to the young woman, Jemima did her best to comfort her. 'He won't hurt you anymore. You're safe now Summer.'

'Fffrr.' It was obvious to Jemima that Summer was trying to tell her that her child was in danger, but the damage to her mouth and nose was making it all but impossible to speak.

Guessing what she was trying to say, Jemima did her best to reassure her. 'Freya's safe. We found her. She's on her way to the hospital. You'll see her soon. They're all safe.'

The young woman's shoulders relaxed, and she sobbed with relief. Moments later, when Dan returned with a blanket, Jemima covered her as best she could before helping her out of the vehicle and securing the cloth around her. Sensitive to Summer's predicament, Dan kept a respectful distance, heading off to move the car closer to the women as Jemima saw to her immediate needs.

'If I help you, do you think you'll be able to get into our car?' Jemima was by no means certain that Summer would be up to doing that. But the young woman nodded. She was keen to distance herself from the vehicle that Taylor had shoved her into. 'The ambulance won't be long. There's no need to rush. We'll go at whatever pace you're comfortable with.'

CHAPTER 22

Jemima was torn. With only herself and Dan at the scene, her priority was to take care of Summer. Until the paramedics arrived to treat her injuries and transfer her to hospital, there was no option but to stay. Though she knew that every second spent with his victim increased Taylor's chances of escape. What's more, given his ruthless disregard for everyone, there was the possibility that he could harm some other unsuspecting person. But for the moment, all thoughts of tracking down Douglas Taylor were on hold.

'Have you alerted the paramedics?'

'They're on their way,' confirmed Dan.

'Contact the others. Tell them to get over here. We need to focus our resources on this area. Taylor would've had to have set out on foot from here. Of course, he might've found another vehicle by now. But if he hasn't, he couldn't have gone far. Especially since the blood on the airbag shows he's injured. Get a dog unit out here too, there's a lot of ground to cover, and it's still early enough for the canines to pick up a scent,' said Jemima.

'Will do,' said Dan. As he walked away from their vehicle tiny clouds of dust rose from the ground as he repeatedly scuffed his shoes across the surface. Dan was a practical man.

Glad to be doing something, instead of standing around like a spare part. He was more than capable of making arrangements to enable them to move the manhunt forward. Busying himself with these tasks enabled him to stop thinking about what he'd like to do to Taylor should he be the one to apprehend him. Though he knew deep down that it was wishful thinking, as when it came down to it, he couldn't allow his emotions to get in the way of a textbook arrest.

The ambulance was the first to arrive. Siren blaring. Lights flashing. As the paramedics approached, Jemima filled them in on what had happened.

Jemima turned to Summer and squeezed the young woman's hand. 'Once we've managed to get Douglas Taylor in custody, I'll come and see you at the hospital. But you've no need to worry, Summer. You and Freya are safe. He'll not get to you again.'

Summer gave the slightest of nods, to acknowledge that she understood. One of the paramedics helped her into the back of the ambulance.

'Where are the others?' asked Jemima. With Summer taken care of, her attention was back on the case.

'Between three and five minutes out. ETA for the Canine Unit is ten minutes,' confirmed Dan. 'I wonder if that cyclist saw anything?'

'Cyclist?' Jemima had no idea who he was referring to.

'You know, the one with a death wish. You almost hit him.'

'Oh, him. Doubt it. Speed he was travelling he couldn't long have passed Taylor's car, and I've a feeling he wouldn't have taken the time to stop to check the accident site out. Seemed far too self-obsessed.'

'Guess you're right,' said Dan.

'Umm, anyway, no point in us standing around here. As we've a few minutes until the others get here, let's drive further up the lane and see if there's any obvious place Taylor might have headed for. He's never going to get far on foot. Not quickly anyway. He'll be on the lookout for another vehicle. So, if there's a property close by, or some sort of public car park, it'd be a good place to start. I know we passed a path that the cyclist headed down, but once we head off-road there'd be any number of potential hiding places. We'd need the dogs to check it out.'

As the ambulance pulled away, Jemima started the engine and set off along the lane. Having travelled two hundred yards further, and negotiated yet another bend, they came across a house. It was set back a short distance from the lane, and the driveway was empty. Due to the narrowness of the lane, Jemima pulled on to the crumbling concrete driveway. 'Let's check this out. Could be there's no one home. Then again . . .'

They stepped out of the car and got their first real look at the property. It was a reasonable size, in need of maintenance, with an unappealing facade. Even from a distance it was apparent that it was a fixer-upper.

With no doorbell visible, Jemima rapped on the door. When there was no answer, she knocked harder, as Dan attempted to look through the windows. With no sign of life at the front of the property, they made their way around to the rear, where a high wooden gate blocked the way. Dan pressed down on the latch mechanism, which yielded, allowing the gate to swing open. Whoever lived in this property was lax about security.

They entered the garden, mindful of the fact that apart from a hunch they had no good reason to set foot on the property. A cursory glance showed the garden to be mainly laid to lawn, and well maintained, which suggested that this was not a derelict property. There was a large shed at the far end. Its door was shut and there were no visible windows.

'Guv.' Dan nodded towards the rear door of the house, where a pane of glass close to the locking mechanism was broken. There was little doubt that the glass had been knocked out in a hurry, as jagged edges were visible. Closer inspection revealed broken glass lying on the floor just inside the property. Someone had trodden on it, as some of it had been crushed to powder.

'We're going in. We've reasonable suspicion a crime has been committed, and that the occupant might be in danger,' said Jemima. With tasers at the ready they opened the door and set foot inside. 'Police!' Her voice was loud and assured. When there was no reply, they moved through the kitchen to begin systematically searching the place. The door at the far end was shut. The sound of a motor was audible somewhere on the other side.

Jemima nodded at Dan. With both officers ready to deploy their taser should circumstances require it, the sergeant reached out and opened the door. As it swung inwards, the sound became immediately louder. It was easy to see that this was the main living area. There was a TV fixed to the wall, a sofa opposite it, and further down the room, a table and a couple of dining chairs, one of which had toppled over and had sustained damage.

Following a quick visual sweep to establish any imminent threat, Jemima's gaze dropped towards the direction of the motor, and she quickly established that it was a vacuum cleaner, lying on its side. Closer inspection revealed that the dining chair had specks of blood on it. It had also spattered across the sofa, though was insufficient to suggest that someone had been seriously injured. It more likely indicated that someone had been attacked and quickly overpowered.

Jemima headed towards the door at the far end of the room, leaving the vacuum cleaner switched on, as it would help mask any sound they made as they searched the remainder of the property. An open doorway revealed a small, empty bathroom, with an avocado-coloured suite that had gone out of fashion decades earlier. One of the doors of a discoloured bathroom cabinet, with a cracked mirrored panel was open. Its contents were strewn across the floor. There was an overpowering smell of cologne, a bottle of which had smashed with some of the glass having landed in the ceramic basin.

'What's the chances of this not having been caused by Taylor?' whispered Dan.

'Oh, it's him, all right,' said Jemima. 'Too much of a coincidence otherwise. Question is, is he still on the premises?'

Satisfied that there was nothing more to find on this level, Jemima pointed upwards. Dan nodded his understanding, and they made their way out of the bathroom towards the stairs. This was a scenario they had faced so many times throughout their partnership. Stepping into the unknown as they faced down danger. The clock was ticking, and with no sign of backup they had no option but to carry on and search the entire building.

Jemima took the lead, tentatively placing her weight on each step. Dan followed close behind, aware of the likelihood that in a rundown building such as this, one or more of the treads might creak and give away their position.

They were almost halfway up the staircase when they became aware of a thudding sound from somewhere on the floor above. It was the first sign they'd had of someone else being in the house. Jemima readied herself. At the top of the stairs there were two doors, one closed, the other open. The detectives glanced at each other as memories of what had happened in a remote cottage in the Brecon Beacons flooded to the fore.

Back then, they had been faced with the same choice. Dan had entered the room with the open door, while Jemima had headed the other way. In the ensuing events, Dan was seriously injured, and Jemima was left fighting for her life.

As the senior officer, it was Jemima's decision, and she wasn't about to make the same mistake again. This time they would go in together. Be there to back each other up. After all, if Taylor was in one of those rooms, two against one increased the odds of them successfully ending the standoff.

The thudding sound became faster, and once at the top of the stairs they ascertained that it was coming from the room with the closed door. It was the obvious choice to look, but Jemima decided to check the other room first. Just in case it was a double bluff and Taylor was waiting for them to go to the other room and then attack them from behind while they were distracted by whatever they would inevitably encounter behind the closed door.

Moments later, they were satisfied that there was no one in the room with the open door. Walking the few steps towards the entrance to the other room, they stopped outside and listened. The thudding was frantic, and now they could hear someone squealing.

Jemima flung open the door, as both officers were ready to take down Taylor before he had a chance to disarm them. However, there was no sign of him. Instead, they discovered that the noise was being made by a middle-aged woman, who was bound, gagged and bleeding. She was secured to a radiator so that she was unable to free herself.

Satisfied that there was no one else in the room, Jemima set about freeing the woman, as Dan called for yet another ambulance. Once freed from her restraints, the woman clung to Jemima as though her life depended upon it. Sobbing and spluttering, she tried to tell them what had happened. Jemima helped her stand and led her the few steps to the bed, where the woman sat down heavily.

'Take your time. You're safe now,' said Jemima, as she cradled the woman. 'What's your name?' She had already established that the woman's wounds were superficial.

'M-Moira. Moira McWhirter. He attacked . . . m-me w-when I . . . w-was cleaning,' she sobbed.

As Jemima comforted the woman, Dan disappeared from the room, only to return shortly afterwards, with a cool, damp flannel, which he handed to Jemima.

'Thanks, Dan. Could you make her a cup of tea? Plenty of sugar too,' said Jemima as she set about dabbing the woman's face.

'Y-you're both very k-kind. I thought I would've b-been stuck there 'til my son got home.'

'Do you both live here?' asked Jemima. She sensed it might calm the woman to talk about normal things. Though she knew that she'd have to question her about the incident soon.

'N-no. This is my son's house. I live further up the lane. Pop in once a week to give this place a good clean. Greg works too hard. Never has time for housework. Needs his downtime.'

Jemima nodded supportively. 'Are you able to tell me what happened today?'

'I don't know how he got in. I'm always security conscious. Make sure to lock the door again as soon as I've got here.'

'The intruder smashed one of the glass panels in the rear door. The key was in the lock.'

'I didn't hear anything. Hoovering. He hit me over the head with something.'

'I believe it might have been one of the dining chairs. What did he want?'

'Cash and a car. I told him that there wasn't any cash here. My Greg doesn't keep cash in the house.'

'So he left with nothing?'

'No. Greg's got a racing bike. He said he'd take that.'

'Do you mean a motorbike, or a bicycle?' Jemima knew the answer even before she asked the question.

'Bicycle. He took some of his clothes too.'

'The clothes your son wears when he rides the bike?'

Moria nodded. 'He's got all the fancy gear. Trains at the velodrome in the Sports Village.'

Dan returned with a mug of tea. 'Are you able to hold this?' he asked.

Moira nodded and reached out with shaky hands, which she wrapped around the ceramic and manoeuvred it towards her mouth.

'Did you get a clear look at the intruder's face?' asked Jemima.

'Yes.'

'Was it this man?' Jemima showed Moira a photograph of Taylor.

The woman almost tipped the tea as she nodded and began to weep once more. Jemima reached out and grabbed the mug before the woman scalded herself.

'Taylor was the man on the bike,' she said to Dan. 'Call Gareth and the others and tell them they need to cover the exits for that particular path. He won't want to remain in this area. He's looking for a way out.'

'I thought there was something wrong when he turned on to that path,' Dan said. 'But I guess he must've been desperate to get off the road to reduce the risk of us spotting him, and that path was his nearest exit point. Even though he had to double back on himself. You never see a road bike on a bumpy track like that; it won't be so fast offroad, and he'll have to stick to the tarmacked paths if he wants to keep the bike with him. He'll be looking to find a motorized vehicle at the earliest opportunity.'

'Precisely. Tell them to look for carparks and nearby properties where he can steal one. And advise the Canine Unit of the start point. Though as we now know he's on a bike, I don't hold out much hope of the dogs picking up a scent.'

'Will do, Guv. Oh, and the paramedics should be here any minute.'

'Thanks, Dan. I'll stay with Mrs McWhirter until they arrive.'

'You're a good girl,' said Moira, as she reached out and squeezed Jemima's hand.

CHAPTER 23

Douglas Taylor was leaving a trail of devastation in his wake. Hardly surprising for a man who only appeared to value his own life. No one doubted that as long as he was able to do things to his own advantage, he wouldn't care who got hurt along the way.

With Moira McWhirter on her way to the hospital and her son, Greg, notified of what had occurred, Jemima's attention turned once again to finding Taylor. In normal circumstances she would have coordinated the next steps of the operation. But given Mrs McWhirter's vulnerability she had felt compelled to put the older woman's needs first. Especially since she had clung to Jemima for support and comfort after the terrifying ordeal she had endured.

Jemima knew that Dan was more than capable of sorting out what needed to be done. She'd instructed him and trusted him implicitly. It would also boost his morale to have her demonstrate her faith in his abilities. Plus, Dan wasn't so comfortable with the touchy-feely emotional side of things. And the last thing Moria McWhirter would have needed was to feel that she was being a burden.

'Gareth and the others have split up to try to cover potential exit points off the trail,' said Dan. 'I've also contacted central control and asked for all available units to head to the area, as it's not a given he's going to stick to the path to get back to the road. He might ditch the bike and go by foot.'

'What about the Canine Unit?'

'They've made a start. Got Taylor's scent from the driver's seat and airbag. They're taking the dogs down the path from the entry point he accessed.'

'Well done, Dan.'

'I've also arranged for some of the team that were with us at the property to send up drones over the area. Thought it might come in useful, given the expanse and potential hiding places.'

'Excellent thinking. Seriously, well done.' Jemima wasn't saying this to massage her sergeant's ego. She was genuinely impressed with his initiative.

'Thanks.' Dan smiled and stood a little taller. 'What's next for us? Are we heading in there or what?'

'As things stand, I don't see any point in us joining the search. Taylor's got a time advantage. Plus, we can't rule out the possibility that he knows that area like the back of his hand. He's kept his captives in that house for years, while he's no doubt got to know the surroundings.'

'So, what are we going to do?' Dan was perplexed. In all the years they'd worked together, Jemima had always insisted on being hands-on. More often than not she'd be the first one into the fray. Leading from the front.

'We're heading back to the incident room. Jolie Perkins suggested that Taylor had advance warning that we were coming for him.'

'You mean we've got a leak?' Dan's eyes widened as the realization dawned.

'We must have, and I intend to find out who's behind it. If Taylor slips through the net, which seems highly likely, then until we find out who's been feeding him information, any attempt to reach him is going to be compromised.'

'You don't think it's one of our lot?'

'I've no idea. I wouldn't have thought so. Then again, after what happened with the Rory Lawson case and the Marquess Club, we all know that we can't close our minds to corruption on the force,' said Jemima.

'Please God, don't let us go there again,' said Dan. 'They were a scary few days. You, me and Gareth against the world.'

'Don't forget that it almost cost Kennedy his life,' added Jemima. Her tone of voice left no room for doubt that she was deadly serious about finding out who was responsible for the leak. 'Anyway, you get to drive,' she tossed the keys to Dan. 'I'm going to contact central control to find out if there've been any recent reports of a vehicle being stolen in this locality. The stolen bike is a means to an end. I'd put money on him heading for a car park or some other remote property to nick one.'

Moments later she got the news she was expecting. 'Yep, about ten minutes ago. We got a report of a white BMW stolen from . . .' The location was less than five miles from the property they had just left. 'Vehicle registration mark,' the operator relayed the details using the phonetic alphabet.

'It's gotta be Taylor. Dan, if you take a left here, you might be able to cut him off. Keep an eye out. I've a few calls to make.'

Dan gulped as he felt his heart rate increase. He didn't like driving at speed at the best of times and had lost count of the number of times he'd said a silent prayer as he'd sat helpless in the passenger seat as Jemima pursued a suspect. But as he was the one currently behind the wheel, every split-second decision and reaction would be down to him if they happened to come across the stolen BMW. He was dreading the possibility of a high-speed pursuit. All his skill and training courses didn't seem to count for much now.

Jemima selected a contact and pressed speed dial. The phone was picked up almost immediately. 'Jemima? Anything wrong?' Kennedy sounded concerned.

'I think we've got ourselves a leak, Ray. I've no idea who's responsible, but I hope it doesn't compromise things at your end.'

'What's happened?'

Jemima filled him in on the recent developments.

'Well, I can categorically confirm that the leak wouldn't have come from this end. Only Frank and I know the details. It's standard operating procedure for us to keep the troops, as it were, out of it. They don't ever get to know client details. It's a forces mentality. They do as they're told and don't question orders,' said Kennedy.

'At least that narrows down the possibilities,' said Jemima.

'And to put your mind at rest, we arrived at the secure location without incident,' said Kennedy. 'I'm confident that there's no way anyone will find out where we are. We transported our charges in the back of a windowless van. Even they've no idea where they are. So, I wouldn't worry about Taylor coming after them. Even if he found our location, which he won't, he wouldn't get through our security measures. Hell, I doubt the Royals are as well protected.'

'That's good to know, Ray. It's a weight off my mind, and despite Taylor being tipped off, you'll be pleased to know that we rescued everyone else too. They're all being triaged at the hospital.'

'Do you need us to protect them?'

'Couldn't afford you, Ray. With Taylor still on the loose, there's no second-guessing what he might do next.'

'Guess not. But the difference is that as he knows you're aware of his identity; he's no reason to silence the others.'

'I agree, but the leak suggests he's not working alone,' countered Jemima.

'Fair point. Just let me know if you change your mind.'

'Before you go, it's just occurred to me, Lydia Leysham didn't contact anyone, did she?' asked Jemima.

'We confiscated her phone when we arrived at the hospital. I checked the call log myself and there were no calls or texts received that day.'

'And she doesn't have another phone?'

'Absolutely not. We frisked her,' said Kennedy. 'Now go do your job. Find your leak, and put a stop to that sick bastard, Taylor too. You're a bloody good detective, Jem. So go do what you do best and leave the protection side to us.' The line went dead before Jemima had a chance to respond.

Jemima had barely had time to draw breath before her phone rang. It was Gareth. 'Guv, we've found the bike abandoned in some bushes not far from where a white BMW was reported stolen. There're no cameras anywhere near the place, but it's too much of a coincidence to think that someone else nicked that car, so close to where Taylor abandoned the bike.'

'It's him all right,' said Jemima.

'What do you want us to do?' asked Gareth.

'Get yourselves back to the station. You'll be more use there going through traffic camera footage to see if we can track his journey. Dan and I are hoping to intercept him.' She relayed their latest location and explained where she thought Taylor might be heading. 'Get on the blower and arrange for other available units in the vicinity to be . . .' Jemima stopped mid-sentence as she did a double take. They'd just approached a junction and were about to turn left when a white BMW whizzed past.

'Shit! That's him! Step on it, Dan. Don't lose him.'

Dan gripped the wheel even tighter. The engine squealed as he accelerated, leaving a trail of rubber on the surface of the road.

Keeping a cool head, Jemima told Gareth exactly where they were. 'Get all units over here. We need to cut him off before he reaches the main road.'

'Will do, Guv,' said Gareth.

Jemima reached out and flicked the switch for the blues and twos. She knew that a high-speed pursuit would test Dan's nerves. He was a good copper, but his various phobias, including travelling at speed, did not sit well with his chosen career. It was unfortunate that on this occasion she had opted for him to be the one in the driving seat. Now all she could do was to offer gentle encouragement, while keeping a lid on any frustration she might feel if he didn't act as decisively as she would have done if she was the one behind the wheel.

Jemima glanced sideways and saw that Dan's knuckles were white. His jaw was clenched so tight that a pulse was visible. She believed he was up to the task, but just hoped that he'd hold his nerve and trust in his own abilities.

'You've got this Dan.' Jemima had no idea whether her partner had heard her few words of reassurance, and she sure as hell wasn't going to repeat them. Given the speed they were travelling, it was in everyone's interests that he remained entirely focused on the road ahead.

As they arrived at a straight section of the lane, Taylor's BMW came into view once more. The sight of it spurred Dan on, and he pressed the accelerator harder. But no sooner had the BMW appeared than it disappeared once more as Taylor took a bend far too fast. Dan eased off the accelerator and took the bend with ease. They were now travelling along a particularly hazardous section of road. The carriageway narrowed as one bend followed another, providing all the challenges of a slalom course that they could have done without. It proved impossible not to flinch as shoots from overgrown hedgerows loomed large and relentlessly whipped the sides of their vehicle.

Moments later there was no mistaking the sound of a collision up ahead. At first, they couldn't see anything, but Dan applied the brakes and slowed down. As he relaxed his grip on the steering wheel, he glanced across at Jemima. His brow was slick with sweat.

Seconds later as they rounded yet another bend, they were confronted with carnage. Jemima's seatbelt was unbuckled, and the passenger door open even before Dan had brought the vehicle to a stop.

'We need an ambulance now!' She glanced over her shoulder and shouted the instruction to Dan, who was just getting out of the car. Given his aversion to blood, he was better placed to organize the basics, and there was no doubt in Jemima's mind that there would be plenty of blood.

The high-speed pursuit had come to an end, though not in the way any of them had foreseen. The white BMW had collided head-on and at speed with a monstrous tractor which had been travelling in the opposite direction.

Jemima reacted without missing a beat. She needed to reach Taylor and do everything in her power to try to keep him alive. It was already apparent that someone had tipped him off. If he died before telling her who that was, then there was every possibility that that person would get away without having to face any consequences.

Jemima winced as she neared the crash site and saw the full extent of the damage. The tractor was large, robust and despite having been hit at speed had sustained only superficial damage. The driver remained frozen inside the cab, staring blankly at the carnage below. Even from this distance the man's haunted expression was apparent. He was obviously traumatized by being caught up in such an unexpectedly catastrophic event.

'Are you injured?' Jemima shouted and waved her hands to get the man's attention. She repeated the question twice before she received a response. Even then it was merely a shake of the head as the man was so shaken up that he was unable to speak.

'Stay where you are!' called Jemima. 'The emergency services are on their way. They won't be long.'

He nodded once to confirm his understanding. Though if Jemima had blinked, she would have missed it.

Turning her attention to the car, she saw that the front section was raised off the ground and the bonnet was unrecognizable as it had concertinaed considerably. If Taylor had survived the impact, he would have sustained severe and extensive damage to his legs and torso.

She didn't want an up-close view of what it looked like inside the car. No sensible person would. But the ambulance hadn't arrived and as a police officer she had sworn an oath to preserve life. Which meant that you didn't get to pick and choose. When a scumbag like Taylor required help, she had to put her personal feelings aside and do whatever she could to help.

Jemima swallowed hard, dreading what she was about to encounter. She knew from experience that some sights would be imprinted on your brain forever, and sensed this would be another of those times.

The front of the vehicle was so distorted it proved impossible to open the door. A quick glance inside informed her that it would require cutting equipment to separate Taylor from the vehicle's mangled mechanisms.

The driver's window had shattered, and she reached through the gap to feel for a pulse. Taylor's head lolled sideways, a significant splinter of glass protruding from his right cheek. It was impossible to tell where the steering column ended, and a human body began.

The sound of approaching sirens announced the arrival of more skilled reinforcements, but Jemima reached forward, nonetheless. Taylor had all the appearance of a corpse, but as Jemima moved her fingers over his neck she felt a pulse. It was weak. Irregular. But it was there. The monster was alive and unconscious.

CHAPTER 24

There was nothing more for Jemima or Dan to do at the scene. It was down to others to do their best to save Taylor's life, but Jemima was not surprised when a call came through as she drove them both back to the station, to say that Taylor had been pronounced dead at the scene.

Dan hadn't uttered a word the entire time they'd been in the car. Jemima knew her partner well enough to appreciate that he was blaming himself for what happened. By a quirk of fate, he'd been the one behind the wheel when they spotted Taylor making a bid for freedom. A high-speed pursuit was one of Dan's fears. But to have things end so badly . . . Well, it was a big ask for anyone to come to terms with something like that.

Dan held his head in his hands and eventually moaned. 'It's my fault. It's all my fault.'

'You're not to blame, Dan. Yes, you were driving. But Taylor made his own decisions. He did that to himself. If he'd had the balls to stay and face the music, he wouldn't have left Summer for dead. Moira McWhirter wouldn't have been attacked and left scared half to death, and Taylor wouldn't have stolen another vehicle and driven so recklessly.

'So, let's get this clear, you didn't make any of those decisions. Douglas Taylor did. And in the end his luck ran out.'

'I guess,' muttered Dan.

'You need to dig deep and pull yourself together. We've things to do. Taylor's gone. He's not going to hurt anyone ever again. But he was tipped off and we need to find the leak. Otherwise, there's someone out there who's been enabling him, and we can't allow that person to get away with it. Those women and kids deserve justice. There's no way they should have to spend the rest of their lives looking over their shoulders worrying that whoever's been hiding in the shadows is going to come after them.'

Dan sighed. 'Yeah, you're right. We put this to bed once and for all. The world's a better place without the likes of Taylor in it. Let's push on and get it done.'

'We will, but not today. We're way past the end of the shift, and let's face it, we're running on empty. There's no way we'll be able to put this to bed in the next few hours. Best we round everyone up back at the station. Pool our information, then call it a day. We'll be far more productive after some downtime.'

* * *

That evening proved a welcome respite to the day's events. Finlay was already asleep when Jemima got home. James had just finished his homework and was keen for his mother and Mason to join him in a game of Cluedo. It was fun to do something normal — even if it was trying to solve a fictional murder. To laugh. Chat. Listen to amusing anecdotes. Seeing James so at ease and happy with his life was the best remedy to the horrors she had encountered at that house in the Wetlands. It was obvious that Mason loved her and the boys, and that feeling was reciprocated by all of them. The life they had right here, right now; the love, the security, the support network, was all the four of them needed. They had undoubtedly come together in an unconventional way, but they had bonded to become a loving family.

CHAPTER 25

Jemima glanced at everyone as they assembled for the team briefing. From their body language and facial expressions, it was immediately apparent that it had been a good call not to have pushed on at the end of the previous day. The break had done them good, which should help each of them to bring their A-game to that day's shift.

Douglas Taylor had demonstrated his resourcefulness. There was no doubt in Jemima's mind that the man had been both smart and ruthless. But he'd somehow been tipped off that they were about to raid the property, and that was evidence of him being in cahoots with someone with close links to the investigation.

They were on the back foot. For all they knew, the person who had leaked the information could be of a similar mind-set to Taylor. Which raised the possibility that there might be other women and children out there, being held captive too.

Taylor was dead, but they needed to crawl over every aspect of his life. Familiarize themselves with every available scrap of information about him. Get to know what the man had been like before he took this path. Because somewhere in his past, there would be a link to the person responsible for leaking the information which enabled him to escape.

'Mack, Levi, I want you to head over to the property. Liaise with forensics and establish if they've found anything useful that might help us identify the leak. I also want to make sure that every inch of that property and the grounds are examined as we need to find the body of Tabitha Leysham's son, Marcus. At the very least that little one should be returned to his mother so that she can mourn his passing in whichever way she chooses.'

As both officers headed out, Jemima continued. 'As for the rest of us, we've got to find the source of that leak, but first off, Nancy, what, if anything, did you establish about L&T Holdings?'

'I tried to contact Companies House just before it all kicked off yesterday. It should have been a simple search, but their website was down, and no one was answering the phone.'

'Chase it up. The registered owners of that property will have had dealings with Taylor, and right now we need all the information we can find on him.'

'I'm on it,' said Nancy, as she sat down and logged on.

'Gar, I want you and Dan to undertake a deep dive into Taylor's financials. We've got his bank details from when he was employed as a PA by both Bianchi and Fontaine, and as I recall he kept the same bank account throughout that time.'

'Let's hope he's a creature of habit, but if he's not, there'll be records of where he transferred standing orders and direct debits to. Leave it to me. I'll find his financials.'

'Excellent. Once you do, we're looking for regular payments into or out of his account. Someone tipped him off about us closing in on him. If they're that close, there could easily be a financial link between them.

'But before you get started on that I need the name of your contact at the hospital, Gar.'

Gareth raised his eyebrows questioningly.

'I need access to their security tapes,' said Jemima. 'I want to check something out. See if I can come up with anything which will help us identify who leaked the information to Taylor. It might come to nothing, but I'm taking a belt and braces approach.'

* * *

Once at the hospital, Jemima headed straight for the security hub.

'Can't seem to get rid of your lot at the moment.' The head of security chuckled.

'Believe me, if I had a choice I wouldn't be here. But it's my one hope of getting a lead,' said Jemima.

'I've set up a monitor for you in a separate room. Thought you wouldn't appreciate interruptions from my lot. It's got the recordings of the timeframe you asked for.'

'Thanks, I appreciate it. And I'll be able to access feeds from every security camera, should I need to?'

'Absolutely. I've selected the one closest to the room in question, but if you'll allow me, I'll just give you a quick demonstration of how you change the feed you're viewing. That way, you should be able to track anyone around the hospital. Of course, we only cover the corridors, not individual rooms. So, if your suspect is doing whatever it is you're interested in anywhere other than a corridor, you won't be able to get them bang to rights. At least, not by our security tapes.'

'If only I had a clear idea of who my target is,' said Jemima.

'Sounds like you could be on a hiding to nothing. But good luck anyway.' He was about to head out of the room when Jemima had a thought.

'Do you have cameras covering public payphones?' she asked.

'Yes. Though not close enough so that you could see the number being dialled. That would be an invasion of privacy.'

'How many payphones are in the building?'

'Give me a few minutes and I'll have the answer.' He headed out of the room.

Jemima set about familiarizing herself with how to view the footage, and quickly accepted that this would turn out to be a time-consuming task. Not that she would allow that to put her off. As she felt that something needed to be done, she'd knuckle down and get to it. She'd fought against the odds for much of her life, and the lesson she'd learned is that a defeatist attitude didn't get you anywhere. You made your own luck in this world. It required effort, backbone and a thick skin. Sometimes it worked out. Other times it didn't. But what every successful person knew, is that failures were a route to success. If something didn't work out, you amended your strategy and kept on trying. Chipping away until you reached your goal.

The trouble was, they were up against it. Convinced that no one on her team would have leaked the fact that they had identified the property where Taylor was holding the women and children, there was only one other person who could have passed that information on to Taylor. Though, if Jemima was correct with this line of thought, it was a betrayal of the worst possible kind.

Jemima hoped that she'd got this wrong. But she was determined to get to the bottom of things. The leak needed to be found and quickly. Then again, given the nature of her job, with every case she'd investigated there had never been a time when Jemima wasn't up against it. She'd pitted her wits against, and in many cases fought physical battles, with some of the most heinous people. Every one of those criminals had posed further danger to the public if they weren't identified and taken off the streets. Douglas Taylor had been no different, and nor was his accomplice.

Jemima looked up as the door opened and the head of security entered the room.

'There are ten payphones in all, and these are their locations.' He placed a printout on the desk beside her. 'They're the camera feeds you'll need to access.' He pointed out the relevant information.

Until Jemima had something else to go on, she was prepared to do the grunt work by diligently trawling through the security footage. An hour later, Jemima rubbed her eyes and yawned. The air-conditioning unit was clunking away doing a poor job of keeping the room at a reasonable temperature. It was stuffy and cramped, and her head ached.

Jemima had learned over the years not to second-guess anyone's motives as you only got to see what they wanted you to see. And she knew from personal experience that even those who had convinced you that they had your best interests at heart could sometimes not be trusted. Why Lydia Leysham would betray her daughter in such a heinous way, Jemima couldn't fathom. The woman had seemed genuinely concerned for her daughter's well-being.

Ray Kennedy had already confirmed that Lydia's mobile had been confiscated for security reasons. He'd also told her that he'd personally checked it for calls made, received, and text messages. Jemima had no reason to doubt her former mentor, as he was one of the most trustworthy people she knew.

Jemima felt a weight in the pit of her stomach. As she studied the footage, she started to think that she must have got it wrong, as Lydia remained at her daughter's side. Then her heart rate increased as the door to Tabitha's room opened. The security tape showed Lydia having a word with one of the officers standing directly outside. They spoke for a few seconds, then Lydia headed along the corridor.

As Jemima followed Lydia's progress along the corridor, and down to the concourse she switched cameras numerous times. At first, she was convinced that the woman must be heading to one of the shops or the coffee outlet. But then it happened. Lydia looked around, as though concerned that someone might be watching her. It was obvious from her mannerisms that the woman was wrestling with a dilemma, as she paced back and forth like a caged beast. From the clarity of the surveillance footage, Jemima spotted Lydia's shoulders relax, as tension left her body. It was apparent the woman had reached a decision. She turned and headed towards one of the pay phones, then dialled a number and spoke to someone. The conversation was lengthy.

Having witnessed this ultimate betrayal, Jemima experienced a surge of anger. Throughout her childhood, her own mother had treated her abominably. Routinely doling out psychological abuse, always covertly, until Jemima felt worthless and helpless. And here was another mother betraying their offspring. And Tabitha's experience was far worse than anything Jemima had endured.

If Jemima were to see Lydia Leysham any time soon, she knew she would quite happily rip the woman's head from her shoulders. Not only had she let her own daughter down, but she'd also compromised every woman and child whose life had been blighted by Douglas Taylor.

CHAPTER 26

There was no time to lose. Jemima needed answers, and she wanted them now. The seat skidded across the shiny floor as she pushed it away and raced out of the room.

George Templeton, the head of security, was the first person she needed to speak to. Having offered to help her in any way he could, he was best placed to establish the number dialled by Lydia Leysham. As she entered the main security viewing suite, she found George sitting in front of a monitor, eating a doughnut. A dollop of raspberry jam had dropped on to his otherwise pristine shirt. Though Jemima knew better than to alert him to the fact, as it would inevitably delay her getting the information she needed. As he looked at her questioningly, she got straight to the point.

'Show me the footage,' said George. It seemed the man was used to eating and working at the same time, as he carried the remains of the doughnut with him and munched as he walked, licking his fingers clean when he eventually took his last bite.

Jemima led the way back to the room she had recently vacated, unlocked the door and showed him the image frozen on the monitor.

'Leave it with me. I'll get on to it immediately. Should be relatively straightforward as we've got the time displayed, and I know just the person to ask. I'll get the number she called for you. Now go take a break,' he ordered. 'I work better on my own.'

Jemima didn't need telling twice. She was more than happy to leave this to George while she took the time to see to her own needs. As she headed in search of coffee, she rang Ray Kennedy once more.

'This is becoming a habit, Jemima,' said Kennedy.

'Sorry, Ray, but I thought I'd better update you. I think Lydia Leysham might be the source of our leak.'

'Was she, indeed?' Kennedy's voice was stern. 'So how do you want to play this? Do you want me to tackle her?'

'Not at the moment, Ray. I just wanted to give you the heads up. I've established she used a hospital pay phone to call someone. Currently I've no idea what number she dialled, or who she spoke to, but I've got someone checking it out.'

'Sneaky thing to do. Nasty business if she turns out to be the person responsible for alerting Taylor. To choose him over her daughter, well that's exceptionally cold.'

'My thoughts exactly,' said Jemima. 'I've no idea what the set-up is at your end, but would it be possible to isolate Lydia from Tabitha? I don't know whether she'd risk harming her. But as things stand, I don't think she should be trusted, and if she's determined to do something, I'm sure she'll find a way.'

'Don't worry about it. I'll put her in an isolation room until I receive further instructions from you. Tabitha is our priority. Lydia might very well be footing the bill, but she's excess baggage.'

'Do me a favour, Ray and make up some plausible excuse for getting her out of the way. I don't want her suspecting that we're on to her this early in the game. It's best she thinks she's got away with it for now.'

'Leave it with me. Speak to you later.' Kennedy wasn't one for pleasantries, and the line went dead before Jemima had a chance to thank him or to say goodbye.

* * *

Having returned to the room, she could see George through the door's central glass pane. As he was still on the telephone, she thought that perhaps he was getting the runaround. Though as she opened the door, she appreciated that it wasn't the case.

'Love you more . . . No, you hang up . . . No, you hang up.' George blew kisses into the mouthpiece, stopping abruptly when he realized that unbeknown to him, Jemima had entered the room and was standing behind him, looking less than impressed. 'Gotta go, sweetie. See you later.' He disconnected the call. Before Jemima had a chance to say anything, he explained. 'That was my wife. She's the one in the know. That's why I said to leave it to me. I know what they're like and you'd only have got the runaround if you'd taken things down the official route. Far quicker when you have a direct line to the top.'

Jemima smiled for what felt like the first time in a long while. She had anticipated the worst. It was easy to become cynical about everyone and everything when you were working a case like this. Just when she thought that George had been messing about instead of doing what he said he was going to do, she had found out that he really had played a blinder and saved her a great deal of hassle by his act of kindness.

Eager to establish who Lydia had been calling, Jemima dialled the number, only to be connected to an automated voice saying, '*Welcome to the Tesco mobile voicemail service. The person you are calling is unable to take your call. Please leave your message after the tone.*' With no personalized voice message, it was impossible to know who she had been contacting.

Lydia had gone against Jemima's instructions of not contacting anyone. Of course, she didn't know for certain that she had leaked information about a police operation. But as far as

174

Jemima could tell, she was the only person who was privy to the information to have made a telephone call. Which made her the most likely person to have tipped off Taylor.

* * *

Back at the station it was time to check up on everyone's progress before making enquiries to find out whose telephone number this was. It would be another soul-destroying task. Though no more soul-destroying than the other things they had been doing.

As she headed towards the incident room, she decided that it was time to bring Lydia Leysham in for questioning. She dialled Ray's number.

'I've changed my mind.'

'You want me to tackle her?'

'No. It's best you keep to your original remit and guard Tabitha. But I'd appreciate it if you brought Lydia in so that I can formally question her.'

'Sure thing. Leave it with me. Though it would've been good to give the old interrogation skills an airing. I miss that side of things.'

Jemima smiled, as she momentarily reflected on the numerous occasions she and Kennedy had interrogated suspects together.

She entered the incident room to find that everyone was working diligently and made a beeline to Nancy's desk. 'Any progress on L&T Holdings?'

Nancy sighed. 'I'm still waiting on Companies House to tell me who the directors are,' she said. 'They've been giving me the runaround all morning.'

Dan interjected before Jemima had a chance to say anything. 'It's the typical public sector story. Things are fucked up and their search facility's down. Been that way for weeks. Nothing in this bloody country works. You can bet your life the lazy bastards are all, "working from home". More likely sat there watching porn on their computer while the rest of us pay their wages.' Dan's frustration and contempt was undisguised.

'Mate, you really need to take a few days off when we've put this case to bed,' said Gareth. 'No point getting worked up. It doesn't change a thing.'

Jemima was concerned. Dan's outburst was out of character. 'I need your help for a moment, Dan,' she said.

'Sure thing.' The sergeant got up and followed her out of the room.

'Are you OK?'

'Yeah, why?'

'It's just that Gareth's right. You did get a bit worked up in there. And I know that yesterday's high-speed pursuit is a tough one to come to terms with. There's no shame in needing to step back for a couple of days.'

'I'm fine. Honestly. But thanks for asking. I'm just sick and tired of the way things seem to be going down the pan. We're up against it, doing everything we can to take detritus off the streets and make the place safer for ordinary people. Yet there are so many lazy bastards, who seem to be getting paid for doing nothing, and make our job harder than it should be. It just winds me up, that's all.'

'I know what you mean, but it's out of our control,' said Jemima. She squeezed his arm supportively. 'You good to get back to it?'

'Yeah. You don't need to worry about me. I'm frustrated, as we all are, but apart from that, I'm fine.'

'What about Taylor's financials?' asked Jemima, as she re-entered the room and turned her attention to Gareth.

'Got lucky there. He obviously doesn't follow Martin Lewis's advice to change bank accounts regularly to get better interest rates and new customer deals. Our man was still using the same bank. The interesting thing is he'd been getting regular payments of four thousand a month paid into his account without fail.'

Jemima raised her eyebrows. 'That's a substantial amount. Especially for someone who couldn't risk spending much time away from that house. What the hell was he doing to make that much money?'

'I've no idea, but I intend to find out. Though, what's interesting is that those monthly payments started a few weeks before Tabitha's abduction, and have continued ever since,' said Gareth.

'That's too much of a coincidence. Any idea who's been paying him?'

'Not really sure on that one yet. Still working on it.'

'Any updates from the forensic search of the house?'

'Nothing that's going to be a quick win,' said Gareth. 'They've been through everything and bagged things up. Levi and Mack are logging it in as we speak. It's a long shot that we might eventually be able to trace the surveillance equipment, but it'll take time so I wouldn't hold your breath on that one.'

Jemima's phone rang, cutting her conversation with Gareth short. She glanced at the display and saw that it was Ray Kennedy. As she answered the call, she headed to the far side of the room so as not to disturb the others.

'How's it going, Ray?'

'Thought I'd let you know that we've just loaded Lydia into the back of the van and we're about to leave. Beneath that hoity-toity superiority there's an alley cat waiting to be released.' Ray chuckled.

'Take it that it didn't go well when you told her you were bringing her in?'

'That's an understatement, Jem. She was already playing up about us isolating her from Tabitha. Seems to think that because she's footing the bill, she gets to call the shots, but that's not how we operate.'

'Does she know why she's being brought in?' asked Jemima.

'Only in the broadest of terms. I kept it vague. Just said there'd been some developments you needed to discuss with her. Anyway, gotta go. Should be with you within the hour.' The line went dead.

'Guv, over here!' Gareth gestured to her. It was apparent from his expression that he had something important to tell her.

'You found something?' She raised her eyebrows expectantly.

'I've just established that those regular monthly payments into Taylor's account were from L&T Holdings, but even before they became routine, he received some payments from them.'

'How many payments, and what time frame are you talking about?' asked Jemima.

'Well, that's where it gets interesting. When he worked for Fontaine and Bianchi there were no payments from L&T Holdings. But prior to that there were some ad-hoc payments of a few hundred here and there. For a period of about two years or so.'

'Interesting. Great work, Gar. We really need to know who's behind L&T Holdings, because it's clear that someone at that company has been bankrolling Taylor,' said Jemima.

'Nancy, please tell me you've got something on them?'

'Still no joy from Companies House, but I've been trawling the internet to see what's out there. I've got a company number and a registered address in Cheltenham. They deal in properties. Mainly commercial, but some residential. Their website shows details for an operations manager, one Charlotte Winstanley. So far, I haven't been able to contact her.'

'Keep trying and arrange for the local station to send a couple of their uniforms to check the place out,' said Jemima.

She was frustrated that seemingly every step of the way, their progress was like wading through treacle. But she had a hunch that once they established who was behind L&T Holdings, the case would crack wide open. The company's Cheltenham base was interesting, as it was in the area where Taylor had previously had connections.

Levi and Mack were back in the incident room having finished booking in the evidence collected from the property. 'I want you both to follow up on the surveillance equipment from the house. Use the serial number of each piece of equipment and get back to the manufacturer. From there you should be able to trace them to the retailers and hopefully find out who purchased it. Could be that whoever's been bankrolling Taylor paid for the kit too.'

'Wouldn't be surprised if L&T Holdings turn out to have purchased it,' said Gareth.

'That's precisely what I'm thinking, and there's a chance we might get more information on who's behind it. After all, we have proof that L&T Holdings are transferring a significant amount of money to Taylor each month, and let's face it, it's more than many people's salaries.'

'It's a possibility that he's on the payroll and that he's been legitimately working off-site. After all, home working became an acceptable thing for a lot of people when we had the Covid lockdowns,' said Dan.

'Agreed, but it's unusual that the same company owns the house he lives in, isn't it? What if whoever's in charge of L&T Holdings has been paying him so that he could keep those women and kids hidden?' The room was silent, and as Jemima scanned the faces of the rest of her team, she noted their surprised expressions.

'Guess anything's possible,' said Nancy. She didn't sound convinced.

'I know it sounds far-fetched, but I want it checked out.'

'Will do, guv,' said Mack. He gathered up his belongings and headed to the door. Levi nodded his agreement and followed Mack out of the room.

'Nancy, you were going to look into Taylor's family. You'd established that his father's name was . . .' Jemima glanced at the evidence board for confirmation. 'Benedict Sebastian Taylor. What have you established about him?'

'Nothing, guv. I haven't had time to crack on with it.' Nancy's cheeks reddened. 'It's on my list of things to do, but other tasks keep taking priority.'

Jemima masked her frustration. She knew that what Nancy had said was true, but they still needed to find out more about Douglas Taylor's life. 'Fair enough, I know I've been asking you to juggle a lot of balls and something had to give. In that case, Dan, I want you to follow up on Benedict Sebastian Taylor, and any other family members. Especially ones living in and around the Cheltenham area. See if there's any connection to L&T Holdings. And while you're at it, look into the father's financials. See if there's anything of interest,' said Jemima.

Dan was busily scribbling down the list of tasks Jemima was asking him to work through. 'Will do,' he said.

'Nancy, once you've finished, give Dan a hand. We've got to keep the momentum up. Tie up loose ends. It's the only way to stop whoever was helping Douglas Taylor from getting away with it. If any of you need motivation, just keep picturing those women and kids, and the godawful way they were forced to live. Each of them deserves justice. And it's down to us to ensure that they get the chance to live out the remainder of their lives without having to look over their shoulders waiting for whichever sicko was in cahoots with Taylor to come out of the woodwork and make a play for them.'

Everyone nodded their agreement. 'Oh, and just so you're aware, Ray Kennedy is on his way in, with Lydia Leysham. We need to know who she called on that hospital payphone, and one way or another she's going to tell me what I want to know.'

'Rather her than me,' said Dan, as he shared a knowing glance with Gareth. Both men laughed. They'd worked with Jemima for long enough to know that it was unwise to make an enemy out of her. She was a genuinely good and kind person. Most of the time she was reasonable and level-headed. But when push came to shove with a suspect, or anyone she believed was trying to pull the wool over her eyes, she'd have their back against the wall in double-quick time. Sometimes this was physically. Often, it was verbally.

It bothered Jemima that Lydia Leysham could have been the source of the leak. Having been a police officer for many years and throughout that time encountered some of the most evil people alive, Jemima considered herself to be a reasonable judge of character. She acknowledged that she didn't get it right all the time, but in general she could spot a so-called wrong-un a mile off. And from everything she'd seen of Tabitha's mother, Lydia had seemed genuinely concerned about her daughter's welfare.

With the rest of the team hard at their allocated tasks, Jemima set about finding out as much as she could about the Leysham family before she came face-to-face with the matriarch once more. If there was any dirt to find, she wanted to know about it, because if Lydia was working against them and instrumental in allowing Douglas Taylor to evade capture, she was going to stop the woman in her tracks.

Jemima soon ascertained that there was little personal information readily accessible online about Lydia. She came from a monied family. Her father had been a highly successful entrepreneur and CEO of a multimillion-pound business. And Lydia herself was no slouch. She had an MBA and had been a board member of her father's company for the last twenty-three years. In addition to this, she also gave freely of her time and money to various good causes.

After half an hour or so of following various trails, Jemima gave up trying to dig up dirt on the woman. If her research was to be believed, Lydia Leysham was a saint. No one had a bad word to say about her. In this day and age, when everyone was ready with an opinion, it was extremely unusual to find an individual who was so universally liked.

CHAPTER 27

As Jemima was about to start delving into Edgar Leysham's life, her phone rang. It was Ray Kennedy. He informed her that they would be at the police station within ten minutes. It gave Jemima enough time to ensure that there was an interview room free and arrange for a uniformed officer to attend while she interviewed Lydia.

While Lydia was escorted to the interview room, Jemima took the time to have a word with Ray, who confirmed that Tabitha was doing well. After thanking Ray for his help, she headed to the interview room to speak to Lydia. Stopping outside the closed door, she took a deep breath before opening it and stepping inside.

Lydia Leysham gave Jemima a look which left her in no doubt that the woman was incandescent with rage. Throughout their previous encounters the woman had appeared anxious, but nevertheless had somehow found the strength of mind to remain dignified. On this occasion, Jemima had not even had the chance to close the door behind her before the woman leapt out of her chair and pounded the desk located between them with both of her fists. Her eyes narrowed and expression darkened as she focused her anger on Jemima. 'Why the hell have you brought me here? I should be with my daughter!'

'Sit down!' ordered the constable. He took a step forward, ready to forcibly restrain her if he needed to.

'It's fine, Constable,' said Jemima, reassuring him that she could handle the situation by herself. 'Perhaps you could get us both a cup of tea?' She turned to Lydia. 'Or would you prefer coffee?'

The offer of a beverage clearly confused Lydia and had the effect of taking the wind out of her sails. Jemima had banked on that: from what she'd previously observed, Lydia Leysham was conditioned to conform to social etiquette.

Jemima certainly wasn't in the business of offering a beverage to someone she was about to interrogate. But she felt that this was one occasion when it might just wrongfoot Lydia and get the woman to drop her guard.

'T-tea. Two sugars. Th-thank you,' stammered Lydia. In a matter of seconds, the woman's belligerence had abated.

Jemima was pleased that the simple offer of refreshment had seemingly made the woman less hostile. She was still prepared to push her however hard she needed to in order to get an answer to the question, and to find out whatever else she was hiding.

As the police constable left the room, Jemima pulled out a chair for herself and sat down.

'Sit, please Lydia.' Her tone was polite and reasonable. She gestured at the seat the other woman had recently vacated.

Lydia complied. Jemima appreciated that her chosen approach was working. She smiled inwardly, knowing that Dan and Gareth fully expected her to go in there and give the woman hell. She acknowledged that further down the line it might just come to that. But as things stood, Lydia appeared to be amenable to her carrot approach.

'Why am I here?' Lydia's complexion was pale and blotchy. A far cry from the way she had previously looked. Her eyes were bloodshot, with dark shadows beneath them. It aged her considerably. Her facial expression and the way in which she uttered those four words, suggested that she was exhausted and genuinely confused.

'Because we had no other choice.'

'Surely, I'm not a suspect? I'm the mother of a victim. Desperately trying to come to terms with what has happened to my daughter. Doing my best to stay strong for her while I grieve for the loss of a grandchild I never got to meet. The entire situation is horrendous. If that wasn't enough, I've been treated appallingly, by a man I'm paying to protect my own daughter. He stopped me from spending time with her. And from what I can ascertain, you've enabled him to treat me this way.'

'You're not the victim here, Lydia. Tabitha and the others who were abducted and kept in captivity are the victims.'

'Yes, that monster took my daughter. He raped her repeatedly then killed her child . . . My grandchild!'

'Yes. That's exactly what Douglas Taylor did. And given his three-strike rule, he would have murdered Tabitha too, if she hadn't had a stroke of luck and managed to escape from that hellhole he kept them in.'

'Is that his name?' The breath caught in Lydia's throat and her eyes filled with tears. 'Have you caught him yet? Please tell me that monster is in captivity and that he'll never get out again.'

In that moment, Jemima decided to lie. Until she'd got the information out of her, there was no reason to tell Lydia that Taylor was dead. 'No, we haven't arrested him. But surely that's down to you?' Jemima watched as the accusation sunk in and the woman's expression changed. Even before Lydia responded, Jemima was starting to sense that perhaps she had got it wrong.

'Is this some sort of sick joke? Because if it is, it's not amusing.'

'I assure you that it's not a joke, Lydia. We know for a fact that someone tipped Taylor off about us raiding that property. That warning enabled him to escape before we arrived.'

'You surely don't think that I said anything to him?'

'The thing is, Lydia, only a handful of people knew that Tabitha had given us details which could lead us to where the others were being held. And you were one of those people.'

'Oh, I see.' Lydia pursed her lips as she shook her head.

'You see what, Lydia?'

'You can't possibly acknowledge the fact that one of your own was in cahoots with that dreadful man. So you suggest it has to have been me. How pathetically predictable. You people close ranks and blame the victim's family. Well, you won't get away with it. I won't allow it. I'll cause such a stink. You'll see.'

'That's not the case, Lyd—'

'Don't insult me with your lies,' she interjected.

'Enough! I don't have time for this,' Jemima's tone hardened. She'd played nice, but it was clearly getting her nowhere. It was time to change tack and shake things up.

Lydia stiffened and sat back in her seat, extending the distance between them.

'Yesterday I spent a significant amount of time examining CCTV coverage of the hospital to establish how the leak could have occurred.'

Lydia went to say something, but Jemima held up her hand. 'I haven't finished.'

The woman thought better of it and closed her mouth.

'I sent you the image of the house. You showed it to Tabitha and knew that we were planning on raiding it. You sold your daughter out, along with every other one of Taylor's victims. You were the leak, Lydia. You gave Taylor advance warning of what we were about to do. You allowed him to escape.'

Lydia's expression darkened. Her mouth opened as she was about to counter the allegations.

Jemima was having none of it. 'Don't you dare interrupt me. You will listen to what I have to say!' Jemima slammed her fist on the table and glared at the woman.

Lydia flinched and pushed herself backwards in the seat. She wasn't used to displays of aggression. Throughout her life, she was generally the one calling the shots. But social etiquette was adhered to, and things were done with decorum. Yet suddenly she had found herself all but trapped inside a police interview room, where it had quickly become apparent that the normal rules of engagement no longer applied. She was so far out of her comfort zone. All she wanted was to get back to Tabitha. To support her daughter.

Sensing the woman's fear and confusion, Jemima cracked on without missing a beat. 'I tracked your movements, Lydia. You made a phone call using a hospital pay phone to this number. And before you made the call, you looked around repeatedly to ensure that no one had seen you. Hardly the actions of an innocent person.' Jemima placed a piece of paper on the desk and pushed it towards Lydia. 'Whose number is this? Who were you calling?'

'This is ridic—' A tone of indignation had returned to her voice.

'Stop wasting my time!' Jemima leapt out of her seat. 'This is your last chance. Tell me now. Or at the very least you'll be charged with wasting police time!'

Lydia paled as she realized that there would be no fobbing Jemima off. 'It's Edgar's phone. I was calling Edgar. I had to let him know that I'd be uncontactable.'

'Edgar? You rang your husband? And you expect me to believe that?'

'Of course I'd ring him. Given our social standing and our work commitments there are things which he would need to either rearrange, or at the very least inform people that I would be indisposed for the time being.'

'That sounds very formal. And is that all you told him? Didn't he ask about Tabitha?' asked Jemima.

'Well, I might have mentioned that she had started to remember things and that you were hopeful of locating the property where she was held captive.'

'Why didn't you call him from your mobile?'

'I wanted to speak to him out of earshot from Tabitha.'

'That still doesn't explain why you didn't use your mobile.'

'I know. Please, don't make me explain. This is highly personal and extremely embarrassing,' pleaded Lydia.

'Answer the question.' There was no disguising the anger in Jemima's voice.

'It's just that Edgar's not been answering my calls. Things haven't been right between us for a very long time. But since Tabitha's been found . . . Well, he hasn't even wanted to see her.'

'Didn't you think that was strange?'

'Not really. Edgar's been run ragged throughout the last few months. He has a lot of responsibility on his shoulders. There are many people reliant upon him.

'Edgar's not her biological father. Though for the purposes of her birth certificate he is named as her father, and he's brought her up as his own. They were very close when she was young, and we were a happy family unit until Tabs reached her teens and her hormones kicked in. Her antics were testing, to say the least. We both did our best, but by that stage, Tabs knew that she wasn't biologically Edgar's, and she wasn't averse to bringing it up whenever tempers flared.

'Edgar was stoic, far more so than I would have been. Tabitha did everything she could to get a negative reaction out of him. She disliked the fact that given our social standing Edgar expected her to behave in an exemplary manner. He was a hard taskmaster, expecting her to excel at her studies and to behave like a lady.

'It was too much to ask. He felt she'd let him down and he distanced himself from her. Claimed she was an embarrassment. Which to a certain extent she was. But teenage angst is part and parcel of family life. A rite of passage, if you will. She would have grown out of it eventually.'

Jemima's mind raced through the implications of what she'd just learned. If Lydia was to be believed, it appeared there was a rift between Edgar and his daughter.

'Who is Tabitha's biological father?'

'A man named Jeremy Fancourt, but you'll be wasting your time if you go down that route. Jeremy and I had an affair with each other, after I married Edgar. But Jeremy died in a skiing accident shortly before Tabitha was born.'

Jemima decided that for the moment she would not push Lydia for further information into Edgar's relationship with Tabitha. Choosing instead to try to establish whether he was linked to Douglas Taylor. 'Does the name L&T Holdings mean anything to you?'

'No. Is it important?'

'I wouldn't ask if it wasn't,' said Jemima.

'I suppose Edgar might have heard of it. He has numerous business interests. But it means nothing to me. Tabitha's disappearance put a strain on our relationship. In an ideal world Edgar and I would have divorced. But as I've already indicated, we have responsibilities. We share the same house for appearance's sake, but thankfully it's large enough to enable us to live separate lives. Though we're adept at playing the devoted couple whenever necessary.'

The door to the interview room opened as the constable returned with two cups of tea. 'Stay here and make sure that Mrs Leysham doesn't go anywhere,' said Jemima, as she rushed out of the room.

CHAPTER 28

Jemima returned to the incident room. All eyes were on her as she walked through the door, as her arrival made a welcome break from their tasks.

'Well?' asked Gareth.

'Lydia Leysham has just confirmed that the call she made on the hospital payphone was to her husband. She told him that Tabitha had revealed details about where she was incarcerated and that we were hopeful of identifying the property and raiding it.'

'The parents were in on it with Taylor?' Dan's jaw dropped as he tried to get his head around the shocking nature of this possibility.

'I don't know about that. Lydia admits to revealing information to her husband. But that doesn't necessarily mean that she was in on anything.'

'If it's so innocent, why did she use a hospital payphone instead of her mobile?' asked Nancy.

'Apparently, all's not well in their marriage. She claims it's been a marriage of convenience for many years, and if she'd called him on her mobile, it's likely he would have rejected the call.'

'Well, he didn't go to the hospital to visit Tabitha,' said Gareth.

'That's right. He didn't. The other bombshell that Lydia dropped is that Tabitha isn't her husband's child. It wasn't a secret. Both Edgar and Tabitha were aware of the fact. Tabitha's biological father died before she was born.

'Lydia claims she rang her husband to make him aware that she'd be uncontactable. She wanted him to advise various business contacts and others who relied upon her.

'I'm going to ask the local police to pick up Edgar Leysham so that we can question him. His demonstrated antipathy towards Tabitha is concerning. I don't buy into the narrative that he's too busy or important to drop other commitments to rush to Tabitha's bedside. Any parent, biological or otherwise, who cared about their child, would have visited her in hospital. But the man has avoided all contact. Lydia has already told me that Edgar and Tabitha were at loggerheads throughout her teenage years. He also knew that we were closing in on Taylor's location. Which makes me wonder if he was the one who tipped him off.'

'I've just established that Benedict Sebastian Taylor is linked to L&T Holdings,' said Dan.

'What's more, he was at school with Edgar Leysham. They attended the same posh boarding school and were on the rugby team together. There's a photograph of them together on the school website,' said Nancy.

'Let me see.' Jemima headed towards Nancy's desk.

Gareth, who was busily checking something on his machine while the others continued to update Jemima, suddenly thumped his desk. 'I've found it! I've bloody found it!' He raised his arms triumphantly.

'What?' asked Jemima, as she turned her attention to him.

'Nancy's spot on. They were at school together. But there's so much more. Look! They're presenting the school with a cheque for £100,000, for an upgrade to their sporting facilities. It's not just the photo. Read the caption.'

Everyone gathered around Gareth's screen, to see the photograph of Edgar Leysham and Benedict Sebastian Taylor. The caption beneath the image read, '*Lord Leysham and Benedict Sebastian Taylor, founders of L&T Holdings, present their former school with a substantial cheque to enable upgrades to sporting facilities.*'

The implications of this latest set of revelations were a lot to get her head around. It now seemed possible that both Edgar Leysham and Benedict Taylor might be complicit in Douglas Taylor's crimes.

Jemima hoped that Edgar Leysham's social status would not prove problematic. A man like that would inevitably have powerful friends. People who routinely operated out of sight. Pulling the strings to ensure the so-called 'right result' for those they believed mattered. Since the revelations at the Marquess Club, the scales had fallen from Jemima's eyes. She was now far too seasoned a detective to have remained an idealist. She had come to realize that good people were few and far between. Especially across the spectrum of public service which had become a cesspit of corruption. Justice had long since become a lottery with the odds significantly stacked against victims.

Jemima exhaled noisily before she spoke. 'Well done everyone. This changes things. Someone give Mack and Levi a bell. Tell them to leave what they're doing and get up here. It's time to change our approach.'

'I'll do it,' said Nancy, who wasted no time picking up the phone.

'We also need search warrants for L&T Holdings and Benedict Taylor's home address.'

'On it,' said Dan, as he picked up the phone.

'What about the Leysham home?' asked Gareth.

'Not at the moment. He's likely to have all sorts of people in his pocket, and I don't want to risk him knowing that we're coming after him. For now, let him think it's just the business we're interested in. He knows that we identified Douglas Taylor, so he'll guess we'll have looked into his financials. In which case a search warrant for the business premises won't come as a surprise, and there's every chance he'll try to lay all the blame on Benedict.

'I'm going to have another word with Lydia. I won't be long. In the meantime, get on to the locals and tell them that we need them to locate and detain Benedict Taylor and Edgar Leysham. They're to be brought in for us to question them in relation to an ongoing investigation and that no matter what either man might say or threaten, they mustn't be allowed to speak to or contact anyone until we arrive.'

Having passed Lydia into Jemima's custody, Kennedy had also handed over a bag of her personal belongings. Jemima decided it was time to take these to the interview room. As she walked through the door, Lydia Leysham looked up and met her gaze. Her demeanour had changed in the short time since their previous encounter.

'Do you really think Edgar could be responsible for what happened to Tabs?'

Jemima sensed that the woman had spent the time mulling things over. After all, it wasn't an easy thing to be confronted with evidence of the unthinkable. No matter how much the bonds of her marriage had disintegrated over the years, it must still be unpalatable that someone she had once willingly shared her life with could betray her trust by doing something so maliciously evil.

The door clicked loudly behind her. It sounded ominous as Jemima's anticipated response hung heavily in the air. Huxley closed the gap between them, placing the bag of Lydia's personal effects on the table. Lydia ignored this. Focused entirely upon Jemima, who pulled out a chair and sat down. 'Well?' she asked, as she pressed for an answer.

'I'm not going to sugarcoat it, Lydia. It's certainly looking that way. We've evidence that directly links Edgar to your daughter's abductor, Douglas Taylor. Your husband founded a company, L&T Holdings, with Douglas Taylor's father; that company has been making substantial monthly payments to Douglas Taylor for the past eight years.'

Lydia's hands shot to her chest as her face contorted and she groaned. The sound was deep, protracted, and agonized.

'Do you need a doctor?' Jemima was worried that the woman might be having a heart attack. When Lydia ignored her, she repeated the question, placing a hand gently on her shoulder.

Lydia stared blankly at Jemima, who repeated the question for a third time. Lydia shook her head, took a deep breath, and began to compose herself. It was as though her brain had finally processed the information and she accepted that she had to deal with it. Her expression cleared, as she adopted a firm resolve. 'No, no, really, I'm all right. Self-indulgent, as usual, but this latest news has been a revelation. Believe me, if it turns out that Edgar was behind this horrendous ordeal, I'll do everything in my power to destroy him. I'll give him nowhere to hide. Shout it from the rooftops if I must. My allegiance is to Tabs, and the other victims. They've all been forcibly subjected to a living hell, and I'll make sure Edgar doesn't walk away from this.'

'In that case, you'll consent to us undertaking a thorough search of your home,' said Jemima. 'It's essential we establish exactly what we're up against. And we need to find and apprehend your husband, and his friend Benedict Taylor.'

There was no hint of uncertainty in Lydia's response. She had come to a decision and was prepared to back it up with action. 'I pride myself on being good in a crisis. Tell me what you need, and I'll ensure it'll be done.'

Fifteen minutes later, Jemima walked out of the interview room with all the information she needed. Lydia had given written permission for the police to enter and search the Leysham's home and outbuildings. She had supplied the code to disable the security system, and informed Jemima of the location of, and combination to, a hidden safe.

CHAPTER 29

With details and photographs of Edgar Leysham and
Benedict Sebastian Taylor circulated to police forces, and
ports throughout the UK, an order was issued to find and
apprehend them in connection with an ongoing investigation
into abduction, false imprisonment, rape and murder.

Jemima returned to the incident room to find that Levi
and Mack had joined the others. Each of them seemed rein-
vigorated and ready for whatever they were about to face.
Everyone stopped talking as they gathered round to find out
what their next move would be.

'Are arrangements in place with the local force?' asked
Jemima.

'They're up to speed with the situation,' confirmed Dan.

'Excellent, because we're going to undertake three
simultaneous property searches. Gareth, I want you and
Nancy to take the L&T Holdings office. Every electronic
device is to be recovered, along with paperwork. The two of
you are best suited to combing through that lot and making
sense of the data files. Dan, I want you and Mack to head
to Benedict Taylor's address. You know the sort of things
we're looking for. Levi, you're with me. Lydia Leysham's
given us written permission to undertake a thorough search
of the property, grounds and all outbuildings, so we don't

need a search warrant. Keep in touch and update everyone on anything of interest.'

It was almost ninety minutes later when Jemima and Levi arrived at the turn-off for the Leysham family home. There were two squad cars waiting for them, as with each of the three searches being undertaken, they needed more officers to help them with the task. Jemima briefed the local officers and made sure that they knew they were to keep their body cameras on so that they could not be accused of planting evidence should they find anything. When she was certain that every officer knew what was expected of them the convoy set off down the approach to the property. It was the first time Levi had set eyes upon the place, and he let out a long whistle of appreciation.

'It's not as grand as it first appears,' said Jemima. 'When you get up close, you'll realize it's rundown in places.

'Remember to keep your eyes peeled for Leysham. We haven't heard that they've apprehended him yet, so it's not impossible that he could be hiding out somewhere on the premises.'

Jemima and Levi searched the house as other officers took the grounds and outbuildings. It was a painstakingly slow process. They weren't just on the lookout for Edgar Leysham; they were also trying to find any documentary evidence definitively linking him to Douglas Taylor and the property used to imprison the women and children. As payments had been made via L&T Holdings, it would be all too easy for Edgar to claim he had been completely unaware of what was going on. He'd pretend to be shocked that L&T Holdings had made those payments, and claim it was all down to Benedict Taylor. A man desperate enough to help his son, regardless of the cost to anyone else. But Benedict's complicity didn't necessarily mean that Edgar was innocent.

Leysham's legal team would milk that uncertainty for all it was worth. Muddy the waters until there was reasonable doubt and the jury would be unable or unwilling to come to a guilty verdict. And Jemima had an unshakeable feeling that Edgar Leysham was as guilty as hell. His absence from Tabitha's hospital bedside screamed just that.

Jemima had to find the evidence against him, and then tie it up so tightly that the man and his expensive lawyers had no wriggle room for him to worm his way out of it.

'According to Lydia there are two studies on the ground floor,' said Jemima. 'I suggest we begin with those. We'll take all electronic devices and any paperwork which might help create an audit trail. Look for photographs too. I know these days there's less chance of people having snaps lying around the place, but you never know.'

They were still searching the studies when one of the groups of local officers came into the house. 'Checked the barn, greenhouse and shed, ma'am. Nothing of interest. Do you want us to give you a hand inside?'

'It'd be great if you could make a start upstairs. What about the others, how are they getting on?'

'They're patrolling the grounds, just in case Leysham's hiding out there. They're also looking for any obvious hidey-holes where he might have stashed anything incriminating in a hurry. If he knew you were on to him, it would be foolish to get caught with anything on his person. It'd incriminate him straight off.'

'That's my thought too,' said Jemima. 'He's been in control until now, and he must've felt untouchable. This will be a new experience for him. Given his social standing I'd guess he's a well-known face in these parts.'

'Oh, he is, ma'am,' interjected one of the officers.

'Which means he'll want to keep his head down and couldn't easily hide anything without risking someone recognizing him. He won't have the luxury of anonymity like an ordinary Joe Bloggs. Which makes life harder for him and in turn gives us the upper hand. So, if he had kept anything incriminating in this house, it's more than likely to still be here. We just need to find it.'

As the search continued, Jemima's phone rang. It was Dan. 'Just letting you know that we've got Benedict Taylor. The plods picked him up outside his house. He'd been doing a bit of retail therapy. Bought himself some new shoes and designer jeans.'

'Doesn't sound like the actions of a man who has something to hide,' said Jemima.

'Precisely. Unless it's one hell of a double bluff. From the little I saw of him I didn't get the impression he was putting on an act. In my opinion he came across as completely nonplussed to discover that we were searching his house and that there was an alert out for him to be detained for questioning.'

'Have you finished there?'

'More or less. Haven't found a thing. Interestingly, there were no photographs of Douglas. Don't you think that odd?'

'Absolutely. I know our boys are still young enough to be dependent upon us, but even when they grow up and leave home, I can't imagine not having photographs of them. Or some other keepsake,' said Jemima. 'Has he been informed of Douglas's death?'

'Not yet.'

'Good. Keep it that way. I want to be the one to tell him when we interview him. That way I can gauge his reaction. I'm hoping to finish up here soon. Text me the address of the station they've taken him to, and I'll see you there.'

Every document was removed from the safe and bagged as evidence. As were notebooks, journals, diaries, correspondence and photographs. Artwork was removed from walls and examined to ascertain whether anything had been hidden behind them. Rugs were removed and furniture tilted to establish whether anything had been hidden underneath. There were no fitted carpets, which sped up their search. Toilet cisterns were checked, bath panels removed, cupboards and drawers emptied, clothes, shoes and ornaments searched. Yet on the face of it there didn't seem to be anything incriminating.

Jemima tugged her hair in frustration as she walked from room to room once more. 'We must have missed something.'

'I don't think we have, Guv. We've been over everything with a fine-tooth comb. There's nothing,' said Levi.

It was then that Jemima's eyes focused on a large ornate inglenook fireplace, at the far end of the room they were standing in. 'What about that?'

'It's been checked,' said one of the local officers. 'Doesn't look as though they use it. There are some logs stacked up, but they look purely ornamental.'

'Did you search it thoroughly?' asked Jemima.

'We pulled all the logs out. There was nothing, ma'am.' The officer was bleary-eyed, his shoulders sagging, not used to putting in this amount of physical effort and keen to call it a day.

'But the logs are stacked neatly,' said Jemima. Had the fireplace really been searched?

'We did pull them out ma'am. Every single one of them. But we put them back afterwards. Didn't want to risk tripping over them,' said another officer.

'Fair enough, but I want to check it myself,' said Jemima. As she said it, she spotted both officers roll their eyes in despair. She let their obvious disrespect pass without comment; she didn't want to antagonize them unnecessarily. Her team were on their patch, and she would need their cooperation, or that of their colleagues, for a while yet.

'Levi, give me a hand.' Jemima bent down as she began to pick logs off the pile and passed them to him. When the fireplace was empty, Jemima crawled forward until she was able to reach up inside and feel around. As she moved her hand, her fingertips reached what she thought might be a ledge. Though her arm was not long enough for her to know for certain.

'I think there might be some sort of ledge in there, but my arm's not long enough.'

'Allow me, ma'am,' said one of the local officers. At six feet four inches, he was the tallest officer by far.

Jemima shuffled back to allow him access and waited with bated breath.

'Well bugger me! There's something there. Sorry, ma'am. We weren't as thorough as we should've been.' His tone had changed from veiled exasperation to one of contrition. As he brought down his arm, everyone saw that he was holding a sealed package wrapped securely in plastic.

CHAPTER 30

Yet again they found themselves inside another police station. This time in Cheltenham.

Since taking charge of this newly formed squad, Jemima was beginning to lose count of the number of police stations she had visited. Though what she and the rest of the team had soon realized was that no matter where the building was located, every police station was noisy, utilitarian and had seen better days.

Jemima and the team gathered to update each other on what evidence they had found at the three properties. Gareth was the first to speak.

'We confiscated every electronic device and paper record at L&T Holdings. It'll take us days if not weeks to go through it, and that's only if Nancy and I get more support to help us. I suggest that as soon as this briefing session is over, we transport it back to base, because it's not going to be practical for us to undertake such a lengthy thorough forensic investigation from here.'

'I agree,' said Jemima. 'I'll have a word with Olsen. Get him to arrange additional resources. I've no doubt that Leysham will bring out the big guns when we go after him, so we need every scrap of evidence to build a watertight case against him.'

'Thanks, Guv. It's going to be a mammoth task.'

'We've also got names and contact details for staff who work at the company. The receptionist was the only one there. She confirmed that Benedict was in as usual up until yesterday, but he had today off,' said Nancy.

'What about Leysham?'

'Hasn't shown his face there for the last four days. Not that that's unusual. Apparently, he oversees things remotely. Just pops in if he needs to sign something. She had no idea where he was.'

'Gar, I want you and Nancy to include the electronic devices we recovered from the Leysham property. They are all catalogued so there'll be no risk of mixing them up with the company stuff.

'Levi, give them a hand to load them up so that they can take everything back to our operational centre. Then come back here because there'll be things for you to do.' It made sense for Levi to be the one to help them with this task. Having spent his time with Jemima, there was nothing he could add to the briefing session that Jemima didn't already know.

'Will do, Guv.'

Turning her attention back to Gareth, Jemima continued. 'Give me a bell when you arrive, and I'll update you on progress at this end.'

Gareth and Nancy didn't need telling twice. With the scale of the task ahead of them they knew they were on the clock. Collecting their personal possessions, they headed out of the door while the briefing session continued.

'Anything of significance at Taylor senior's house?' asked Jemima.

'Nothing,' said Mack. 'No documents. No safe. Not even any photographs of his son.'

'Umm . . . Well, we found this package hidden inside the chimney at Fortisham Grange. It was placed up high enough so that there was little chance of it being noticed.'

'Have you taken a look at it?' asked Dan.

'Not as yet, but I'd bet my life it's important. OK, I need to set things in motion with Olsen. In the meantime, I'd like you two to open that package, photograph and document the contents, and we'll go from there,' she said.

Jemima took a deep breath as she dialled Olsen's number. There was no love lost between her and her senior officer. He was the polar opposite of Ray Kennedy, who had been all about the team. Olsen appeared to be pure ambition and self-interest through and through.

Ten minutes later she returned to the others, pleasantly surprised that the superintendent hadn't made life difficult for her. In fact, he had recognized the urgency of the situation and had been supportive.

'So, what have we got?' she asked. Dan and Mack were using a laptop to search a location using street view.

'Paperwork for a property purchased a couple of years back. It's in the joint ownership of Edgar Leysham and Charlotte Winstanley.'

'Where have I heard that name?' Jemima's eyes narrowed as she tried to recall the information.

'No idea,' said Dan.

'Is that it?' Jemima pointed at a cottage in what appeared to be a village setting.

'No. Give me a sec,' said Mack. 'Almost there.' Moments later they were staring at a quintessential chocolate box cottage with a thatched roof, located close to a village green. 'It's located in Hazelwood. Which is apparently a village in Monmouthshire.'

'Wouldn't take long to get to the wetlands property from there,' said Dan.

'I've got it,' said Jemima. 'Charlotte Winstanley's the operational manager at L&T Holdings. And I seem to remember that when Dan and I first visited the Leyshams, someone named Charlotte was just leaving the property. She'd had a meeting with Edgar Leysham.'

'So why the hell would Leysham hide documents relating to a property they've purchased?' asked Dan.

'Oh, wake up and smell the coffee, man. For someone in our line of work you're so naïve,' laughed Mack.

Dan stared blankly at him.

'Makes perfect sense if she's Leysham's mistress, and he bought the property in joint names as a little love nest,' explained Mack. 'He wouldn't want his missus to know about it. And possibly he doesn't trust his bit on the side enough to give her the deeds to the property.'

'I think you might have just cracked it, Mack,' said Jemima. 'So, while Dan and I interview Benedict Taylor, I'd like you to see what you can find out about Charlotte. When Levi gets back from helping the others load the evidence, get him to do some research on that village, because I've a feeling we'll be visiting that cottage soon.'

* * *

Benedict Taylor was surprisingly calm for a man who had returned home to discover that his house had been raided by the police and who had been subsequently brought in for questioning. His lawyer had arrived, and the two men were sitting together awaiting their arrival.

Jemima entered the interview room ahead of Dan. She pulled out a chair and sat down. It was the first time she had set eyes on Benedict, and she was surprised to see that he shared no physical similarities with his son. With the formalities out of the way, she began. 'Firstly, I'd like to stress that at this stage of our enquiries you are not under arrest.'

'So why is my client here?' asked the lawyer.

'I'm about to get to that,' said Jemima. 'Have you seen or heard the news in the last few days, Mr Taylor?'

'No. Can't say I have.'

'I'm sorry to have to inform you that your son, Douglas, was killed in a traffic collision yesterday.'

Benedict sighed. Jemima allowed him a moment to compose himself, though the man didn't appear to be too visibly upset.

'Do you understand what I've just told you, Mr Taylor?' His lack of emotion was puzzling.

'Yes, I understand perfectly. You must think I'm cold-hearted, but really, I'm not. You see I stopped having any sort of relationship with Dougie a very long time ago. I haven't seen him in, oh, it must be about ten years or so.'

'Why was that?'

'Well, the first thing you need to know is that my late wife and I adopted Dougie. He was the only child of her best friend, who tragically took her own life. She was a single parent. No one knew the identity of the boy's father, and it wasn't as if we didn't try to find out.

'We took Dougie in when he was nine years old. Fostered him at first, then adopted. My wife insisted upon it. He was never the easiest of children, and quite frankly being the age he was and his troublesome nature, if we hadn't taken him, he would have ended up in care until he was old enough to fend for himself.

'We tried our best, but he was hard work. Always seemed to resent everyone and everything. We sent him to boarding school, the same one I attended. Thought it might instil a bit of discipline into him. We were forever getting calls to say that he'd been causing trouble. I had to pull a few strings to ensure that he remained a pupil there.'

'Let me stop you there, Mr Taylor,' said Jemima. 'You say that you've had nothing to do with Douglas in the last decade.'

'That's correct,' interjected Benedict.

'So how do you explain that for many years Douglas has received regular monthly payments of a substantial amount, from L&T Holdings? It seems to me that you've employed him in some capacity.'

'Excuse me?' Benedict's brow furrowed as he tried to make sense of what he'd just heard. 'You've got that wrong. I wouldn't employ him. Why would I? He doesn't have the sort of skillset that would be of benefit to L&T Holdings. You must have made a mistake.'

'It's no mistake, Mr Taylor. See here, I have a copy of Douglas's bank statements going back over that period,' she selected the relevant documentation from the folder she had brought with her to the interview room.

Benedict picked up the paperwork and studied it carefully. He shook his head. 'That explains it. Though I can't imagine what the hell he was playing at.'

'What who was playing at?' pressed Jemima.

'I agree that these payments to Dougie came from L&T Holdings. But the account number they were paid from is not our general account. Go check it out for yourself. We donate a significant amount of money to charities. This account number is the one set up for that purpose. You need to speak to Edgar Leysham about that. He's the one with sole access to that account. It was his baby. His way of us giving back to society. I was always too busy with day-to-day matters, whereas Edgar likes being seen as a benefactor. It was too much hassle for me, so we agreed on a separate account. He dealt with the decisions about who received what when it came to charitable contributions. Though what the hell he was thinking going behind my back to pay that amount of money to Dougie, God only knows.'

'And you have paperwork to back up the fact that Edgar was in sole charge of that account?'

'Absolutely. You'll easily be able to verify my claims. Though what I don't understand is why Dougie being killed in a traffic collision has led to you raiding my home and questioning these payments? On the face of it, Edgar's decision to pay Dougie that exorbitant amount of money on a regular basis seems highly questionable. I can't begin to imagine why he did it, and it does make me wonder if something was amiss. Edgar and I have known each other for most of our lives, as school chums and business partners, but we move in different social circles. I've not once met his family. Nor he mine. Or at least, I thought he hadn't.' Benedict appeared to be completely nonplussed. 'I would have expected Edgar to have mentioned something like this to me. Not just gone ahead without my knowledge. Believe me, I'll be having words with him once I get out of here. I need to get to the bottom of what was going on.'

'Did you know that Tabitha Leysham has been found?' asked Jemima.

'Really?' At hearing those words, Benedict's expression changed from perplexed annoyance to one of delight. 'No, I didn't, but thank heavens for that. I can't begin to imagine what Edgar and his wife must've gone through over the years. So, where was Tabitha? Run off with some lad, I suppose?'

'She'd been abducted, Mr Taylor.'

'Abducted?' His jaw dropped and he appeared to be genuinely horrified. 'But that's dreadful. She disappeared years ago. Is the poor girl all right? Have you apprehended the person responsible?'

'It was Douglas.'

'What was Douglas?'

'Douglas abducted her, and other women too.'

'Dougie? Dougie? You must be mistaken. I appreciate he had his demons. But no.' Benedict shook his head in denial. 'No, you must be mistaken. Dougie wouldn't do anything like that . . .' His voice trailed off as the words sank in. He appeared to be utterly bewildered. Minutes passed in silence as they allowed him time to take things in. When he next looked up there were tears in his eyes. 'There were others?'

'Yes.'

'Oh, my . . . Th-this must be d-down to me. I should have b-been firmer with him. Kept a closer eye. N-not pushed him away. I had no idea. No idea whatsoever. I'd have put a stop to it if I'd known. Turned him in myself.' Benedict Taylor was a broken man, horrified by what Douglas had done.

'No one's blaming you, Mr Taylor,' said Jemima. She was convinced that the man was genuinely shocked by what he'd just learned.

'Will you tell me what he did with that poor girl?'

'He kept her, and three other women locked up inside a remote property.' Seeing how upset the man was, Jemima decided it was best not to mention the children.

'Where?'

'The Wetlands area in Newport, South Wales.'

'But how could he afford a house in the first place? The last I heard of him, he was some sort of personal assistant . . .' The man's thought process was almost transparent. 'This is where you tell me that the money from that account was used for him to pay rent on that property?'

Jemima shook her head. 'No, Mr Taylor. I'm afraid not. You see, L&T Holdings owns that property.'

'But we don't own any properties in that location.'

'This is the Land Registry record,' said Dan. He handed the document to Benedict, who by now was shaking so much that he was unable to hold it. Leaving his solicitor to take it instead.

'It's true, Ben,' said his solicitor after he studied it carefully. 'It's here in black and white.'

'What the hell has Edgar done? Was he in on this with Dougie? His own daughter?'

'It's certainly looking that way,' said Jemima.

'But I've always thought of Edgar as my friend. Turns out I didn't know him at all.'

'I know this has been a lot for you to take in, Mr Taylor, and I appreciate how upsetting it must be. But I have one more question. Are Charlotte Winstanley and Edgar in a relationship with each other?'

'Charlotte? Edgar? To be honest, if you'd asked me that yesterday I'd have laughed you out of the room. But the truth is, I don't know. I don't think I know anything anymore.'

CHAPTER 31

Benedict Taylor was released without charge. The man was broken by what he'd learned. Though, surprisingly, not because his son had died, but because of learning of his sick reign of terror, and the fact that his friend and business partner had funded and aided Douglas's acts.

'Gareth called to say they'd reached the station. He said to tell you that there was a team of ten officers waiting for them,' said Mack.

'Olsen came good, then,' said Dan. 'First time for everything, I suppose.'

'Before we do anything else, I need to give Gareth a call,' said Jemima. She wanted him to prioritize investigating the account from which the monthly payments were made to Douglas. If Benedict had been truthful, and Edgar had sole access to the account, then it was definitive proof that Leysham had been in league with Douglas.

Having updated Gareth, Jemima turned her attention to the others.

'I've filled them in on what we learned during the interview,' said Dan.

'What progress have you made?' asked Jemima. She looked at Mack and Levi.

'We've established the exact location of the property,' said Mack. 'Presumably we're going to raid it?'

'That'll be our next move. My thinking is that it's the only place Leysham could safely go to ground, and he was determined to hide the paperwork relating to it,' said Jemima. 'So where exactly is the village?'

Levi spread out a map and pinpointed the location.

'Shouldn't take too long to get there,' said Jemima. 'We'll follow this route.' She sketched it out with her finger. 'What do we know about the village?'

'More of a hamlet really,' said Mack. 'A handful of properties. Not even a church or a village pub.'

'So, we're talking remote. That's good. Less chance of anyone interfering or getting caught up in the operation. Saying that, I hope to God that its remoteness doesn't mean that it's being used in the same way as the Wetlands property,' said Jemima. This possibility had only just occurred to her, and it caused a shiver to run down her spine.

'Don't think so, Guv,' said Levi. 'We've looked at it online. Got it up on this screen if you want to take a look.' They followed Levi to another desk, where a laptop was open. 'See for yourself. It's a standard cottage if there is such a thing. No high walls, gates or hedges. One way in and out. And the entire front of the structure is visible from the road.'

'Looking promising so far. Do we know the layout of the property?'

'Unless they've modified it since it was purchased three years ago. We found it on one of the property websites. This is what it looked like.' Levi toggled to another window and the four of them saw what the internal layout had been at the time of marketing.

'Excellent work you two,' said Jemima. 'Right, let's head over there and get this thing done.'

'Do we need the Armed Response Unit?' asked Dan.

'I don't believe we do. From everything I've learned about him, Leysham isn't the type to be waiting there with a firearm. He likes pulling the strings. Making things happen with his money and connections. Apart from that, he'll want to play the innocent card. Once we arrest him, he'll be lawyered up faster than we can blink. His sort considers themselves to be above the law, and the likes of us are just hoi polloi. Something to wipe off the bottom of their shoes. I've no doubt there'll be all sorts of threats issued, about how our careers will be over if we don't get back in line. But it won't wash.'

'What's hoi polloi?' asked Levi. He frowned in puzzlement.

'Not heard of that one then, eh mate?' Mack laughed and shook his head, 'It's us. The common people. Plebs.'

'Okaaay,' said Levi. He sounded unsure. 'Thought it was some made-up word.'

'No, it's real,' said Dan.

A few minutes later they were headed in two cars towards the Monmouthshire village. Jemima was once again in the passenger seat, as she wanted to speak to Olsen to update him on what they were about to do. Keeping the superintendent informed was something she routinely did. But given the privilege card that Leysham would inevitably play, she didn't want the resultant stink that he would cause to come back to bite them. It was better to alert Olsen so that he was prepared whenever the phone call came through to him.

'I take it there'll be some sort of commotion at the property which will give you cause to believe that there could be imminent danger to life?' asked Olsen. His voice boomed over the speaker phone.

'Absolutely, sir. Otherwise, I wouldn't dream of forcing an entry,' said Jemima.

'In that case, crack on, Chief Inspector.' Olsen disconnected the call.

'Has he had a personality transplant?' asked Dan.

'I'm beginning to wonder, but it seems for once he's got our backs.'

A few miles out from the village, they cut the flashing lights and sirens. They were useful when speed was important for ensuring that other road users got out of the way, but the last thing they wanted was for Leysham to get wind of their arrival. Best that they took him by surprise, before he could make a run for it, or destroy any evidence he still had with him.

Both police vehicles pulled up on the edge of the village. The property was still out of sight. Each officer put on a stab-proof vest and ensured that they had a utility belt with a baton, and a canister of CS gas. To make it clear who they were, they each wore a police issue jacket.

'Be sure to switch your bodycams on. We need an irrefutable record of everything that goes down,' said Jemima. 'Leysham might not prove the greatest physical threat, but we don't know anything about Charlotte Winstanley's physical capabilities, and there's also a chance that there could be others present at the cottage who might weigh in on Leysham's behalf.'

Everyone nodded their agreement.

As usual in these situations, Dan was the one to carry the battering ram. His build and general fitness level meant that he was slower than the others, but over the years he had perfected the knack of putting a significant amount of power behind the implement when slamming it against a door.

As it was, there was no need for them to pretend that they had heard something suspicious to give them a valid reason to force entry to the cottage. The door to the cottage was open and the sound of raised voices was easily heard from the pavement.

'What the hell have you got me involved with, Edgar?' The woman's voice was shrill.

'It's nothing. Honestly, Charlotte. Tabitha's been found, and Benedict's lad was involved in her disappearance.'

'Benedict's son? But how's that even possible?'

'I don't know. I'm at a loss to explain it. All I know is that Benedict will blame me.'

'Why would he do that? I've known Benedict a long time. Far longer than I've known you, and he's too honest for his own good.'

'There are things you don't know, Charlotte. Benedict's lad, Douglas, well he was holding my Tabitha at a property that was owned by our company! I literally had no idea about it.'

'Do you really expect me to believe you?'

'Why wouldn't you?'

'Perhaps because until Tabitha went missing you did nothing but complain about her. Saying she was an embarrassment and a liability. I even remember you saying that you wished she was dead, and then, hey presto, she went missing. If memory serves me, that was a few months after you started making those ridiculous monthly payments to Douglas.'

'That's right, I did, but I told you at the time that the lad was doing consultancy work for me on the QT. I knew that Benedict wouldn't approve. He was so hard on the lad, and I just thought the boy deserved a chance.'

'So, he deserved a chance, and Tabitha didn't? Do you seriously expect me to believe that guff? I'm starting to think that you're the one who's dodgy, Edgar. It's taken me long enough, but I'm beginning to see that you've been using me.'

'Don't be ridiculous woman!' His voice was angry.

'You've spent years telling me how special I am. Saying you'd leave your wife for me. But it was a pack of lies.'

'I bought you this house!'

'You can't even be honest about that! You didn't buy this house. You took money out of the company. You're always moving money about. Telling me to look the other way. You've been bleeding Benedict dry, and he's known nothing about it.'

'You shouldn't voice baseless accusations like that. It's slanderous.'

'It's the truth, Edgar. We both know it is. And as for Benedict helping his son, well he washed his hands of him years back. He's said on many occasions that Douglas was a bad lot and there was no helping him. That's why he cut ties with him. So don't you go badmouthing Ben, trying to get him into trouble, because I won't have it.'

'You won't have it! Just listen to yourself. Who the hell do you think you are? You'd be nothing without me. Noth—'

'I'm going, Edgar. Leaving you. The truth is, I should have done it years ago.'

'You're going nowhere, you gold-digging bitch. At least, not until you've calmed down and thought about things rationally. The way you're acting, your histrionics will land us both in trouble.'

'I'm perfectly calm and rational, Edgar. And don't you dare talk down to me. My cases are packed and I'm leaving you. There's no further discussion to be had. I've seen you for what you are, and I don't like what I see. I must have been mad to have fallen for your lies. But no more, Edgar. I've had—'

The conversation ended abruptly, as the sound of something heavy crashed to the floor. By overhearing the discussion, Jemima had learned a lot in the last few minutes. Though she realized that perhaps they should have interrupted the couple sooner, as it seemed that the verbal altercation had suddenly turned physical. She just hoped that she hadn't left their intervention too late.

Reaching for her baton, Jemima raced into the cottage to find Edgar Leysham standing over Charlotte, who was sprawled unconscious on the floor. Leysham's arm was raised as he gripped a poker, ready to bring it down on her head once again.

With no time to think, Jemima acted instinctively. Leysham was so focused on finishing Charlotte off that he failed to notice the police presence. Launching herself at lightning speed, she swung her baton across Leysham's midriff with tremendous force. At the moment of contact his arm was at forty-five degrees, and speedily closing in on his target.

Leysham's ribs cracked; he was winded and lost his balance. He groaned as an agonizing pain shot through his torso, causing him to lose control of the situation. The poker clattered to the floor. He clutched his ribs and looked around wildly, like a wounded animal desperate to find a means of escape.

His breath coming in short gasps, he attempted to charge at Jemima, but she was having none of it. Still gripping her baton, she swung it like a backhanded shot in a tennis match. It caught him side-on.

This time, Leysham went down and didn't get up until Levi had cuffed him. The young officer yanked him up unceremoniously and shoved him towards a chair. 'Sit down,' he ordered.

'Take your hands off me,' snarled Edgar. 'I will not be treated in this disrespectful manner.'

'You forfeited any right to deference the moment we walked in and caught you red-handed trying to murder this woman. You're no different to any other criminal we deal with.' Jemima glared at him. 'Read him his rights, Levi.'

'It'll be your word against mine, and I am an influential man. A Lord. I'll tell everyone how you viciously assaulted me.'

Levi ignored the threat and read him his rights.

As Jemima looked around, she saw that Mack was checking on Charlotte's condition. 'Has anyone called for an ambulance?' she asked.

'Dan's sorting it,' said Mack. 'She's unconscious but breathing. I've checked and her airway's clear. Help me get her in the recovery position.'

Jemima bent down and helped manoeuvre the unconscious woman into a safer position, and they waited there until the ambulance arrived.

Edgar Leysham's injuries were painful but not serious. He was treated at the scene, read his rights, then taken to the police station where he called his lawyer, Cedric Fortescue.

As it was late and everyone was exhausted, Jemima left instructions that once Edgar had finished conferring with his legal counsel, he was to be confined in a holding cell overnight, to be questioned the following morning.

CHAPTER 32

They arrived at the station that morning each looking more energized than they had done twelve hours earlier. The evidence against Edgar Leysham had mounted up while they slept. The night shift had worked diligently, tracking money transfers on the various accounts to which Edgar had sole access.

There was still plenty for Gareth and the others to follow up on, while Jemima and Dan went to interview Edgar.

Leysham's bloodshot eyes suggested that he hadn't managed to get much sleep, though it was immediately apparent that tiredness hadn't diluted his arrogance and sense of entitlement. When they walked into the room, his lip curled contemptuously as though they were something he needed to wipe off his shoe.

With the formalities out of the way, Cedric Fortescue was the first to speak. 'I want it on record that I will be lodging a formal complaint about the appalling way you have behaved towards my client. Lord Leysham has been treated as though he is a common criminal. Forced to endure a night in the most basic and unhygienic cell, where he has been kept awake by all and sundry and offered only inedible refreshment.'

'Your client has been treated no differently to any other person held at the station.'

'That is my point, Chief Inspector. Lord Leysham is a man of importance and deserves respect.'

Despite feeling her hackles rise, Jemima was determined not to play the man's game. Instead, she ignored the comments and began the interview in earnest.

'Lord Leysham, you were arrested for the attempted murder of Charlotte Winstanley, which occurred at a property in the village of Hazelwood, Monmouthshire, yesterday evening.'

'I don't hear a question in that statement,' said Fortescue.

'When we entered the property, you were found with a poker in your hand and your arm raised ready to strike the unconscious Ms Winstanley once more. Why did you attack her? Why did you want to kill her?'

'Really Chief Inspector. This is preposterous. Do you really expect anyone to believe that Lord Leysham, a man of exemplary character, known for his good deeds and charitable works, would have attacked an employee in such a way?' asked Fortescue.

'Please answer the question, Lord Leysham.'

'I've instructed my client not to answer any questions put to him. As you well know, under law he has the right to remain silent. We have evidence of injuries inflicted upon my client when you assaulted him, and once this interview has ended, we will be filing a complaint against you personally.'

'That's your right,' said Jemima. 'However, you might wish to reconsider once you've viewed the footage from the bodycams that each of us were wearing. They form both a visual and auditory record of the event in question. They picked up a heated argument between your client and Ms Winstanley prior to our entry. During that conversation they referred to other events we intend to question your client about.'

Edgar opened his mouth and quickly closed it again without saying anything, as Cedric Fortescue turned to face his client. The solicitor's previously smug expression suddenly evaporated as it became apparent to him that his client had not been truthful.

Jemima and Dan sat in silence and watched as they played the bodycam footage to Fortescue and Leysham. Edgar soon shut his eyes and his chin tilted ever so slightly towards his chest. Whereas the solicitor's muscles tensed, clearly shocked at the realization that he had been duped by his client.

'Would you like some time to confer with your client?' asked Jemima.

'It would be appreciated,' said Fortescue, his tone immediately more conciliatory.

Jemima would have loved to be privy to their upcoming conversation, but that was never going to happen. Instead, she and Dan would use the time to get an update from Gareth and the rest of the team. What she was about to learn would seal Edgar Leysham's fate.

* * *

When they returned to the interview room some forty minutes later, there was a noticeable change in the dynamic between the two men.

Fortescue was the first to speak. 'Given the nature of the evidence, I've advised my client to answer your questions.'

Probing Edgar about his attack on Charlotte took little time, as they already had sufficient evidence against him.

'As you're aware, we have a recording of you telling Ms Winstanley that you were making regular payments to Douglas Taylor for consultancy work he was contracted to undertake for your company. What work was he undertaking?'

'It was confidential.' Edgar's voice was level, but there was a noticeable flicker of uncertainty in his eyes.

'Given the fact that eight years ago, Douglas Taylor abducted your daughter and held her against her will, I suggest that you tell us why you regularly paid him four thousand pounds a month. Payments which began shortly before Tabitha was abducted,' said Jemima.

'I had him on a monthly retainer. Douglas had a skillset that was very useful to our business.'

'That's interesting,' said Jemima. 'Our investigations have shown that Douglas was a PA, though he wasn't that successful as he failed to remain in post with various employers. So, what crucial skillset did Douglas possess, which made him so indispensable to your business that you had him on such a large monthly retainer for eight years?'

'You wouldn't understand, and as I said, it's confidential.'

'Our investigation shows that the money was paid to Douglas from an account within L&T Holdings for which you were the sole signatory. Indeed, we've been informed that that account was set up by yourself, purely for donations for charitable purposes.'

As the pressure mounted, sweat erupted across Edgar's brow, and he shifted restlessly in his seat.

'We have also discovered that the property in Newport where your daughter was being held, along with other women and children, had been purchased from funds from that account. The account which only you had access to.'

'What other women and children?' Edgar's voice had risen by almost an octave. His eyes were wide and as he looked repeatedly from one officer to another. 'I knew nothing about other women and children. Whatever that man has done has nothing to do with me.'

'It has everything to do with you,' said Jemima. Edgar's shock at this revelation seemed genuine, as it appeared that Lydia hadn't shared this information with her husband. It lent credence to her claim that their marriage had been on the rocks even before the revelations of yesterday. 'You purchased the property via L&T Holdings and remained the registered owner along with Charlotte Winstanley. Yet our investigation has shown no evidence of that property ever being listed as part of the L&T Holdings portfolio. Your monthly payments to Douglas were, in your own words, a retainer for his supposed useful skillset. Yet you're unable to tell us what that skillset was.'

'I-I,' Leysham faltered. The man was clearly out of his depth and unable to think on his feet.

'I'll make it easy for you, Lord Leysham. We've already checked the accounts and staffing records at L&T Holdings. Douglas Taylor was and never has been on the payroll, nor is there any record of him ever having been paid a monthly retainer. Indeed, your business partner was unaware of the arrangement you had with his son.'

'It's not as bad as it seems,' said Leysham. 'I admit that I purchased that property in Newport. But I bought it for Tabitha. So that she would have somewhere to live. She'd found out about my affair with Charlotte and was threatening to tell her mother. I couldn't allow that to happen. Lydia's the one with the money. Not me. If she had proof that I was having an affair, she'd have filed for divorce, and I'd have been left with nothing. I couldn't allow that to happen. I have a reputation to protect.'

'Some reputation.' Dan shook his head in disgust. 'You had your daughter abducted to save your so-called reputation. Are you seriously expecting us to believe that?'

'No of course I didn't have her abducted. I merely asked Douglas to help relocate her. The money was to go to Tabitha. To make sure she was looked after. A few weeks after he took her Douglas told me that they were in a relationship. It seemed best to let things play out. If Tabitha was happy, then Lydia didn't need to know about Charlotte.'

Jemima couldn't hide her disbelief at the story. The man was delusional if he thought they were going to believe his lies. 'And you were content to allow your wife to suffer for all this time without knowing where her daughter was? Not only that, but to lie to the police when they investigated her disappearance?'

'Really Chief Inspector, you're making it sound worse than it is,' said Leysham. 'I truly believed that Tabitha was happy. She certainly wasn't happy living at home. I thought

I was doing her a favour, and it was the only way I could think of to stop her from telling her mother about my affair.'

'If you thought that Tabitha was happily living with Douglas Taylor, why didn't you mention it when we informed you that she'd been found?'

'I suppose I panicked.'

'You're lying. Why did you contact Douglas to let him know that we intended to raid the property? Your actions were not those of an innocent man. They were the actions of someone desperately trying to cover his tracks.'

'I didn't contact him.'

'Earlier, when we left the room, I was advised by one of my team that a phone registered to Douglas Taylor received a call shortly before we raided the property in question. That call came from a number which we know belongs to you. It's the number your wife rang when she informed you of the fact that Tabitha would be removed from the hospital and transferred to a secure facility.'

'Lydia told you that?'

'Yes. Your wife is keen to help us bring those responsible for what happened to Tabitha and the others to justice. She said she'd do whatever it takes.'

When Edgar Leysham eventually realized that he wasn't going to get away with it he issued a barrage of expletive-ridden threats worthy of many a hardened criminal. Hours later, and the man's furious verbal rampage still rang in Jemima's ears. It was incredible that despite the things he'd done, he absolutely believed his wealth and status should place him out of reach of the law.

He was formally charged and remanded in custody for the attempted murder of his former lover, Charlotte Winstanley, and the role he had played in the abduction of his daughter and enabling the false imprisonment of the other women. It was unlikely that they would find sufficient evidence to implicate him in the rapes and murders committed by Douglas, but they were determined to give it their best shot. Benedict Taylor gave a sworn statement contradicting Edgar's narrative that Douglas had been on a company retainer. Benedict, like others who knew Edgar, was keen to distance himself from him.

For the next few days, Gareth was like a dog with a bone. He'd already found plenty of evidence to prove Leysham's guilt, but plenty wasn't enough. After what the man had done to ruin his daughter's and the other victims' lives, Gareth was determined not to call a halt to his fact-finding mission until he had gone through every available piece of information. And his obsessive mission eventually paid off, for as he delved deeper into the company's financial accounts, he came across the evidence that Leysham had purchased the entire security system which had ultimately ensured that the women and children remained captive for years on end. There was little doubt in any of their minds that this would be the final nail in the man's coffin. It wouldn't take away the years of pain and suffering that each of the victims had been forced to endure, but it might give them some relief and force the presiding judge to impose the harshest available custodial sentence.

EPILOGUE

For the last few weeks, it seemed as though in the little spare time she had, Lucy had talked about nothing else. Then again, she often joked about how apart from in immediate family settings, social occasions passed her by. Growing up, she made the most every opportunity. Before the kids came along, even if she'd put in a fourteen-hour shift in her drive to make a success of the business she had founded, she'd still find the time and energy to glam up and party with the best of them.

Though the last few years had been tough. Before his accident, Ellis had been away for long stretches at a time. Working on film sets. Sometimes on another continent. In general, their work-life balance suited them both, as they were both high achievers, with careers they enjoyed. Lucy was caught on a treadmill as she became a victim of her own success. Ambition and drive motivated her to keep pushing harder to take her corporate hamper business to the next level. But every time she reached a particular goal, she set herself another and focused on that.

On those rare occasions when she had time to sit and think, Lucy appreciated that perhaps she needed more fun in her life. She joked about approaching middle-age as a pseudo-Cinderella. Albeit a high-flying, work-obsessive big-earner, who employed a live-in nanny to look after her kids as well as her sister's two. And whenever she quipped about this, Jemima's response was that if Lucy was Cinderella, then that must make her one of the ugly sisters.

An opportunity for the siblings and their partners to escape the humdrum and go out for the evening came when Mason suggested they attend a charity ball at a city centre venue. It was a cause close to his heart — raising money for a teenage mental health charity.

In the lead up to the event it was as though the sisters had regressed to their student days. Pampering and preening. Spending time on their appearances, rather than grabbing the closest thing to hand and hiding behind jeans and oversized jumpers.

Jemima and Mason took the boys to Lucy's house, where they would spend the night being looked after by Eloise. As they waited for the taxi to arrive, Lucy and Jemima sipped a pre-event cocktail, looking glamorous and sophisticated in their evening wear. Mason and Ellis scrubbed up well too. Both men looked the part in their tuxedos.

Jemima was pleased to see Lucy looking so relaxed. She'd been raving about the event for weeks. Then again, she was a social butterfly. Seemingly comfortable in any situation. Spreading her magic. Captivating even the most aloof and socially awkward with her uncanny ability to make them feel as though they had been her friend forever.

Jemima understood why her sister made such an effort to enjoy social gatherings. After all, Lucy had always been a sociable person. Yet her chosen career meant that she often spent large swathes of time alone in her plush garden office, either sat at her computer, or on the phone.

With almost two hundred attendees, the event was sold out, and the room for pre-dinner drinks was packed to bursting.

'There's so much wealth packed into this room,' said Lucy. She gestured at some of the designer evening wear and plethora of jewellery worn to impress.

'You could afford those things too,' said Jemima.

'Could think of better use of money,' said Lucy.

'Me too.'

'I'm sure I went to school with him,' said Ellis. He pointed at someone in the distance. But before the others focused on the man in question, he was hidden by the throng. 'Can't think of his name, but I'm sure it'll come back to me.' Ellis's brow furrowed as he tried to recall it.

Mason took Jemima's arm. 'I'd like to introduce you to a couple of people.' He gently steered her away, and she spent the next twenty minutes in conversation with Mason's acquaintances.

A microphone crackled into life and there was the sound of chinking glass as the host for the evening made an announcement. 'Ladies and gentlemen, dinner is almost ready to be served. If you'd like to make your way into the dining room, you'll be escorted to your table.'

Having said their goodbyes to the group of people they'd been conversing with, Jemima glanced around in the hope of spotting Lucy and Ellis. But with the crowd heading in the direction of the dining room it was impossible to locate them.

Jemima and Mason joined the back of the queue and were some of the last people to enter the dining room. Each table had six place settings, with name cards to indicate their allocated spot. As their table was towards the far end of the room, they were forced to weave through the dining area. As they eventually approached the table, Jemima spotted Lucy and Ellis in conversation with another couple who were seated facing away from the entrance. Lucy glanced up, smiled and pointed to the two empty seats which had been allocated to Jemima and Mason.

As they reached the table they were greeted by their fellow diners. It was then that Jemima realized who Lucy and Mason were speaking to. Mark Derbyshire was a defence barrister. In court he was a formidable man, operating at the top of his game. Jemima had heard many an officer groan when they learned that they had to give evidence in a trial at which he was the opposing counsel. He invariably kept the police on their toes and exploited every chink in their armour. Though it was difficult to deny that the man was easy on the eye.

Mark's wife, Mariella, was a GP. Jemima had first met the woman under horrendous circumstances, when years earlier, Mariella had discovered the unconscious form of Millie Rathbone at the bottom of the stairs when she called around to the Rathbone's house. The police had been called, and a gruesome discovery made. The Rathbones had been the Derbyshires' neighbours. Sally Rathbone was Mariella's longtime best friend, and a GP at the same practice in North Cardiff. She was also Millie's stepmother.

Since the conclusion of that case, Jemima had occasionally encountered Mark Derbyshire when giving evidence in court cases, but their paths rarely crossed. Though throughout the ensuing years the two women hadn't encountered each other again.

Jemima was astonished to see the Derbyshires, and it was apparent from their expressions that they were equally surprised. Jemima's initial impression of the couple was that Mark looked exactly as she remembered him. Mariella was still an attractive woman, though it was noticeable that she had aged. Her hair, which was her natural colour, was flecked with the odd grey strand. And when she smiled, faint lines appeared around her eyes and mouth, which Jemima was certain hadn't been there when they had last seen each other.

Jemima introduced Mason to the Derbyshires, and they took their seats. Mason sat between Jemima and Mariella.

'Well, this is absolutely marvellous,' said Ellis. 'I'd no idea that you and Mark knew each other. Mark and I were at the same school. Haven't seen each other for years.'

'We've lots to catch up on,' said Mark. 'But tell me, how do you know each other?'

'Oh, we're family. Simple as that. Jem's my sister-in-law. She and Lucy are sisters.' Ellis smiled.

'And you're married?' asked Mariella. The question was directed at Jemima and Mason.

'No. We live together, but we're not married,' replied Mason.

'Try before you buy, eh? I like your style,' said Mark. He chuckled then winked at Mason.

'Mason's a vicar,' said Lucy. Her tone was stern.

'Sorry about my husband,' said Mariella. Her cheeks had flushed. 'He frequently embarrasses me. Likes to be provocative.'

'Comes with the territory in my line of work. I'm sure the inspector knows that.' He glanced at Jemima and smiled.

'Chief Inspector now,' said Lucy. 'Heading up a new initiative, no less.' She reached across and squeezed Jemima's hand. 'We're extremely proud of what she does.'

'Absolutely,' echoed Mason.

'Wow, you've brought along your own fan club,' said Mark. 'Well, here's to you keeping me in business.' He raised his glass to Jemima.

'Enough shop talk, darling. This is a social occasion, after all.' Mariella squeezed her husband's arm to reinforce the message. 'So, Mason, from your accent, I guess you're American or Canadian?'

'Canadian.'

'I guess it's quite a change, living in Wales?'

'Actually, it's much the same as home, insofar as it's a small village church. Though the weather's different. More rain. Less snow.'

'So how did you meet Jemima?'

'A young woman was murdered in my church.'

'Ah, well so much for my clumsy attempt at steering the conversation away from crime,' laughed Mariella.

Ellis was at a loss to understand why there was tension. Yet there was a noticeable change in the atmosphere since Jemima and Mason had arrived. Not that either of them had said or done anything to cause this to happen. The problem seemed to be with Mark, who was clearly antagonistic towards them. Yet Mason hadn't encountered the Derbyshires until that evening. So, he guessed that Mark and Jemima must have had a few confrontations when they had encountered each other at court.

As they were all stuck together as a group for the duration of the meal, Ellis was keen to keep things on an even keel. If they could just get through that part of the evening without the occurrence of a major altercation, then they could go their separate ways for the next part of the event. In order to dial down the tension, he set about engaging Mark in conversation once more, while the others spoke happily among themselves. Though it was a relief when dinner was served.

As they eventually made their way into the room where a band was playing, Mason whispered into Jemima's ear. 'What's up with that Derbyshire guy? He seems to have a problem with you.'

'You think?' It was a rhetorical question. 'I guess it's because we're on the opposite sides of the law. We've had some tense encounters over the years. It's the same with all the defence counsels. To be successful in that game you have to have a ruthless streak and play to win.'

'Play to win?' interjected Mason. His voice sounded incredulous. 'Surely it's a question of morals? I understand that even those who have committed crimes deserve to have a fair trial, and high-calibre representation, but nothing will ever improve in society until people start facing up to their actions and accept they must face the consequences and change their behaviour.'

'Believe me, I get where you're coming from Mason. I really do. But that will never happen. I think your theory explains why you're all about saving people's souls. Trying to prick someone's conscience to think about doing the right thing.'

'It's about being a better person. Which isn't an easy thing for any of us,' said Mason.

'I know. But out there, on the streets, there are very few people who think about what's right or wrong. People just do what they believe is in their own interest, and to hell with the consequences.'

'That's a very cynical outlook, Jem.'

'It's something us police officers see day-in day-out. It grinds you down, but you learn to detach yourself and deal with the fallout of people's bad decisions. It's our role to find the criminals and build a case against them, in the hope that if the case goes to trial, the jury will see that the evidence presented by the prosecution speaks for itself. But people like Mark Derbyshire are paid ridiculous amounts of money to muddy the waters. He's focused on getting them off. No matter the consequences. He's in it to win.'

'How can you be so calm and detached?'

'It's just the way the system operates. Anyway, forget about Mark Derbyshire. We're here to enjoy ourselves. After all, those tickets cost a fortune.'

'Fair enough. Do you fancy a dance?'

'You bet I do,' said Jemima.

The next few hours were spent happily enough, as Mason and Jemima danced the night away. The unpleasantness of earlier became a distant memory as they focused on the music and the intimacy brought about by being in each other's arms.

The dance floor was busy, as were the fringes where groups of people sipped drinks, laughing, and chatting among themselves. It was a happy, upbeat atmosphere. A pleasant change from many evenings when Jemima came off-shift, exhausted, and increasingly disillusioned with whichever case she was working. Without a shadow of a doubt, Mason was the best thing that had happened to her. She was yin. He was yang. And Mason was determined to drag her into the light. He made her feel alive in so many ways. Like two sides of the same coin, together they were complete.

As the latest offering of the band came to a close, Jemima glanced across and was surprised to see that Lucy had been dancing with Mark. As the music finished and they pulled apart, she saw Mark run his fingers down the inside of her sister's forearm. The effect on Jemima was visceral and immediate.

'What's the matter? Are you all right, Jem?' Mason sensed that all was not well. He held her shoulders, firmly but tenderly and stared into her eyes as he waited for an answer.

At first, she didn't hear him. She was too wrapped up in her own thoughts. For a moment she had been transported back to that awful time in the alley. When she had been knocked out. Dragged to her feet. Then raped. She remembered at the end of the ordeal, her rapist had run his fingers down the inside of her forearm. She'd had a nagging feeling ever since then that the act was important. That it would help her identify her attacker. Yet, until now she'd had no idea of its significance.

'I'm not feeling too good. Do you mind if we go home?' She avoided looking into Mason's eyes. Knowing that if she did, he would inevitably spot the tears that were welling up ready to fall.

'Yeah, of course.' He kissed the top of her head. 'Do you want to let Lucy and Ellis know that we're heading off?'

Before Jemima could answer, she noticed Lucy heading in her direction. 'I'm afraid I'm going to be a party pooper, sis. I'm going to find Ellis and we'll get off.'

'Jem was just saying the same thing,' said Mason. 'Hardly surprising the hours you girls work. Tell you what, you ring for an Uber and I'll find Ellis.' Mason headed out in search of him.

Jemima waited until Mason was out of earshot, then grabbed her sister's arm and headed away from stragglers on the dance floor. 'It was Mark. I'm certain it was him.'

'What was Mark?' Lucy looked and sounded perplexed. As she studied the expression on her sister's face, she suddenly realized what Jemima was saying. 'Mark Derbyshire raped you?' Lucy's eyes were wide, and her voice squeaked.

It was all Jemima could do to nod. 'But it's one thing knowing it. Quite another thing proving it. So don't say anything. Just act as though everything's OK.'

'You'll get him for this, Jem. I know you will.' Lucy drew her sister towards her and embraced her tightly.

'Damned right I will, Luce, and I guarantee he won't see me coming. That sick bastard's not going to get the chance to rape another woman. One way or another, Mark Derbyshire's going down.'

THE END

THE JOFFE BOOKS STORY

We began in 2014 when Jasper agreed to publish his mum's much-rejected romance novel and it became a bestseller.

Since then we've grown into the largest independent publisher in the UK. We're extremely proud to publish some of the very best writers in the world, including Joy Ellis, Faith Martin, Caro Ramsay, Helen Forrester, Simon Brett and Robert Goddard. Everyone at Joffe Books loves reading and we never forget that it all begins with the magic of an author telling a story.

We are proud to publish talented first-time authors, as well as established writers whose books we love introducing to a new generation of readers.

We won Trade Publisher of the Year at the Independent Publishing Awards in 2023. We have been shortlisted for Independent Publisher of the Year at the British Book Awards for the last four years, and were shortlisted for the Diversity and Inclusivity Award at the 2022 Independent Publishing Awards. In 2023 we were shortlisted for Publisher of the Year at the RNA Industry Awards.

We built this company with your help, and we love to hear from you, so please email us about absolutely anything bookish at feedback@joffebooks.com

If you want to receive free books every Friday and hear about all our new releases, join our mailing list: www.joffebooks.com/contact

And when you tell your friends about us, just remember: it's pronounced Joffe as in coffee or toffee!